D1098092

Executive

Simon and Schuster / New York

Privilege

A WASHINGTON NOVEL

Lynne Cheney

Designed by Irving Perkins
Manufactured in the United States of America
1   2   3   4   5   6   7   8   9   10

Library of Congress Cataloging in Publication Data

Cheney, Lynne.
    Executive privilege.

    I. Title.
PZ4.C5184Ex [PS3553.H3495] 813'.5'4 78-27325

ISBN 0-671-24060-9

To Dick, who has shaped my life—
and even one or two of my opinions.

Prologue

A GRAY-HAIRED butler laid the Presidential News Summary neatly atop the *Washington Post*, the *New York Times*, and the *Wall Street Journal*, then stood back to make sure the entire stack was precisely lined up beside the single place set at the table. All of the lines ran parallel or perpendicular, as nearly as he could tell, but still the total effect left him dissatisfied. He moved a water glass slightly, but was still not pleased. It was the color that was bothering him, he decided. The white tablecloth was what kept everything from seeming right. The President himself preferred it in the dining room of the White House's family quarters. "Matthew, it's just too dark in here," he would complain, whenever a darker color, like the Williamsburg blue, which Matthew preferred, was on the table. "All these dark colors," the President would say, gesturing at the antique wallpaper with its fantasy of early American scenes, "and those heavy drapes. It's too much. Let's lighten it up in here." But the china was white, too, and the white-on-white effect did not please Matthew's eyes. It lacked elegance, he thought. And he suspected that the First Lady agreed with him.

He shook his head in resignation and went into the kitchen, where he took up a careful watch at the door. So good was his timing that he had to wait only a moment or two before the President came striding into the dining room for his usual, solitary weekday breakfast.

Zern Jenner entered the room head down, walking rapidly. Various observers had noted over the years how his pace quickened when he was in the East. At home in Montana he would amble along, his face lifted and expectant, his eyes seeking out the eyes of anyone he might encounter, all quite in contrast to the way he was moving now. No politician since Huey Long, one columnist had observed, was so adept at changing his body language to suit the regional circumstance. Like his stride, Jenner's dress was also eastern today: a three-piece dark suit, shirt just discernibly blue, tie striped in red. But the West was undeniably in his face, in the fan of wrinkles around the eyes, which came from years of squinting into the wind and sun.

The butler picked up a silver pot filled with coffee and entered the dining room, too late to help Jenner with his chair, but in time to see him angle the stack of newspapers so that he could read while he ate. The butler poured coffee into a white china cup decorated with a gold presidential seal, and the President began on his breakfast and the news summary at the same time.

Running his eyes down the right-hand side of the news summary's table of contents, Jenner nodded in approval at the diversity of sources it was drawn from: the wires, the networks, even this morning's *Washington Post* and *New York Times*. It had been just about a year since Jenner had casually mentioned that he thought it might save him reading time if the fat Washington and New York papers were included in the summary on the morning they came out instead of in the next day's report. And so now White House staffers worked early morning hours to get them in. The *Dallas Morning News* was also listed, and the *Chicago Tribune,* and the *Omaha World Herald.* There was even, he noted with pleasure, an editorial from the *Billings Gazette.*

But when he got to the left-hand column his reaction was far different. As soon as he saw the story listed second, he set his coffee down hard, sloshing some of it over into the saucer. Frowning, he leafed quickly to the news summary's third page, where he read an article condensed from the *Washington Post,* and then he pulled the *Post* itself out from the stack of reading material. Ignoring the lead story about student rioting in Japan, he concentrated on the off-lead story, the one the *Post*'s editors had decided was the day's second most important. "Jenner's Daily Log Shows President's Priorities," it was headlined.

So intent was the President on the *Post* story that he seemed to have forgot the butler's presence.

"How would you like your egg, sir?" the elderly gentleman asked, when he thought the President had reached a stopping place.

"Skip it this morning," the President answered curtly.

The short response did not at all offend the butler, who was used to Presidents and their distractions. He had, after all, borne witness to LBJ's towering rages and Richard Nixon's icy aloofness. By comparison, Jenner's occasional rudenesses were nothing. Had anyone been watching the butler walk back to the kitchen, it would have been obvious that the old gentleman's dignity was intact.

For his part, Jenner noticed the butler's absence no more than he had noticed his presence, so concerned was he to know exactly what information the *Post* had obtained. But as he continued to read, his anxiety lessened, and by the time he had finished, most of his equanimity had returned. Somebody had leaked last week's

Oval Office log, but the *Post* hadn't seen in it what he had feared. Instead, *Post* reporter Nicholas Frye had focused on political activities, on how often the log showed Jenner meeting with those who would be key figures in the next campaign. The President's eyes went over the lead sentence again: "A confidential document obtained by the *Washington Post* seems to indicate that President Zern Jenner is already spending a significant portion of his time on his reelection effort." No harm in that, the President thought. And maybe even some benefit. It might be of help to have party regulars across the country see that he was thinking of next year's elections.

The story would probably keep rolling for awhile. Hell, he was sure it would, it was such a natural for all the Washington reporters who were constantly trying to figure who was in and who was out at the White House. They would analyze and reanalyze his meetings. They would scrutinize them down to the microsecond to see which advisers he was spending the most time with. But as soon as they had realigned the White House pecking order for the ten thousandth time, that would be the end of it. It would stay a Washington story.

Leaning back in his chair, he gazed at the windows which faced Pennsylvania Avenue, his blue-gray eyes seeming to study the heavy-security draperies. But his thoughts were elsewhere, and the image of window and drape wasn't really registering. He was still thinking about the *Post* story, about how fortunate it was that Nicholas Frye hadn't seen any more in the daily log than a little politicking in the Oval Office. It'll stop there, he told himself. Then, standing abruptly, pushing back his chair and ignoring the butler, who rushed in from the kitchen to stand in attendance, he decided that it would indeed stop there. He, Zern Jenner, President of the United States, would make damned sure of that.

Chapter 1

RUDY DODMAN, *Newstime* magazine's thirty-two-year-old White House correspondent, was in the habit of reading the *Post* while he dressed. After opening the louvered shutters on the windows and spreading the *Post*'s front section out on the bed in the Dodman's small Capitol Hill row house, he would skim through the newspaper as he moved between the closet and the dresser, the dresser and the night stand. After eight years in Washington, he had become an expert at reading while he was buckling his belt or tying his shoe or putting in a cuff link.

But on this particular autumn morning, as soon as he had unfolded the paper, it absorbed all his attention. Reading slowly and carefully, he sat down on the edge of the bed, the intensity that he gave to the newspaper seeming to come naturally to him. "It's your eyes," his wife Nancy had said to him more than once. "Maybe it's the color—that almost icy blue. Or maybe it's that when you look at something, you look so steadily. Whatever it is, when you're serious, there's sure no mistake about it." Then she would tease him because he got involved so easily. "Just because you're so serious," she'd said once, "doesn't mean I have to take you seriously, does it?"

This morning, as most mornings, Nancy Dodman had been trying to sleep through her husband's dressing and reading, trying to sleep until she heard their son, two-year-old Mac. But when Rudy broke his usual routine and sat down on the bed to read, she gave it up, opened her eyes, and raised her dark curly head from the pillow. "Tell me about it," she said.

"Somebody's leaked part of Jenner's log to the *Post*," said Dodman, continuing to read.

"The log. What's that? A record of his phone calls?" She rolled over, stretched, and yawned. A small woman, she was saved from being cute by a face with just a touch of the exotic in it. Her nose was slightly flat and her hazel eyes slanted upward. The bedsheets and comforter she had wrapped around her, a green-and-white Oriental print, suited her well.

"That's part of what the log is, but only part," Rudy explained, marking the place where he was reading with his finger. "Practically everything the President does is recorded, from what time he arrives at a fund-raising reception to how long it takes him to sign a jobs bill. It looks like what the *Post* has is a section of the log recording Oval Office visitors for a week, who saw him, for how long, and when."

"Mmmm. So why's that important?"

"It's important because nobody on the outside ever

sees the log, or has any real idea with whom Jenner's spending his time. Usually, the only meetings they tell us about are the ones they want us to know about."

"I get it," Nancy said, sitting up. She made a pair of quotation marks in the air with her hands and solemnly intoned, "A Rare and Candid Glimpse into the Inner Workings of a Presidency."

Rudy laughed. Nancy's grasp of the nuances of Washington political journalism was, he decided, exceeded only by her irreverence for it. "Woman, when will you learn a little respect?"

"Never, I hope," she answered, pulling on a gaudily striped robe and sticking out her tongue at him. Then she started down the hall to where Mac had begun to make morning noises, but just outside the bedroom door she stopped and put her head back around the corner. "Besides I keep you from getting too tangled up in your Washington underwear."

He threw a pillow at her and missed, knowing well that she had a point. Washington did have a rarefied atmosphere, and living in it for awhile it was easy to forget what the world looked like from Bangor or Waco or Poughkeepsie, easy to forget that the rest of the country didn't take Washington nearly so seriously as it took itself. More than a few politicians and journalists had fallen into that trap, he reflected. But then they weren't married to Nancy.

He reached for his cigarettes and lighter and got back to the paper. The tone of the article, which *Post* reporter Nicholas Frye had written, was almost uniformly negative. Frye emphasized how many meetings President Jenner had had with his political aide Dale Basinger, how many hours the President had spent with the chairman of his party. He implied that time thus spent on politics was time misspent, time which the taxpayers were owed. Which was, Rudy thought, more than a little

13

disingenuous on Frye's part. Did any political reporter really expect that with election year approaching the President of the United States would be ignoring his reelection campaign?

There was so much Frye had missed, Dodman realized, as he turned to an inside page and examined the portions of the log the *Post* had reprinted. There were so many hints he hadn't taken and leads he hadn't followed. For one thing, where was Vice President Robert Boyston? The Jenner administration billed him as a top policy maker, but the log showed that during one entire week he had not had a single meeting with the President. And why was Malcolm Ewing, the Deputy Director of the Domestic Council, spending so much time in the Oval Office? He was in for an hour every day at one P.M. and several other times during the week besides.

By the time Rudy put down the paper, he practically knew the log by heart, but he made a mental effort to put the thought of it aside while he shaved and dressed. Usually his best insights came that way, when he knew all the facts but wasn't concentrating on them. Besides, there'd be plenty of chance to think about the log later; in fact, there'd be no choice. Nobody in town would be talking about anything else.

When he finished dressing, he picked up the *Post* and took it downstairs. In the kitchen, Nancy was drinking a cup of coffee at the counter, while Mac, sitting in a Victorian high chair, played with a bowl of cereal. Rudy handed Nancy the paper, and she started reading the Frye story.

"I don't understand why he hasn't done more with it," she said after a minute. "This business of 'the President is playing politics,' is really a cliché."

"I don't get it either. What's really important, it seems to me, is what this log shows about who's who in the administration. Boyston's never in the Oval Office, for

14

instance, and Ewing's in there all the time. Who would have figured that?" He paused for a moment. "And there's something else here too, something about this story that gives me that old feeling in the gut."

"Maybe you're just hungry," Nancy offered, maintaining a straight face, "or do you call that male intuition?"

"What you call that," he said, menacing her with a roll of paper towels, "is having a feel for a story."

Mac, apparently tired of being ignored, held up a hand which he had decorated by neatly affixing a Cheerio to the tip of each wet finger.

"Five," he announced.

"Now are you positive about that, son?" Rudy said, leaning over the high chair. "It most distinctly looks like six to me."

"Ru-dee! Do you want to addle that poor child's brains?" Nancy demanded.

"O.K., O.K., I give up. It's five, all right." He kissed Mac on the cheek and ruffled his fine gold hair, hair which insisted on standing straight out from the child's head.

"He looks like a dandelion turned to fluff," Nancy observed.

Rudy thought his son looked more like a cartoon character who had stuck his finger in an electric outlet, but he kept that observation to himself. Before he made his way to the phone, he pretended to be a roaring monster whose insatiable appetite demanded vast quantities of Cheerios. Mac was still giggling as his father dialed a number in Chevy Chase.

"Jack, Rudy here," he said, when *Newstime* bureau chief Jack Sasser answered. "I'm glad I caught you because I'm not going to make our meeting."

"I figured as much," Sasser responded, "which is why I'm still sitting here with the paper. As soon as I saw the *Post*, I figured you'd head for the White House. Do you think they'll have anything to say about the leak this morning?"

"I don't know. They may wait to see what sort of reaction the story gets first."

"Or they may be so involved with searching for the source of the leak that they'll be too busy to brief about it."

"Sure, can't you just see all the suspects on the staff sitting outside the press secretary's office, each waiting his turn to defend himself?"

"Have you got any theories about Ewing?" asked Sasser in a more serious tone. "What do you think about all the time he's spending in the Oval Office?"

"I think I'm surprised. It'd be easy enough to explain, if he were in there with Basinger and the other political types. Jenner's relied on Ewing's political judgment a lot in the past, ever since the Senate days. But Ewing's not in those political meetings. He's in there by himself, usually for an hour at a stretch and usually at one o'clock every afternoon. I don't know, maybe there's nothing to it. Do you remember how right after Jenner was elected word went around that Ewing had fallen out of favor? To put that down, Jenner declared that Ewing was his best friend in the world, or something to that effect. Maybe the two of them are just sitting in there having a friendly chat. I can't figure what's going on."

"Well, if you do find anything out, call me."

Jack ended a lot of his conversations that way, Rudy reflected. The *Newstime* bureau chief might like to talk about the long view he took of the city, about Washington in the historical context, but that didn't keep him from wanting to be the first to know anything new. Rudy signed off with a promise to call right away if there were any developments.

As he hung up, his gaze fell on Nancy, who was still intently examining the reprinted Presidential log, and it

16

occurred to him, not for the first time, how easy it was for both of them to get caught up in his work. Despite Nancy's staunchly proclaimed independence, it happened. Despite her awareness of the absurdities of politics, it happened. It even happened although they often talked about how to keep it from happening.

He walked over to her and put his arm around her. "What're you going to do today, Nance?" he asked, trying to change the focus of attention.

And she understood what he was doing—only too well, he realized, as she looked up at him knowingly. She was not the type to play a game in which they were both aware of the goal, but earnestly pretended they weren't.

"You know exactly what I'm going to do," she said. "Take Mac to Montessori. Work on my thesis at the library for a couple of hours. And then tonight you are going to hear about everything I find out. You are going to be buried in details about Immanuel Kant. You are going to know more about Immanuel Kant than you ever dreamed in your wildest dreams you'd want to know." She rubbed her cheek against the jacket of his chalk-striped suit and said, almost to herself, "Malcolm Ewing . . . We met him at a party once . . . Isn't he the one who's really a psychiatrist?"

Chapter 2

SEVERAL AFFAIRS ago, Sarah Hoff, *Newstime*'s junior White House correspondent, had been involved with a man who owned a sound gallery in Georgetown. Taking apart and rebuilding stereo equipment was an obsession with him, or so said Sarah, who tended to be as exaggerated and talkative about her personal life as she was precise and discreet about her work. He was always leaving a half-dismantled machine lying somewhere around her apartment, she told friends. The real reasons for their breakup had been complicated and had caused Sarah more than a few tears, but her friends had never seen her cry, nor did she intend for them to now. And so she affected an air of unconcern, leaving the definite impression that she had got rid of her stereo builder simply because she couldn't stand the idea of living any longer with the tangles of colored wire he scattered everywhere.

In her DuPont Circle apartment, however, one memento of him remained. Almost as though he'd been determined to live up to her stereotype of him, he had spent one of their last Sunday afternoons together busily wiring her clock radio into the bedroom TV set. And so it was that every morning the first voice Sarah heard was that of the anchorman for CBC "Morning News." On this particular morning, she partially awakened to a story about student rioting in Japan; she kept her eyes shut through an account of a tribe of Indians in Montana who were claiming ownership of vast stretches of coal-rich lands; she came fully to consciousness only with the story that CBC was running third—the leak of the Jenner log.

She sat straight up, pulling the sheets around her, long-limbed and graceful, though she was a large, full-bodied woman. She listened as the anchorman explained how the log afforded a particularly intimate look at the President and the presidency and, attuned as she was to the inner workings of the White House, she immediately saw the possibilities. There had been attempts in the past to show how Presidents spend their time. One of the networks had done an hour-long "Day in the Life of Zern Jenner" a year or so ago. Writer John Hersey had done minute-by-minute accounts, based on observing both Harry Truman and Gerald Ford over a period of several days. But always the man being observed had known he was being watched. What the log would show was how the most powerful man in the world spent his time when he didn't know he was being observed.

She brushed her long dark-blonde hair back from her face and watched as CBC switched to their White House correspondent, a self-possessed thirtyish brunette who treated the leak of the President's log as a story with special significance for women. "What Jenner's log shows," the correspondent was saying into the camera, "is that the President is spending little time listening to women. No matter how many token appointments to high position they receive, they will have little influence on policy-making so long as they are systematically excluded from the Oval Office."

Was it really possible, Sarah wondered, that the CBC correspondent thought the woman's angle the right one for this story? Her point might be valid—though "token appointments" and "systematically excluded" were overstating things a bit. But given that she had only a minute or two to make a point about the story to millions of viewers, surely this wasn't the most significant approach she could have taken. Was she, however knowledgeable she might appear, simply naive? Or had it been necessary for her in order to get air time to come up with an approach quickly? Any approach, so long as it was attention-getting and sounded authoritative. Somebody had said once that if television had been there to cover Moses coming down from the mountain, the report would have been, "Today God presented Moses with ten commandments, the two most important of which were . . ." But this coverage on the Jenner story was even worse than that. It was more like, "God gave Moses ten commandments today, and never mind what they were. He should have given them to an equal opportunity audience."

Sarah wondered if Rudy still wanted her to get into the White House and cover it this morning for the magazine while he went to the *Newstime* offices. She reached for the phone on the wicker bedside table and tapped out the Dodman's phone number.

"Nancy? Is Rudy there?"

Nancy explained that he had left about ten minutes ago. "I heard him tell Jack he was going to the White House."

There was no need for the conversation to go on, but whenever she encountered Nancy Dodman, Sarah found herself talking too much. "How's your thesis coming, Nancy?" she asked, thinking as she did that her conscience must somehow be connected with her tongue. Her relationship with Rudy Dodman was so proper that it could be chronicled on the lead pages of *Newstime*, but that was through no fault of her own, she knew.

Nancy seemed surprised at Sarah's question, and it was a moment before she answered. "It's coming along," she said finally. "I get over to the Library of Congress for a couple of hours every morning, and then write for a couple of hours in the afternoon."

Sarah had no idea what to say next, and after a moment or two, Nancy filled in the awkward silence by asking if there was a message.

"No, thanks," said Sarah. "All I really needed was to know where he was going." As she hung up, she realized that her call to the Dodman house had been as unnecessary as it was awkward. She had found out from it that she didn't have to go to the White House right away. Rudy had apparently changed his plans and had it covered. But whether it was necessary or not, she was heading for the pressroom. It would be buzzing about the log this morning. Even the old-timers, who usually slept all day in the pressroom's overstuffed chairs, would be awake.

She got out of bed and checked the weather from a bedroom window. From an oak wardrobe in the corner, she pulled out a brown tweed skirt, a natural wool cardigan, and a beige silk blouse, which, as more than one man had noted, was an almost perfect match to her thick, tawny hair. As she dressed, she thought back to the

21

phone call and the awkwardness she always felt around Nancy. It was so stupid, she thought, so pointless, all that guilt-induced babbling. There was nothing to feel guilty about and there probably never would be. Not if she left it up to Rudy, anyway. Never in her life, she thought, had she ever met a man more stubbornly faithful to his wife. Never in her life.

SEVERAL MILES away on Volta Place, Bertram Morris was trying very hard not to be irritated. He and Andy Latvala had, after all, been writing a column together for almost fifteen years now. Surely, he told himself, that was time enough for him to become tolerant of Latvala's eccentricities. But damn it! Every time something came up, Latvala was in North Carolina or Texas or one of those other godforsaken places where the University of Maryland's football and basketball teams played. The ostensible reason for his travels—at least the one they gave the IRS—was to gain an insight into politics outside Washington. But it was an open secret in the city that the primary reason for Latvala's travels was to follow the Terrapins to their games away from home. To Bertram Morris, Exeter and Harvard, it was unaccountable behavior, but he knew, though he tried to keep himself from thinking about it very often, that without Latvala, the column would be dead. The pols—the guys in the double-knit suits who got themselves elected state chairmen and enjoyed sitting around the bar with Latvala—wouldn't talk to Morris any more than Morris's Georgetown friends would talk to Latvala. And so, sitting in his federal row house, attempting to get through to Latvala in Texas, Morris was trying very hard to be patient.

On about the fifteenth ring, Latvala answered.

"Andy," said Morris, "have you heard about the *Post?*" They've got a week of Jenner's office log."

"His what?" Latvala asked sleepily.

"His log. You know, the record of whom he sees and when and for how long."

"Ah, well, that sounds good for a column or two. Who's the Old Man been spending his time with?"

"Not Boyston, that's one surprise. But then I suppose we always knew the 'my-Vice-President-my-partner' business was so much nonsense. Jenner scarcely knew the man when he put him on the ticket."

"But Boyston's a popular guy, you know. I talk to a lot of people who think the country'd be better off if he headed the ticket."

"No chance of that. He'll be lucky to stay on it." Morris had a hard time understanding where Latvala found the people he talked to anyway.

"Listen, I'll bet you . . ." Latvala began.

"There's something else too," Morris said, cutting Latvala off. "Crawford's never in the Oval Office either."

"C'mon now, does that really surprise you?" Latvala tended to have a more detached view of their joint endeavors than did Morris. "I've said time and time again that the guys on the inside who are most willing to talk about what's going on are usually the ones who know the least. Sometimes I know they're talking to us just to get back at whoever's cut them out of the action. The stories they peddle make that other guy look bad and them look great, of course. And sometimes," Latvala went on, warming to his subject, "I think they open up to us to get the kind of ego massage they're not getting at work. Crawford's the perfect example. He tells us what he wants us to think is going on, we build him up with a few favorable mentions in the column, and those sweet young things he likes to impress *are* impressed, but mostly because they don't understand a goddam thing about who's really got power in Washington."

One thing Morris had learned over the years was that when Latvala took off on one of these tangents, the best way to bring him back was not to argue with him, but to ignore what he was saying. "The Man is seeing Ewing for an hour every day," Morris said.

The tactic worked. "Now that is a surprise," Latvala observed. "I wonder what in the hell he's talking to him about?"

"Perhaps those Indians in Montana and their claims to coal lands? Ewing spent several years working on the Whitefeather reservation. I remember that much about him. What do you know?"

"Mostly just the bio. An M.D. from Johns Hopkins, a couple of years as a Peace Corps staff doctor in the Philippines. Then he came back and trained in psychiatry, and after that he worked on the Whitefeather reservation where he came to Jenner's attention. He was a lot more prominent during the presidential campaign than he has been since. I seem to remember rumors that he had fallen from grace and Jenner trying to discount them by saying that Ewing was one of the best friends he had in the world."

"What do you know about his personal life?"

"Not much. I think somebody told me he's living in Alexandria with an artist, Wendy something, I think her name was. To tell the truth, I really haven't tried to get close to Ewing, not since he told me one day he thought our seminars were immoral."

"Immoral!"

"Yeah, I asked him to speak at one, and he asked me how the folks attending our seminars got to be there. When I told him that they'd paid a couple hundred for the privilege, he delivered a long sermon about how all citizens should have equal access to public officials. It was immoral—that was his word—for some of them to be able to buy access by forking over to you and me."

"That's nonsense," said Morris, looking through a glass wall that been added to the back of his house, at a small classically designed pool. There were a few leaves floating in the water. He'd have to do something about that.

"I know it's nonsense. I'm just telling you what he said. And saying he's not going to be of much help to us in doping out what that log is about."

"Whom do you suggest we call?"

"Crawford for starters."

"Despite your just explaining to me that he doesn't know anything?"

"Christ, Bert. Sometimes you act like you really don't know how this game is played. You know Crawford's going to be really torn up about how this log makes him look, and he'll have cooked up some explanation for them with enough truth in it so we can use it. Crawford loves those embassy parties," Latvala added, unable to resist this dig at his partner, who also loved the embassy party circuit, "and if he wants to keep his name on the invitation lists, he's going to have to do something to restore his image as a presidential intimate."

Chapter 3

THE USUAL scattered groups of tourists were standing along Pennsylvania Avenue in front of the White House. Actually, the viewing from across the street in Lafayette Park was better. Over there you could stand back by the statue of Andy Jackson and get the whole of the mansion in your viewfinder. Or you could sit down, if you wanted, and rest your feet or feed the baby or check the guidebook to find out when the Air and Space Museum opened. But at some point, almost everyone crossed over to this side to peer through the iron fence at the shining, immaculate building. Maybe, Sarah Hoff thought, it was because the White House seemed almost unreal, so serenely did it sit in the middle of downtown Washington. You felt you had to check it closely, maybe, to be sure that it was a real building that people used, people who worried and made mistakes, who loved and hated the way human beings always had. As well as she knew what went on inside, Sarah realized that when she saw the White House from out here, it did seem to stand apart from the muddle and confusion of everyday life.

Several of the tourists watched Sarah closely as she walked up to the northwest gate and handed her press pass through to one of the security guards in the glassed-in guard house. As she waited, Sarah could feel a small family group near the gate assessing her, trying to figure out if she were somebody they could tell their friends back home about. She turned to look at them with the idea of staring them down, but when she really saw them, she knew she couldn't embarrass them. A mother, a father, two boys in early adolescence, they weren't beautiful people, not by a long shot. But they were so scrubbed and earnest. Sarah smiled at them as the guard buzzed the gate open.

As she walked up the asphalt drive toward the West Wing of the White House, she shoved her hands into the pockets of her heavy sweater, encountering in one of them a piece of salt-water taffy left from the last time she'd worn the sweater. She had to quit eating junk food, she vowed to herself as she neared the West Lobby, turned left, and headed for the special pressroom entrance. As she passed the West Lobby she noted that a marine in dress blues was standing outside the door. Although his presence signaled that Jenner was in the White House, the marine's function was strictly ceremonial. If she tried to walk through the lobby door, he wouldn't stop her; in fact, he'd probably hold the door open for her. But guards inside or the officers in the glassed-in hut just to the west of the lobby entrance would be quick to let her know that she had wandered out of bounds and to direct her down the drive to the pressroom.

It had been a swimming pool once, the place they now called the pressroom. Whenever she went to work at the White House, that fact inevitably popped into her head—as did the stories about Johnson and Kennedy skinny-dipping in the pool. Every part of the White House had a story connected with it, Hoff thought, pausing just outside the pressroom door. The North Portico straight ahead was more than a magnificent twelve-columned entryway, it was a part of the White House that Andy Jackson had added on. Curious that, Andrew Jackson, the unsophisticated man of the people, overseeing the construction of this elegant piece of classical architecture.

She looked up at the mansion's second floor, or the third floor, really, if you counted the level the pressroom was on. She admired the large Palladian window in the private living quarters and thought of the White House's present occupant. He had often been described as a Jacksonian figure, as a simple, straightforward westerner. But that was image, she suspected. She thought the real Zern Jenner to be a complex man who, in spite of his self-proclaimed feelings of oneness with the common people, had probably always thought that he should lead them, that he should be President. What was the phrase in Freud? "The feeling of conqueror," that was it. She was sure Jenner had had that since he'd been a small boy growing up in Montana. And what he'd been willing to do to fulfill that vision he'd had of himself boggled the mind. In his campaign for the presidency, he had worked three years, three *years* of introducing himself to strangers and sleeping in motels and going over the same ground again and again. She opened the door into the pressroom, remembering the *Times* correspondent who had watched Jenner campaign and observed, "Anybody willing to run for President should automatically be disqualified."

As she made her way through the beige and brown pressroom, she noted it was unusually crowded, considering it was not yet 10:30. She spoke to a few of the reporters who were gathered in groups talking, each trying to find out what the others knew without giving away any of his own ideas. Then she found her path blocked by Jane Minnick, or "Crazy Jane," as much of the press corps called her. She was a woman of medium height, in her thirties, a little overweight, but not especially unattractive—except for the efforts she made to be stylish, and those were inevitably disastrous. She had recently acquired a pair of designer glasses with gray-tinted lenses. For some reason, they always sat crookedly on her face, and the light they cast only made her complexion seem more sallow. She had also tried bleaching her hair, but even she could see that the brassy color she ended up with was all wrong, so now it was dyed brown, a dead, flat brown, which absorbed the light instead of reflecting it. She projected an air of being constantly tired and harassed, and if you made the mistake of asking her how she was, she would go on forever about the evil forces trying to do her in. But Sarah tried to be kind. She thought some of her male colleagues were cruel, the way they treated Jane. She remembered how they'd used Jane to help break in Mark Westfield, Jenner's press secretary, when he was new. For months, a group of reporters had penned passionate love notes to Jane and signed Westfield's name to them. The notes had set forth elaborate reasons why Westfield couldn't declare his love openly, the chief being that the CIA was watching him. It was reasoning paranoic enough to fit Jane's perception of the world. And so for months, until the correspondents tired of the hoax and quit writing the notes, Jane mooned around Westfield, while the press corps muffled their laughter over the press secretary's obvious discomfort and his puzzlement over what he'd done to inspire Jane's ardor.

"Sarah, they think I did it," Jane whispered, grabbing her arm.

"They think you did what, Jane?"

"They think I leaked the President's log to Frye."

"Now, Jane, that doesn't make any sense. If you'd had a copy of the log, you wouldn't give it to Frye, you'd put it out in one of the papers you write for."

"But they're following me again this morning," Jane said, with real panic in her voice. "I get so scared, at night especially."

"Now, look, there's just no reason for anybody to be following you. None. But if you really do get frightened when you're by yourself, why don't you call me and we'll talk for a few minutes until you feel better." Even as she was offering her help to Jane, Sarah knew she would probably curse herself later for getting involved. But however imaginary her phantoms were, the woman's fright was real, and Sarah felt obliged to try to help her.

"I will call you," Jane said, still whispering conspiratorially, "But when I do, I won't say it's me. I'll say my name's Scarlet. I can't use my own name, because the phones are bugged."

Sarah disengaged herself from Jane and walked back past the camera platform and downstairs to where *Newstime* had a small cubicle. On the way, she wondered what had originally inspired Jane's paranoia. Whatever its source, Jane's neurosis didn't seem to affect the way she wrote. She wasn't a hard-digging reporter—which probably explained why so many people in the administration granted her interviews. The pieces she did tended to be pretty puffy, but they were written in a polished, beautifully clear and lucid prose.

There was nobody downstairs except in the *Newstime* cubicle where she could see Rudy sitting, scribbling furiously on a yellow legal pad. "Hey there," she said, coming up to him from behind, "I know you're scared I'll get your job, but you don't have to work that hard."

Dodman, who was usually ready for banter, didn't respond to her sally. "You've seen the *Post*, haven't you?" he asked.

"Not yet, but I heard the story on the morning news."

"Look at this for a minute," he directed, handing her a *Post* folded back to the page where the log was reprinted. "Tell me what you notice about Ewing."

She looked over the log quickly. "Well, he's in there a lot, which I wouldn't have known from listening to CBC. Did you see what they did with this story this morning?" But his look told her he wasn't interested in hearing what the network had done, and so she glanced over the log again. "And he's in there every day," she said, noting the places where Ewing's name was entered in the log, "every day at the same time for about the same time. So?"

Rudy stood, came out of the cubicle, and looked around. Even though he didn't see anyone, he lowered his voice. "It's almost like the President has an appointment with him rather than he with the President."

"I don't follow you," said Sarah. "What are you getting at?"

"Is everybody *blind?*" asked Rudy. "Up there in the pressroom, they're talking about maybe Ewing's got a special political mission, or maybe he's on an assignment to keep the Indian situation in Montana from blowing up. How come nobody's mentioning that the guy's a shrink?"

"Rudy, are you *crazy?*" Sarah asked, grasping the implication of his question. And, under the circumstances, her response was so ironic that it made both of them laugh.

"Listen," Rudy said, "I know how it sounds, like I've been reading too much Allen Drury or something."

"Fletcher Knebel, you mean. He's the one who wrote *The Night of Camp David*, the book that has a President going crazy in it."

"Well, anyway," Rudy went on, "it didn't even occur to me at first, it seems so outlandish. And then Nancy pointed out that Ewing was a psychiatrist, and I couldn't quit thinking about it. One o'clock every afternoon he's in the Oval Office, just like Jenner was regularly scheduled for a daily mind-straightening. And then I remembered all those rumors that circulated during the last campaign about how Jenner'd had to see a shrink to straighten himself out after he lost his second race for the Senate. I know it sounds ridiculous at first, but I've been sitting here writing it out, and it does all fit together, if you suppose that Ewing is the President's psychiatrist."

"Tell me more about the rumors during the last campaign. That was before my time." She took off her heavy sweater and extracted the piece of taffy from the pocket.

"Well, if you remember your ancient history," said Dodman, smiling at Sarah, who was perhaps five years younger than he, "Jenner ran twice for the Senate and lost both times before he finally made it on his third try. He's admitted himself how depressed he was after the second loss, how nothing gave him pleasure or seemed significant. How there was just no reason to get out of bed in the morning. And then, as he tells it in his campaign biography, he's supposed to have had some sort of existential awakening. He said he realized one afternoon, as he was out riding on his ranch, that nobody's life has any meaning except what they put into it. As I remember, he used some metaphor about every man's existence being bankrupt unless he is willing to invest meaning in it. And with that revelation, Jenner says, he started running for the Senate again, and this time, the third time, he made it.

"The thing I kept hearing during the last presidential campaign, though, was that Jenner hadn't been able to pull himself together after his second loss, that, in fact, he'd had to see a psychiatrist over a period of several months—as long as a year, one of the stories went."

"Did anybody try to check out the rumors that he'd seen a psychiatrist?"

"Everybody was checking them out, but nobody got anywhere."

"Did anybody ever just come out and ask Jenner?" she said, deciding not to eat the taffy just yet, not while she was talking to Rudy.

"I don't think so," he said. "In the first place, doing that would have implied that he'd lied about it in the biography he wrote for the campaign. You know how rumors fly in an election year, and there seemed to be no more substance to this one than any of them. So there never was a strong enough reason to accuse him of not telling the truth. I talked to Jack about it several times, and we pretty much agreed that asking Jenner about it directly was not a good idea. Usually the only opportunities there were to ask him questions were in public forums, and you can't just stand up and say, 'Senator, have you ever seen a psychiatrist?' A question like that sounds as though it has some basis to it, and it smears the candidate no matter what his answer is."

"I wonder," said Sarah, "if it's possible that you might have got the whole thing a little out of proportion. Thousands of people see psychiatrists. I was in California last Easter, and I think half the population there is in therapy of some kind or other. It was suggested to me more than once, in fact," she said, smiling and holding up the candy in her hand, "that I should see a shrink and break my junk-food habit. Anyway, if Jenner saw a psychiatrist after his second run for the Senate, that wouldn't disqualify him from being President, surely."

"No, not at all, especially if he'd been open about it from the beginning. But to have it come out in the last few months of the campaign would have seriously damaged his candidacy. Think of it in light of the Eagleton incident. Tom Eagleton hadn't just been seeing a psychiatrist, of course. He'd had shock treatment, which is another matter entirely. But that whole affair was so devastating for the McGovern campaign that I think if it had been discovered during the heat of the last presidential election that one of the candidates had had psychiatric treatment which hadn't been previously disclosed, well, I just think it would have called up the Eagleton debacle in everybody's mind. It would have helped fix a loser's image on Jenner, and in an election as close as the last one was, it could definitely have made the difference."

"And, of course, if he's seeing a psychiatrist now, it would make the difference in the next election."

"That's right. I don't think the American public is ready yet for psychiatric sessions in the Oval Office. Except maybe for that part of the public living in California."

Sarah laughed. "O.K., look," she said, "there's just one point I'm not clear on. You think Ewing might be acting as his psychiatrist now. Do you think Ewing was also Jenner's psychiatrist after he lost that second Senate race?"

"I don't know. All I'm sure of is that there were rumors during the campaign that Jenner had seen a shrink, and that there's currently a situation which looks like he might be seeing one now. I suppose one of the first things to do is check to see if Ewing *could* have been his psychiatrist after Jenner lost the second Senate race. I don't even know if the two knew each other then. Or if Ewing was even a psychiatrist at the time. What is he? Early forties maybe? We should check the dates and see when he finished his psychiatric training. And what years he was in the Peace Corps. Then we can see how it all hangs together."

"I'll go over to the office and look through the files and see what I can come up with. I'm also going to get hold of Wendy Greene. She's the artist Ewing was living with, and I think they're still together. She came to a cocktail party I had last year before the Women's Caucus art benefit and we talked a little. I'll give her a call." Sarah volunteered these efforts even though she had no desire to part from Rudy. She had never been precisely clear on what drew her to him, but the attraction was there, and she felt it now, as she usually did, no matter how intense their discussions. As far as his appearance went, he wasn't nearly as spectacular as many of the men she knew. Although he was over six feet tall and solidly built, he had the hint of fragility about him which blond, pale-lashed men often have. And there were so many things about him which were, to Hoff's way of thinking, impossibly old-fashioned. Still, whenever she was around him, she was physically aware of him, always noticing things like how far his hand was away from hers and calculating the odds they might touch.

"That'd be great," Rudy was saying. "I'd particularly like to hear from Wendy Greene. And I think I'll call Jack and see if he wouldn't like to go see Dale Basinger with me. Before I get into this any farther, I'd like to ask Basinger directly what Ewing's doing in there every day. Basinger's one guy on the White House staff I think will deal straight with me about it.

"You know," he went on, running his fingers through his short blond hair, "this morning I was really up for this story, thinking of all the places it might go. And I guess I still am. But now it's all beginning to be a little frightening. The only other time the American people have really had a candid look at what goes on in the Oval Office was with the Nixon tapes. And now if this damn log shows Jenner's talking out his troubles with a psychiatrist, what are the people supposed to think? How much do you suppose it takes to push them over the line to where they no longer have *any* faith in the leaders produced by the democratic process?"

Sarah knew he didn't want an answer so much as he wanted someone to listen. And she did listen, though at the same time she was wondering if she had found a clue to the response Rudy was capable of eliciting from her. There was sex in it, but there was more besides, and perhaps part of it came from his genuine concern with the consequences of his actions, a concern she found very rarely in the men she knew. Most of them seemed to be playing games, the Superstud game, or the Superachiever game, and she played her own kind of game with them, she knew. The Beautiful-but-Brittle-Girl-Reporter game, she supposed you could call it. Rudy loved winning and the risk of losing, and in that way he was as much a gamesman as anyone. But he was also willing to consider what the game really meant. In the macho world of Washington, where calling a politician or reporter "tough-minded" was the highest form of compliment, Rudy cared what effect his actions had. That made him rare.

What also made him rare, she observed to herself, deliberately veering away from a line of thought which was becoming too serious, was that she hadn't slept with him.

Chapter 4

PRESIDENTIAL ASSISTANT Dale Basinger had one of the largest, most elegant offices in the West Wing of the White House. A high-ceilinged room with exquisitely worked moldings, it was of a scale sufficient to hold a large conference table and a comfortable seating arrangement around the fireplace, as well as Basinger's desk. On two walls were tall, elegantly draped windows, and out of those on the west side of the room, one could see the old Executive Office Building, an exuberant Victorian wedding cake of a structure. The windows facing south had high bushes in front of them for security, but what was missed by having the view blocked off was made up for by the carefully tended seasonal plantings in the window boxes: daffodils and tulips in the spring, geraniums in the summer, and now, in the fall, gold and yellow mums. Basinger often marveled at how the flowers around the White House were always at their peak. There was no dismal dying off of greenery here as there was at his home in McLean. Here, one day the flowers were fresh and crisp, and the next day they were gone. And the White House lawns never seemed to have dandelions or crabgrass either, he had noted. How did the White House gardeners do it, he had wondered, especially on the inhospitable red clay which underlay most of the Washington area? Growing grass on that red clay, as nearly as he could figure out after a few weekend efforts at his Virginia home, constituted an unnatural act.

At this particular moment, however, Basinger was not thinking of the well-tended beauty of the White House grounds, but of the two men who had just left his office and of the mission on which they had come to him. Seated in one of the dark green easy chairs in front of the fireplace, he considered that there weren't many reporters he would have made time to see on such short notice, particularly on a day like today, when things were wild in the pressroom because of the leak of the Jenner log, and Joanie, his secretary, was being flooded with calls from newsmen. But when Rudy Dodman and Jack Sasser called and said it was urgent that they see him, he found a way to make space in his day for them. He had come to know them well enough to trust their judgment about whether it really was a matter of urgency, and this time, as usual, they'd been accurate in their assessment.

Like everybody else, they had questions about the log, but their questions were focusing on Ewing. Basinger had given Dodman and Sasser the response that the President had directed that morning be given out to any questions about what certain staff members were doing in the Oval Office. "You tell them it's none of their business," the President had said. "I want you to be that tough—though you can try being a little more polite about it, if you want. You tell them that what goes on between a President and his staff is a confidential matter."

Basinger had known that response wouldn't satisfy Dodman and Sasser, but he'd given it as ordered. What really surprised him—shocked was probably a better word—were the suspicions they had voiced that Ewing wasn't seeing the President as a staffer at all.

"Look, Dale," Dodman had said, "there's one important fact about Ewing which makes his presence in the Oval Office look like something besides a staff matter."

"The guy's a psychiatrist, to put it simply," Sasser had added. "We could quite accurately write a story, 'President Had Lengthy Sessions with Psychiatrist.'"

"Oh, come on now," Basinger had responded.

"Listen, Dale," Dodman had said, "you've got to think how it looks on the log. One hour a day set aside for Ewing—and the guy is a shrink. And you have to remember, too, all those campaign rumors about your man and about how he cracked up the second time he lost a Senate race."

"Are you fellows back to that garbage again?"

"Think of it this way," Sasser had said, leaning forward. "We've got some pieces here and the most logical way to fit them together is to assume Ewing is the President's psychiatrist. Have you got something to tell us which will prove that *isn't* how they fit?"

Basinger had thought about it for a minute. They were wrong, he knew, but it was hard to say precisely how he knew that. Mostly, he supposed, it was just from having observed the President and Ewing close up. They were like a father and his adult son, with the President valuing Ewing's advice and confiding in him from time to time, but still maintaining dominance in the relationship. There was nothing that fit into a patient-doctor pattern. "All I can say is that from everything I've seen, I know that you're wrong."

"That's not enough, Dale," Sasser had said. "I think we need to know exactly what Ewing is doing in there."

"The President was adamant this morning about that. I'll ask him, but I think the odds are he's not going to say what any of his meetings are about."

"At the least," Dodman had said, "he could confirm that Ewing's seeing him on the public's business and not on private matters."

Basinger had agreed to talk to the President, and now, sitting in the green chair by the fireplace, waiting for the call to let him know the President was free, he thought about the man he was going to see. He hadn't known him as long as had many of the others on the White House staff, only since Jenner had decided—about six years ago it was now—to run for the presidency. Basinger had at that time been a partner in a polling firm that had done some political work, and one of Jenner's lieutenants had called him and asked him to come in and talk with the senator. Basinger had come away from that meeting impressed not only with Jenner's incisive intelligence, but also with his ambition. He had the fire in the belly, the hunger for high office that Basinger had come to think was essential if a political candidate were to succeed. Within a week, Basinger had managed to get a leave of absence from his firm, and he went to work full time for Jenner as his personal pollster. Gradually his influence with the candidate—and then with the President—had grown. Not only did he know how to obtain and interpret polling results, it turned out he had another asset, a sort of inner mechanism which told him, even when there were no numbers to read, when a course of action was wise politically and when it was not. He saw contingencies and consequences that others

40

overlooked. He wasn't sure what accounted for his skill, but he recognized, as did the President, what an invaluable asset it was.

And that was the story of how a poor boy from Wisconsin had come to the White House, he told himself. He owed it all to Jenner, really. How many men would have been willing to admit an outsider to the inner circle of his long-time advisers? And now to this man who had trusted him so much, he was supposed to go and say, "Sir, Mr. President, sir, are you stretching out on the sofa and letting Ewing analyze you every day at one P.M.?" Christ, it was stupid. How could he do that? But he knew he would, because even such an absurd suspicion had to be cut off quickly before it grew and festered.

Basinger's phone buzzed, signaling that the President wanted him. He gathered up the notes he had made during his conversation with Dodman and Sasser and headed out the door, through his secretary's office, and down the hall to the Oval Office.

In the anteroom just outside where the President was working, Basinger nodded to Tom Lester, the President's civilian aide, and he stopped for a moment by the desk of Gretchen Burrows, the President's personal secretary. Clearly, she had been crying. The Oval Office log was her responsibility, and though no one suspected her of being the source of the leak, she nevertheless felt to blame for whatever moment of inattention had permitted someone else to copy it. Basinger offered a few words meant to comfort her, and then he walked into the Oval Office.

It would have been a pleasing room decorated almost any way, but Basinger particularly liked the subdued greens and golds that Jenner had chosen. That, and the western art. The President had moved a Remington bronze from the ground floor of the White House to join the one already in the Oval Office, and now the two statues stood on thick pedestals in front of the windows to the rose garden. On either side of the tall rose garden windows, through which one could see the mansion, landscapes of the West had been hung. Basinger particularly liked the Moran painting of the Tetons, which, when it had first come into the White House, had been hanging outside the Cabinet Room.

As Basinger entered the Oval Office, the President was standing behind his desk, looking out tall, rounded windows through which one could see all the way to the Washington Monument, more than a thousand yards away. Jenner was not an exceptionally tall man, six feet perhaps, but Basinger noted, as he had many times before, how the President's lean, rangy build made him appear to be tall. As Jenner turned toward him, Basinger also noted that the President looked tired. His skin fit tightly to his bones and muscle, so that, except for the fan of wrinkles around his eyes, there were few lines on his face. But he was slightly pale, and there were dark circles under his eyes.

Whatever burdens he was carrying, the President seemed to be trying to put them aside for the moment. "You know, Dale," he said, "Washington autumns are one of the country's great underrated phenomena. Everybody talks about Washington springs, but just look at those trees out there, gold and red and orange. They're gorgeous, even looking at them through this." He gestured at the six-inch-thick bulletproof glass the Secret Service had installed over the windows. "Maybe they seem such a marvel to me," he chuckled, sitting down at his desk, "because there were so few trees where I grew up. And in Montana, autumn lasts just a second or two. One minute it's summer, and then you blink and there's a blizzard."

"It really is a glorious day, sir. About fifty degrees now, not a cloud in sight."

"I'd open the doors and let some of that autumn air in here," said Jenner, "except for the damn flies."

Both men laughed, remembering the Jenner administration's first spring when the President had complained about being unable to leave the huge door to the Rose Garden open, because if he did his office was invaded by flies. That presidential complaint led to the White House bureaucracy's producing a twenty-page memo on the subject of flies in the Oval Office. In neatly tabulated appendices, the memo set forth every conceivable solution, from a screen door to devices for electrocuting the flies. It was a perfect example of the overreaction of the bureaucracy to any presidential wish or complaint, however small. Rather than taking any of the actions outlined in the memo, Jenner had decided instead simply to save it to remind himself of the fuss his slightest whim could create.

A red-jacketed Filipino mess steward entered the room. "Can I get you some coffee, sir?" he asked Basinger.

"Thanks. Black, please," he said, and in seconds he was served a steaming cup of coffee in a white-and-gold cup. The cup was precisely placed in its saucer so that the gold presidential seal on the side of it was facing him.

As he watched the steward leave the room, Basinger reflected that it always made him a little uncomfortable to be waited upon. Maybe if you grew up in Oshkosh you never did get used to the idea of servants, even ones as professional as the mess stewards. Basinger knew it wasn't really he that the stewards were concerned with. They saw him only in terms of the President, and they looked to his, Basinger's, needs only insofar as doing so made Jenner's life easier. Their mindset was military— a special arrangement allowed them to enlist in the United States Navy and enter the steward service even though they were Philippine citizens. And their loyalty was to the Commander-in-Chief. Still, there were times when Basinger would have preferred to get his own coffee.

"What is it you need, Dale?" asked the President, breaking into his thoughts.

"I spent some time this morning with Rudy Dodman and Jack Sasser from *Newstime* and, like everybody else, they're poring over the log. They've taken what seems to me a pretty strange tack on it, but I still wanted to talk to you about it." Basinger realized that he was having some trouble getting to the point but, damn it, the President didn't need this. "Well, it's Dodman, I think," he went on, "who's come up with the hare-brained theory that since Ewing's a psychiatrist, maybe, well, that is, he wonders if Malcolm couldn't be treating you. I know it's a crazy idea, sir, but just because it is so crazy, I thought we should kill it right away."

The President shook his head slowly from side to side. "Well, that's damned sure one response I hadn't counted on. What on earth do you suppose started Dodman thinking that way?"

"He mentioned rumors during the last campaign, stories that you'd seen a psychiatrist back in Montana when you lost your second Senate race."

"That wasn't the only rumor going around," observed the President. "There was one story that Mrs. Jenner and I had engaged in some spouse-swapping orgies in Billings. I was supposed to have been involved with Sue Swanton, especially. You've met the Swantons—Mary and I have known them for years. I don't know if you remember or not, but some campaign trickster, apparently operating on the basis of that rumor, fixed it so that at several of our stops, the band struck up 'Sweet Sue' as I got off the plane."

Basinger shook his head. "That's the first I've heard of that. Campaign rumors really can be amazing."

"Wasn't it Mark Westfield who said that a political campaign was the only place he knew where sound traveled faster than light? But anyway, what about Dodman?"

"Well, he took the campaign rumors, put them together with Ewing's background and his one P.M. meetings with you, and decided maybe Malcolm was your psychiatrist. I think the best way to knock down his crazy idea would be to announce whatever project it is that Ewing's working on for you. That way you don't have to dignify the nonsense about his being your psychiatrist with a direct denial."

The President was quiet. The muscles in his jaw flexed as he clenched his teeth, and his relaxed, conversational mood vanished. "Dale, I can't do that," he said flatly. "In fact, it's crucial that I not do that."

"Yes, sir," said Basinger, trying to tighten his words to match the President's. No matter how many times the President pulled these abrupt mood changes on him, they still threw him a little off balance. Early in their acquaintance, he had concluded that Jenner simply did not realize the effect this blowing hot and cold had on people. To have him cordially agreeing with you one minute and abruptly dismissing you the next was disconcerting to say the least. He tended to do it mostly with those who were closest to him, so in a way it was a compliment. But it took more than a little getting used to.

Besides, what could be so special about Ewing's project that the President wouldn't even explain to him why it couldn't be made public? On almost all domestic matters, he, Basinger, was in the President's confidence. "I think I should tell Dodman and Sasser," he said finally, trying to push aside everything except the problem at hand, "that Ewing is definitely seeing you in some official capacity, even though we won't say what it is. If we refuse even to confirm he's in here officially, rather than on a personal basis, we'll just increase their suspicions."

"You can tell them that much," said the President. "You go ahead with that, but we won't go one step farther. I've been thinking about this all morning, and it occurs to me that what we really have here is an issue of executive privilege. I know the lawyers like to use that term to talk about the Executive Branch keeping information from the Courts and the Congress but, as I see it, it applies here too. I'm not being idiosyncratic or secretive to refuse to talk about the daily log to reporters or to set out the details of the meetings I have in here. I have a right to confidentiality from the press just as much as from Congress and the Courts. The national interest would not be served by my telling them about those meetings. How can I expect the discussions in this office to be open and free if everyone has to sit around and worry about how his words will look on the front page of the *Post*?"

"Or in a book," Basinger interjected softly. Early on he had decided he would never write one of those kiss-and-tell books when his White House days were over. A President had to have at least one person around him who he knew wasn't rushing home at night to record every word he had uttered when he was angry, every mistake he had made when he was tired. A President deserved at least one person around him whose silence he could depend on.

The President, deep in his own thoughts, took no notice of Basinger's comment. "As I think back on the other men who've worked in this room," he went on, "it seems to me that the history of the presidency in the twentieth century is the history of a gradually weakening institution. Think how many Presidents have been brought to their knees, even destroyed in this office. Think how rare it is for a President to serve out the two terms the law allows him and then to leave this office with the people still having faith and confidence in him. Gerald Ford was denied election in his own right, Nixon was forced to resign, and Johnson not to seek a second full term. Kennedy was assassinated, and Truman left office under a cloud which took years to dissipate. Hoover was defeated in his try for a second term, Wilson left the White House a broken man, and we could talk about Taft's defeat and Teddy Roosevelt's abortive attempt to get a third term and McKinley's assassination. Only a few men in the whole century have triumphed over this office instead of being defeated by it.

"In fact, it's rather ironic, that phrase 'executive privilege,' because it seems to me the presidency has become an office with very little privilege attached to it. It's almost as though the President becomes a symbol when he's elected, a symbol to be torn down and destroyed when the nation's frustrations reach a certain pitch. Far from being privileged, he can't have any faults, any flaws, because if he does, they'll be magnified and turned on him and used to bring him down." The President swiveled his chair around, stood, and began walking back and forth with a determined stride. "Well, I for one am not going to help in the process of making this office more vulnerable. You can tell Dodman and Sasser that Ewing is in here every day in his role as a presidential aide, but tell them nothing more. I have a right to confidential meetings with the people who work for me, and I'm not going to undermine it by going over the log with the White House press corps and telling them what's going on when."

"I understand, Mr. President." Basinger didn't want to sound sycophantic—there were always enough people around any President willing to tell him what they thought he wanted to hear. But there were a couple of points which needed to be made. "Sir, I don't think you need concern yourself too much with the idea of being destroyed by the presidency. In fact, there's every indication you'll win a second term."

"It's not a personal thing, Dale," said the President, stopping his pacing and sitting on the edge of his desk, a huge walnut affair which had been especially built for Woodrow Wilson. "It's the office itself I worry about. I don't see how, with the presidency weakened, this country can cope with the problems she faces. Pick any article off the front pages this morning. Take the one about the Whitefeather Indians in Montana, for instance. They're bringing a suit which claims they own vast stretches of Wyoming and Montana land, and that land just happens to have tons of coal under it. It's an incredibly complex matter, which could take forever for the courts to work out, and meanwhile there's a good possibility of violence and an even better one of keeping the mining operations from getting started up. I'm going to have to get involved, not because it's Montana, but because this country needs that coal, and because, as President, I just may carry enough symbolic weight to get both sides to step back and take a second look. But what happens in the next crisis like this, or the next after that, if we let this office grow weaker until it doesn't have any kind of moral force?"

The question was rhetorical, Basinger knew, but he felt some sort of response was called for: "Well, at least we haven't got students rioting in the streets," he said, remembering what he'd heard on the morning news about trouble in Japan.

"Yes, but they're rioting about us, don't forget," said the President, immediately grasping the reference to disturbances in Yokosuka. "They're screaming for us to

48

get out of there, and any sign of weakness or vacillation in our government is going to make them scream louder. The moral force I'm talking about isn't just a domestic necessity."

"I understand your point. And I agree that it would be a sign of weakness for you to submit to a grilling on the details of your daily log. But I don't think you can get away with ignoring the fact that it leaked. You're never going to put a lid on stories about it until you at least face down the press corps. I think you should have a press conference in the next day or two. You might think about talking to the press corps in the same way you were talking to me earlier. Explain to them that you have a right to confidentiality, a need for it."

"Maybe," said the President, walking around behind the desk and sitting down in his chair.

"Even if you decide not to do that, you should go ahead with the press conference. If we just keep sending Westfield out to say you won't comment on the log, the conspiracy theories are really going to start to build. Dodman's will seem mild by comparison with what some of those guys will come up with. If you go out and talk to them, though, your very willingness to meet them will help counter the notion we're hiding something, and maybe they'll get off the stories about the log and onto other things."

"You're probably right," the President agreed, leaning back in his chair. His face was still tired, but his manner reflected none of the tension which had marked earlier parts of the meeting. "Tomorrow afternoon's fairly open, Dale. Why don't you see about setting it up then?"

As Basinger started to leave, the President called after him, "Make it the East Room, Dale. This one's sure to draw a crowd."

Chapter 5

"MR. CRAWFORD," his secretary Violet's voice
came over the intercom, "a call from Bertram Morris on
line two. Would you like to speak with him?"

"Yes, yes," Crawford said. "Get him on the line and
I'll be on in a minute." He had been expecting the call
all day. In fact, he was more than a little put out that
Morris hadn't called sooner. He walked across the intri-
cately inlaid parquet floor of his Executive Office Building office and put the *Washington Star*, which he had
been reading, neatly on the sofa table. He'd just let Morris wait on the line a minute or two. That would convey
the message.

Crawford was a man of average height, in his mid-
fifties, who carried the extra pounds he had put on over

the years in about as graceful a fashion as he could have hoped. They weren't all lodged in his gut, but spread pretty evenly over his body, so that reporters tended to describe him as "stocky," even as "portly" on occasion, but hardly ever as "fat." His face, however, was definitely fat, and as it had become fuller and rounder over the years, his features had seemed to diminish in size, giving him a swollen, vaguely threatening look, for which he tried to compensate with noisy attempts at heartiness.

More years ago than he liked to remember, he had come to Washington, fresh from having finished college on the G. I. bill. He'd been thrilled to land a job on the staff of a congressman from his home state of Oregon. It would be good experience, he told his wife, Kitty, for when he went back to Portland and ran for office himself. But time passed, there were children who had to be sent to college, one thing and another, and he had never gone back to Oregon. Instead, he had taken a series of staff jobs on the Hill until finally he had become the legislative assistant to a new senator from Montana, Zern Jenner.

He'd been a great help to Jenner in those early days, combining a seemingly inexhaustible enthusiasm with a meticulous attention to detail. But in the middle of Jenner's second term, something had happened to Crawford, something he couldn't have described if he'd been asked about it, because he tried constantly to distract himself from what was happening. He began to drink too much and to carry on affairs with a number of young women, all of whom were impressed that Crawford worked for Jenner, a man increasingly perceived as having a good chance at the presidency.

The thing that had happened to Crawford was that he had recognized his own mortality. Life, he had come to understand, though not on the most conscious level, is an experience which every day becomes more limited. Every day a few of the doors are closed; every day the number of choices becomes smaller. He was never going to go back to Oregon and run. He was never going to be his own boss. He'd be a staffer until he died or retired, somebody else's errand boy.

The drinking and wenching that followed made him less valuable, but Jenner kept him on through the campaign and then took him to the White House out of a sense of loyalty. There were still times when Crawford served his President well—he had hundreds of contacts in Washington, most of whom were untroubled by the change in him. And with these men and women, Crawford could be effective at presenting the President's case.

But he was not as busy as the many White House staffers whom the President knew to be thoroughly dependable, and so he had had time in the last few years to become a regular on Washington's party circuit. He spent night after night at black-tie dinners on Embassy Row or in Georgetown, sometimes with his wife, Kitty, but just as often he was alone, at least when he arrived. When it was time to leave, he was frequently observed to be in the company of any one of a number of attractive young women.

He finished rearranging the magazines and newspapers on the sofa table and, deciding he had kept Morris waiting long enough, he walked back to his desk and picked up the phone.

"Bertie, how are you?"

"I've been well, Allen, and yourself?"

"Well, it's been hectic around here as always. I keep thinking I'll get off for a few weeks and go play golf somewhere, but something always comes up the President needs me for."

"Listen, Allen, down to business for a minute. Have

52

you got any ideas about the log? What it shows about the Jenner administration, perhaps?"

"It's a damn shame it was leaked," said Crawford, easing into a subject he'd been giving careful thought to all morning. "I think one question you should ask is who leaked it. Somebody on the staff is willing to violate the President's confidence by making it public, probably because they see some benefit to themselves coming out of having that particular section of the log in the newspapers."

"Do you have any theories about who that might be?"

"I've got more than theories," said Crawford, though he did not. "Now just ask yourself who comes out looking good from those pages that were leaked."

"Well, Ewing, I suppose. Nobody thought he was spending much time with Jenner."

"You're damn right," said Crawford. "He comes out looking like the President's chief adviser or something. Now I know for a fact," said Crawford, though he did not, "that those pages that leaked were very unusual. Ewing hardly ever sees the President and, Bertie, you know how often I'm in there. The part of the log the *Post* got doesn't show that. Just ask yourself who comes out the big winner from this leak."

"I see what you mean," Morris said, already building the column's headline in his mind. He could call it "Winners and Losers from the Latest White House Leak." That sounded good.

"Listen, Allen," he said to Crawford, "I appreciate your guidance. Will you be at the German Embassy tonight by any chance?"

"Wouldn't miss it. See you then."

As soon as he hung up, Bertram Morris tried to put a call through to Malcolm Ewing. It was only fair, after all, to give him a chance to comment on a column which would imply that he was responsible for leaking a presidential document. But when Ewing's secretary announced he was not in, Morris went ahead and started writing. If you checked out every last detail, after all, you'd never get a column done.

He puzzled for a moment over exactly which complimentary formula he would use to repay Allen Crawford for his help. Should he call him "savvy Presidential Assistant Allen Crawford" in the column? He'd used that phrase a lot lately. Better go with "Jenner's crafty political operative, Allen Crawford." That formula, together with the column's hint that Crawford spent a lot more time with the President than the leaked document indicated, would tell most Washington insiders that Crawford was Morris's source. Over the years, though, Morris had found that his sources would rather have the complimentary mention than keep their identities secret. Yes, "crafty political operative," that's what he'd use.

Back in the Executive Office Building, Crawford was thinking about the new blonde secretary he'd noticed down the hall. Maybe tomorrow he'd ask her to join him for a few sets of late afternoon tennis on the White House courts, and then drinks and dinner after. That approach had never yet failed.

As she drove down the George Washington Memorial Parkway toward Alexandria, Sarah Hoff went over in her mind what she had found out digging through *Newstime*'s files. The first and most important thing, of course, was that Malcolm Ewing could not have been Zern Jenner's psychiatrist back in the days when Jenner had been an unsuccessful Senate candidate. Ewing hadn't even been a psychiatrist then, the *Newstime* files had showed. While Jenner was unsuccessfully fighting political battles in Montana, Ewing was in medical school at Johns Hopkins, and from there he moved to even more distant parts, serving as a Peace Corps staff doctor in Manila.

Sarah glanced away from the road a moment and admired the autumn sun sparkling on the Potomac. Then, her eyes on the roadway once more, she began to evaluate the information she had collected. The fact that Ewing hadn't even known Jenner until the late sixties didn't prove anything about what he was doing now, really, though maybe it lowered the odds a little that he was currently the President's psychiatrist. Or, to put it another way, if there were the possibility that he had treated Jenner before, the odds would be a little higher that Ewing was treating him now.

But what were the odds you were dealing with, anyway? Had there been, say, a twenty percent chance that Ewing was the President's psychiatrist, and had that gone down to eighteen percent now? Or had you started with forty percent odds? Or sixty percent? Or five percent? The basic situation was so nebulous, that even when you knew you were making progress toward bringing some form and order to it, you couldn't be certain how much progress you were making.

Well, talking to Wendy Greene might help some. She had not called her. She had decided simply to go to her workshop, which, along with many other artist's studios, was located in a renovated torpedo factory in Alexandria. She remembered Greene's saying she was always in her studio on Tuesdays, and Sarah thought she might gain some advantage by appearing unexpectedly.

She drove her car, an aging maroon BMW, along the Parkway and then down Washington Street. At Cameron Street, she took a left and, a block short of the Potomac, she saw a parking place. She maneuvered her car into the spot, got out, locked it, and walked toward the torpedo factory.

Inside, the old building was a catacomb of artists' studios. As Sarah made her way to the shop where Greene worked and displayed her prints, she glanced into a few of the other shops. Some of the things on display were unbelievably bad. One studio was filled with large pieces of what appeared to be linoleum, all of which were indiscriminately splashed with what looked like dirty red paint. But some of the art was quite nice, and the prints hanging on the wall in Wendy Greene's studio were among the finest. The lines were clean and precise. Looking at them, Sarah thought she could feel her own mind beginning to unclutter.

Greene was in the back of the shop where she and another woman were silkscreening. "Be with you in a minute," she called up to the front, without looking up from the print she was pulling. When she had reached a stopping place, she walked up to where Sarah had been admiring her work. She was petite, red-haired, and freckled. Attractive, Sarah thought, when she turned to watch her approach, but definitely not pretty. Still, she handled herself with confidence and ease, and when she asked Sarah what brought her to Alexandria, Sarah found herself being more direct than she had meant to be. She was trying to find out a few things about Malcolm Ewing, she told the smaller woman.

"But why are you asking me?" Greene asked, throwing up her hands. "Malcolm's business is Malcolm's business. Talk to him about it. I'm not going to talk about his work. I try not to pay any attention to politics anyway."

"I would talk to Malcolm about it, except I can't get hold of him. And what I need to know isn't really about politics anyway. It's about him. What sort of man he is. What his interests are. Those are valid things for me to want to know about a man who spends as much time with the President of the United States as he does."

"They may be valid things for you to want to know, but I don't see how I can answer questions like that. The main thing I've never been able to understand about politics is how to tell what you're supposed to say and what you're not supposed to say, what you should talk about, what you shouldn't talk about. I just *say* things. I don't calculate how they're going to affect the future course of the universe. And so, about Malcolm, I try not to say anything at all. And I even make a special effort not to know the details of what he's doing."

"Probably he appreciates that. Most people in the White House are working such long hours anyway that probably the last thing they need is to have to come home at night and talk about it." With reluctant subjects, Sarah had learned, the important thing was to keep them talking, about anything at all, just keep them talking.

"That sounds good, but I don't know if it's true," Wendy was saying. "I think people who work in the White House enjoy so much what they're doing, most of the time anyway, that they wouldn't mind talking about it."

"But there has to be something else in their lives. If they don't do or think about anything else, that's not healthy."

"I don't agree. I know it's fashionable to talk about people who are addicted to their work, to call them 'workaholics,' but it seems to me that often distorts what's really happening. One of Malcolm's most interesting theories is that challenging work—the kind of work that can fill up your life entirely—is essential to mental health for many people, that mental illness begins when an enthusiastic and ambitious person doesn't have work which requires effort and stretching from him or her."

"How did he come to that conclusion?" Sarah asked. She was pleased at the way Greene was opening up, but a little uncomfortable too. Was it fair to draw her out like this? No doubt she was assuming that they were talking personally now, though of course they weren't. The rule among Washington reporters was that no comments were off-the-record unless they were specifically labeled that way. But Greene probably didn't know about the rule. After all, it wasn't engraved on the side of the Washington Monument or anything. So was it fair to hold her to it?

"I think it started when he was in the Peace Corps," Greene was saying. "All those volunteers the United States shipped over to the Philippines were just dying to do good works, and from their point of view, when they looked around and saw ignorance and poverty and disease, there were plenty of good works to be done. But nobody had figured out how, precisely, they were supposed to solve those problems. There were no clearly defined jobs for them, and consequently many of them suffered disorientation, even depression. Malcolm saw the same thing happening time after time, enthusiastic kids becoming hostile or lethargic or worse. He found the situation totally frustrating himself, but some good did come from it. It was from that experience that he really decided to go into psychiatry."

"Does he miss not having been in practice the last several years?"

Wendy hesitated. The question seemed to make her realize that she was indeed talking about Ewing despite her declaration that she would not do so. "Listen, Sarah," she said, "I'm just not going to answer any more questions. I don't know what you're trying to find out. Probably something I couldn't tell you even if I did know what you're fishing for. But I do know it's not right for me to be talking to you about Malcolm."

Sarah had had many an interview terminate less politely, but Wendy, it was clear, was a novice with report-

ers. She seemed uncomfortable with having to tell another human being she would not talk to her,
particularly when that other person was making such
efforts to seem understanding and sympathetic.

"Listen, Sarah," Wendy said, "If there's ever another
time when you want to talk about printmaking or whatever—anything besides politics—you stop by. O.K.?"

As she watched the other woman walk to the back of
the room, Sarah was disappointed she hadn't found out
more. But at the same time a part of her was relieved
that Wendy hadn't given away much at all.

Chapter 6

THE NEXT morning, standing on the asphalt outside the door to the White House pressroom, Sarah was shivering. Yesterday her wool sweater had been more than enough, but today was a different matter. She turned her collar up, crossed her arms for warmth, and made a mental effort to relax and stop her teeth from chattering.

"Basinger's leveling with me," Rudy was saying. "I know that. I know he went to the President just like he said, and the President told him to confirm for me that Ewing's in the Oval Office strictly on official business. But the more I think about it, the more I'm just not sure it's a black and white situation. Have you ever been to a shrink?"

"No, I haven't, but if we don't go inside in a minute, I'm going to need a doctor of some kind."

Dodman looked at his watch. "We'll go in in a minute for the press conference. But you know we can't talk in there. You wouldn't be so cold anyway, if you'd concentrate on what I'm saying. If any guy who's a shrink spends a lot of time with the President, he could very well be treating him, even if neither of them openly acknowledges it. You know, they'd finish the items on the agenda, and the President would talk about his problems, and Ewing would nod, or whatever noncommittal thing it is shrinks do."

"Rudy, that is an interesting idea, but it's just not definite enough to do anything with. We haven't got anything besides rumor and theory, and no idea where to look for hard information. If there were just some possibility Ewing could have treated Jenner back in Montana, then maybe we'd have something to go with. Everything Wendy Greene said about the importance of challenging work to a certain type of personality would fit the way it must have been for Jenner the second time he lost. All that drive and ambition and total frustration at not finding an outlet for it. But Ewing wasn't there then, and I don't think you could argue that Jenner isn't challenged now. If Ewing's concerned about the mental health of people who don't have work that's tough and demanding, then he's certainly worrying about somebody besides the President of the United States. That's the last thing the President's shrink would have to worry about. I just think we ought to drop the psychiatric angle for awhile and concentrate on some other possible reasons for Ewing's being in the Oval Office so much."

"Yeah, I know," said Dodman, stamping out a cigarette on the asphalt. "I even spent a couple of hours this morning writing up questions for the press conference which work off other hypotheses. Maybe the President's going to send Ewing to negotiate with the Whitefeathers."

"Well, it's possible, I guess. You know they must have talked about it. But how could that be an issue that they'd have to meet about for an hour every day?"

"It won't hurt to poke around and see if there's a connection. C'mon. Let's go in."

"I thought you'd never ask," she said, just managing to get the words out before she sneezed heartily.

They walked through the pressroom and then through glass double doors which opened onto a colonnade bordering the Rose Garden. By the time they had reached the entrance to the mansion at the opposite end of the colonnade, Hoff had resumed shivering. Once into the ground floor of the mansion, she felt better. The yards and yards of red carpeting, which she had found a bit overpowering the first time she saw them, were a comfort today. The color even seemed to warm the marble stairs leading to the main floor.

They walked up the stairs and turned right at the top.

"Not your average working conditions," Dodman commented as they entered the East Room.

"It does look like somebody's having a party," Hoff observed, glancing around at the sparkling chandeliers and the delicate gilt chairs which had been set up for the press corps. This was the room where Abigail Adams had hung her wash, back when she and John had first moved into the new mansion. The picture hanging on the east wall of the room, just to the right of the podium which had been set up for the President, was the Gilbert Stuart portrait of George Washington, salvaged by Dolley Madison when the British burned the White House in 1814. But both those facts—the one so full of prosaic simplicity, the other of destruction and panic—were hard to comprehend, Hoff had to admit, when one admired the elegant gaiety of the room as it was now.

Sarah stayed at the back of the room while Rudy made his way forward to the third-row chair assigned to *News-*

62

time. A few seats behind Rudy, in one of the rows where seats were not assigned, Nicholas Frye was sitting. He wasn't one of the White House regulars and very seldom attended news conferences, so Sarah was surprised to see him. He was a strange one, she thought, an intense loner who had few friends in the press corps. Back in the years when the *Post* had been breaking Watergate stories, Frye had worked for the Senate Watergate Committee. When he moved over to the *Post,* more than a few suspicions were aroused that he'd been a primary source of information from the committee for the newspaper. Many of Hoff's colleagues had also felt uneasy about the ethics of Frye's job switch. Wasn't the job with the *Post* a little too much like payment for services rendered? And how could the *Post,* which was death on public servants who used knowledge they gained in government to move into high paying jobs in industry, turn around and hire a public servant whose value to them consisted in part of the government secrets he knew?

One of the favorite pastimes when things were slow in the pressroom was trying to figure out what made Frye tick. Why was he so intense in his dislike for politicians, in his certitude that they were all crooks? Practically everybody in the press corps picked up a certain amount of cynicism after awhile. Most of them became convinced that H. L. Mencken was exactly on the mark when he suggested that the only way to look on a politician is down. But Frye's attitude was something special. So convinced was he that evil lurked in the hearts of public men that some of the reporters had taken to calling him "The Shadow." There were some suggestions that Frye's approach was dictated by ambition. Stories and headlines that impugned the motives of government officials were, after all, more exciting than ones that did not. But another school of thought held that Frye's motivation lay in his past. His father, a historian, had lost his job at a midwestern university when Joe McCarthy accused him of being a Communist sympathizer. The elder Frye had begun to drink heavily and one summer night had driven his car at high speed into a bridge abutment, intentionally or not, no one was ever sure. His son Nicholas, so the theory went, had become his avenger, programmed to wreak destruction on public men as a public man had once done to his father. Hoff's own view was that Frye would have been the same even if Joe McCarthy had never lived. She had encountered the type before, and not always among her colleagues. Frye was one of those congenital cynics who always believed the worst of people. He'd probably suspected his Sunday school teacher of evil motives, Sarah thought.

She took off her sweater, surveyed the room, and judged there were about three hundred people in it. Perhaps fifty were White House staffers. Dale Basinger was near one of the doorways, standing with two of his assistants. Allen Crawford was leaning against a wall, his face heavy and glowering when he thought no one was watching him, but creased with a hearty smile when he felt himself to be onstage. Malcolm Ewing was nowhere in sight, not surprisingly, Hoff thought. As far as she knew, Ewing still hadn't talked to a single reporter since Jenner's log had been published. No one had even seen him. For him to show up at a White House press conference would have been to invite a riot. Hoff could see it all, cameramen and soundmen and reporters trampling one another in the rush to get to Ewing.

Her reflections were cut short by the President's entrance. All the reporters stood as he walked up to the podium. Under the glare of the television lights, Jenner's gray hair seemed silver, his white shirt a brilliant white. His silk tie gleamed.

"I have a short statement," the President announced, brisk and businesslike. "As you all know, a part of my office log has been published in the press. I look on this log as private, and I look on the meetings it lists as confidential.

"Now I want to talk to you for a minute or two about what that means. I hope I don't sound too much like a lawyer when I do, because you all know how I feel about lawyers."

There was laughter from the press corps, most of whom had been covering the White House when Jenner had dared the wrath of the legal profession last year by nominating a nonlawyer to the Supreme Court.

The laughter seemed to relax Jenner. His tone became more conversational, he picked out first one member of the press corps and then another, and he looked straight at the person he had chosen as he spoke. "It seems to me," he said, "that a President has to have complete candor and objectivity from those who assist him. Otherwise he is not going to explore all the alternatives and consequences of a decision before he makes it, and he's going to end up making some bad decisions. Now if the President's advisers can't be sure that what they say to him will be confidential, they're not going to deal straight with him. People just don't work that way. When they know they're speaking for the public record, they shade the truth because they worry about how their statements will appear and about how they will affect them personally. I know this and you know this.

"And I'm not talking about anything new. In 1787, the framers of the Constitution met in private, and then they sealed the records of their convention for thirty years. Most of them said that without this kind of procedure we would not have got the kind of Constitution that we did.

"What I'm saying is that I think it's essential that there be some privacy in the Oval Office—even from the press. If Congress or the Courts had asked me for the log which was printed in yesterday morning's *Post*, I doubt

I would have voluntarily turned it over. And certainly, if I'd been asked to explain it, I would have refused. I would have cited 'executive privilege' and talked about my need for confidentiality. I would also have suggested that if Congress or the Courts can get such information from me, the independence of the Executive Branch from the other two branches of our government is in jeopardy.

"Now it seems to me right and appropriate that I take the same stand with you, the press, the fourth branch of our government. I don't mean to seem hostile or inflexible. I certainly am not going to launch a great search for the source of this leak or start tapping phones as some of my predecessors have done, in order to prevent new ones. But I also want to be quite firm in saying that I will not now, or at any time in the future, discuss with you any of the meetings listed on the log.

"With that established, I'll be glad to take your questions." He nodded toward a neatly dressed, dark-haired woman in the first row. "Diane."

"What subject do you and the Japanese Prime Minister plan to discuss during his visit next week?" she asked, squinting a little in the bright lights.

In the back of the room, Sarah Hoff imagined she could hear several members of the press corps stifling a collective groan. The question was such a softball, such an easy one for the President.

"The foremost purpose of our talks," Jenner was saying, "will be to see what steps can be taken to put the friendship between our two countries on an even sounder basis."

"Will that include talking about the recent anti-American demonstrations in Japan?" With her follow-up question, a harder one for the President, the dark-haired reporter redeemed herself in the eyes of her fellow reporters.

"Yes," answered the President. Everyone waited expectantly for him to go on, and when he did not, there were a few nervous laughs and much general confusion. Hoff wondered why political figures didn't utilize the one-word response more often, so effective was it at throwing questioners off balance. Especially in a press conference with the cameras rolling, time limited, and the reporters competing with one another for notice, there was no possibility of an awkward, lingering silence to pressure the President into expanding his answer.

Within seconds a dozen reporters were on their feet, all shouting, "Mr. President."

"John," Jenner said, recognizing a darkly handsome, heavily browed man in the second row.

"Mr. President, we hear reports that Prime Minister Yanaga may in fact be ready to ask you to shut down certain American bases in Japan. The threat from the Japanese Communist Party, which claims credit for the current anti-American rioting, is sufficient, these reports say, to prompt the Prime Minister into trying to assuage the Communists by meeting a few of their demands, specifically, the ones about closing down American bases. Would you like to comment on that?"

"Well, John, I don't know who your sources are, but I certainly wouldn't agree with all their assumptions. Prime Minister Yanaga's party has been in power since 1948. His party holds more than twice as many seats as the Communists in Japan's lower house. That doesn't sound to me like they pose an overwhelming threat."

Hoff felt some sympathy for the reporter who had asked the question. The President had avoided talking about the issue the reporter had wanted him to talk about—whether the President and the Prime Minister would be discussing base closings—and now, in a split second, the reporter had to decide on a second question which would, ideally, succeed where the first one had failed. It was an exceedingly difficult trick to master, and Hoff was not surprised when the curly-haired reporter who had the floor failed. He let the President's answer distract him from the real issue.

"I'm sure you know, sir," he said, "that while the Japanese Communist Party has fewer than a hundred seats, they are hoping to form a coalition of left-wing parties which would constitute a majority in the Diet. Wouldn't you say that constitutes a significant threat to Japan's ruling conservatives?"

"I think it would be more of a problem, John, if Japan's left-wing parties had a history of being able to cooperate."

A mood of frustration filled the room. The reporters didn't want a history lesson, they wanted to know what the President and the Prime Minister were going to discuss. But there was no time to think the matter through as the seconds of the press conference ticked off. There was only time to react, to jump up, wave an arm, and shout, "Mr. President, Mr. President."

"Jim," Jenner said, acknowledging a slight, pale man directly in front of him.

"Could you please explain to us your position on the demands the Whitefeather tribe is making in Montana?"

As he would have with any problem occurring within the borders of his native state, the President had all the facts about this one ready at hand. He explained how complex the controversy was, going back, as it did, more than a century. "The lands in question were originally bound to the Whitefeather tribe in 1870," he said, "but then seven years later, a year after Custer's defeat at Little Big Horn, Congress voted to strip the tribe of most of the land, some five-and-a-half million acres." He went on to explain that the Indians felt Congress had been motivated by a desire for revenge, and so they maintained that their ownership should be restored, a viewpoint opposed by those who had since become owners of the land and by the coal companies who had spent millions leasing mineral rights to the land. "The matter is exceedingly complex," the President went on, "and it could take years to decide. I am hoping a way can be found to resolve it sooner, and to that end I plan next week to appoint a presidential mediator who will stand in for me in an attempt to bring both sides together and see if a solution can be negotiated."

Pencils scribbled furiously, for the presidential mediator was real news, something the reporters had not heard of before the press conference. The newsman who had asked about the dispute was still on his feet ready with a follow-up question.

"Is it possible that you are considering Malcolm Ewing to be your negotiator in this matter?"

The President didn't answer for a moment. Everyone in the room knew he was trying to decide if the newsman's question overstepped the boundaries he had laid down about the log. Would the question have been asked if Ewing's name had not appeared so often? The President apparently decided to give the reporter the benefit of the doubt.

"On any list of people best qualified to serve in this role, Malcolm Ewing's name would appear. As I know you are aware, he spent almost two years working in a clinic on the Whitefeather reservation, and the bond of trust he established with tribal leaders during that time would no doubt be a great asset."

The correspondent who had asked the question sat down dispiritedly. The President had managed to reply to his question without really settling the matter that was on everyone's mind. What was Ewing doing during the hours he was in the Oval Office? Were he and the President meeting about the Whitefeather claims or not?

As the correspondents in the front of the room jumped

from their seats, waving and shouting again for the President's attention, Hoff, in the back of the room, watched Jenner closely. She saw that the President had noticed Nicholas Frye was on his feet, not waving and calling, just standing very still. Hoff watched as the President's eyes went over Frye, then stopped and came back. When the President called on the *Post* reporter, it was with the air of a man who, though he dislikes fighting, has decided nevertheless to pick up a gauntlet which has been thrown down.

"Mr. Frye," said the President.

Frye was so completely unlike the man who had called on him, that Hoff suspected the reporter cultivated his unkempt dress and slouching demeanor deliberately to set himself apart from public figures like Jenner. In contrast to the President, who was polite and correct, though a bit condescending, Frye was disdainful when he spoke, almost disrespectful.

"I wonder if you'd like to comment on the fact that Malcolm Ewing, a man with whom you seem to be spending a great deal of time, is a trained psychiatrist."

There was a shocked silence in the room as everyone grasped the import of Frye's question. In the back, Hoff stood on her toes, trying frantically to see Rudy and his reaction to finding out he hadn't been the only one to think along such lines. But from where she was standing, she could only see the back of his head. The President's reaction was very clear to her, however. A muscle in his jaw was working as he clenched his teeth. He was angry, as angry as she had ever seen him, angry with an intensity she could feel even from the back of the audience.

"Mr. Frye, I find the manner of your question rude and its implications insulting. Of course Malcolm Ewing is a psychiatrist. That is a matter of public record. He is also, as I have said before, one of the closest friends I have in the world. But I am not seeing him in my office in either of those roles. Now please don't think that by saying this I am retreating from what I said at the beginning of this press conference. If I were seeing Ewing as a psychiatrist or just chatting with him as a friend, those would not be privileged matters. They would concern me as a human being rather than me as President. Or perhaps I should say 'me as a private citizen' rather than 'me as President.' Presidents are human beings after all." Jenner paused for a moment, smiling at his joke in a half-hearted way.

"So, Mr. Frye, I feel I can set your mind at ease on the issue of my mental health without violating the principles I've been talking about. I am seeing Malcolm Ewing strictly in his capacity as a presidential adviser."

Frye had sat down during the President's answer, but now he was on his feet again, almost shouting his follow-up. "Mr. President, have you ever been treated by a psychiatrist?" he demanded.

Jenner hesitated a fraction of a second, then snapped, "No!" He was silent a few seconds more, then he mumbled a thank you to the press corps and strode up the aisle and out of the East Room.

The reporters sat quietly for a moment, as though they were stunned by the President's unusual exit. Tradition had it that a press conference went on for a set length of time until the senior wire correspondent brought it to a close by saying, "Thank you, Mr. President." No one in the room could remember any President ending a press conference in the way Jenner just had.

The silence gave way to murmuring and then to hubbub as the reporters got up from their seats. Sarah pushed her way toward the front to where Rudy had been sitting and to where reporters were crowding around Frye, some of them questioning him indignantly, some of them just curious.

"Hey, Nicky boy," a short baby-faced midwestern reporter was saying to Frye. "What do you know we don't know?"

The tone of the question infuriated Frye. "I'll tell you what I know," he spit out at the shorter man. "I know the President's lying, that's what I know."

"Lying, what do you mean, lying?"

Frye looked disdainfully around him. "None of you seem able to dig it out for yourselves, so why don't you just wait and read about it in the *Post* tomorrow."

Sarah watched as he turned and pushed his way toward the exit. In the confusion he left behind, there were the predictable mutters of resentment, but there was something else too, another almost contradictory mood. Sarah saw it on the face of the baby-faced midwestern reporter who had irritated Frye. She could hear it in the voice of the wire service correspondent next to her. It was excitement, exhilaration, the kind of adrenalin lift which signaled that a hunt was on. The fox and hounds metaphor wasn't a particularly pleasant one, she reflected. But then neither was it pleasant to have to admit that she felt the excitement, the high, in herself.

UP IN the West Hall of the mansion's family quarters, Mary Jenner was watching the network correspondents analyze her husband's news conference. They had chosen a few adjectives early in their discussion, and they kept repeating them. "Evasive" was the one they kept using to talk about the answers Jenner had given. "Surprising" was their favorite when they talked about the way he had walked out of the press conference, though one of the correspondents went so far as to call the abrupt termination part of an "erratic" performance.

She got up and snapped off the television set in irritation. What could Zern have been thinking, she wondered. Walking out that way would just give them one more reason to criticize him.

She was a small, shapely, perfectly groomed woman, dressed exquisitely in a beige wool suit with a black, beige and white silk blouse. As she walked over to the Palladian window, the light picked up the few strands of silver in her dark brown hair. She knelt on the flowered chintz sofa in front of the window and looked down at the West Wing, trying to decide if there were any way for her husband to turn the news conference to political advantage. Finally she concluded that there was not. Zern's behavior made him look temperamental at best. At worst it made him look a fool. What had he been thinking? He should never have called on that insufferable Nicholas Frye. He knew what the *Post* was trying to do, raising all the fuss about the log. And now Frye was implying those things about psychiatrists. If Zern felt he had to call on him, he should have at least made sure he didn't let him get under his skin.

She sighed deliberately, trying to fend off the tension she could feel building inside her. Then she tried to take her mind away from her husband's gaffe and the effect it might have on next year's elections by reciting the sentence which had become a kind of mantra with her. "I will not go back to Montana. I will not go back to Montana," she repeated, her eyes closed.

She opened her eyes, turned so that she could sit down, and decided that she felt a little better. It wasn't that she hated Montana. Not at all. In fact, she had learned to love the state where her husband had grown up. She had learned to love its plains and mountains and the blue sky which stretched from horizon to horizon. True, it had been hard when they had first been married, almost forty years ago it was now, and she, fresh from Radcliffe, had been the easterner, the outsider. But she had coped. She had seen what could be done and did it and put the rest out of her mind, and gradually she was accepted.

No, she didn't hate Montana, but she did hate the failure Zern had known there, and she never, never in her life wanted to go through such a time of failure again. It was the second time he lost that had been particularly traumatic. The second time he had run for the Senate and failed, the spirit had seemed to drain from him. The loss had robbed him of the spark and special brilliance which she had seen in him from the beginning and which she had known promised greatness.

She and he had never been given to examining each other's feelings and motives the way she knew some of their married friends did, and so they hadn't really talked much about why losing was so traumatic for him. She had supported him in the only way she knew how, by encouraging him to action. The past couldn't be erased, but the future would bring other contests, and so he needed to prepare for them. Gradually he had begun to do just that, and he became once again the Zern Jenner she had married. But the memory of the spiritless, disoriented man he had been for those few months lingered. She wanted never, ever to see him that way again.

That was what she meant when she closed her eyes and began the mantra again.

MEANWHILE, IN his spacious office in the Executive Office Building, the Vice President of the United States was screaming at one of his aides. "Where the hell is this thing going!" he yelled. "This wasn't in the plans. Nothing's gone right since this thing started."

The aide, a thirty-six-year-old lawyer, known throughout Washington as "Boyston's boy," adopted his most deferential tone. "We didn't count on Frye, sir, you're right about that. He wasn't in the plans, but that doesn't necessarily mean it's turning bad."

Robert Boyston's only acknowledgment of the young man's comment was a vicious kick he administered to a

74

chair he happened to be pacing by. Whenever he felt the frustrations building, he let them out this way, just the way that doctor had recommended back when Boyston had weighed over three hundred pounds and had held everything in. He thought back to that time frequently, mostly because of the satisfaction it gave him to think what he'd lost in the interim—a hundred and twenty pounds—and what he'd gained—a couple of million dollars and the vice presidency.

"How's the mail," he demanded.

"Not many letters yet. Not long enough since the *Post* ran the story on the log. But lots of telegrams and phone calls. I've pulled a couple of the telegrams, more or less at random, for you to look at."

"Read one."

" 'Dear Vice President Boyston,' it starts out."

"Get to the message," Boyston demanded.

The aide did not even flinch. "I feel betrayed, sir," he read in an emotionless voice.

> When our convention nominated Zern Jenner, I worried that he did not understand the ideals of our party. But then he chose you for his V.P. and I felt better. He said he would listen to your advice, and I know you think the right way.
>
> But now I read he doesn't have you in his office much. One paper even said you might not be on the ticket of our party next time. I have written the President saying this better change if he wants me to support him. In the Bible it says a Beast shall come with two horns like a lamb but shall speak like a dragon, and that, sir is the Beast of Hypocrisy. Warn the President.

"Well, that's pretty much on track, anyway," the Vice President observed. "I was beginning to wonder if all those good people had fallen asleep."

"I wouldn't be surprised if Frye's tactics woke them up so much that some of them started thinking about you for the top spot. It's really not turning out so bad, sir."

"Yeah, but goddam! That Frye's an unguided missile. You can't tell what he's going to do."

The Vice President's secretary, Pam, opened the door to his office and stuck her head in. "Jane Minnick's on the phone again, sir. This must be the dozenth time she's tried to call you today. She says it's very, very urgent."

"That stupid bitch. I'm not going to spend any time talking to her."

Pam hesitated. An outside observer might have thought the Vice President's profanity was bothering her, but it wasn't that. She'd grown used to that a long time ago. "She's crying, sir. In fact, you could say she's hysterical," Pam said.

"Maybe you should speak to her, sir," the aide suggested, motioning for Pam to leave them and shut the door. "Minnick sure enough could turn into an unguided missile."

"You talk to the stupid broad then. I'm not going to waste any more of my time on her." This time it was a sofa leg that caught the full impact of the Vice President's wrath.

Chapter 7

WHEN DALE BASINGER came into his office following his early evening meeting with the President, he was not surprised to find his assistants Jerry Gersten and Hank Davis, and Press Secretary Mark Westfield sitting at his large, polished wood conference table, drinking beer. He was Gersten's and Davis's only link to the President. What they wanted Jenner to hear had to go through him; what they wanted to know about Jenner had to come through him. Westfield, though running the press office, was usually told nothing by the President except what he could tell the press, and that meant he usually knew even less of what was going on than did Gersten and Davis. Consequently, all three of them tended to appear in Basinger's office when a crisis was building. They raided his small refrigerator for beer, then waited for him, hoping to find out what was happening.

"Come in, come in," said Gersten irreverently when he saw his boss in the doorway, and before Basinger could put his papers down, Gersten was asking, "What's the Old Man saying?" Gersten was incredibly young, twenty-three or twenty-four, Basinger could never remember which, and one of his most effective tools for operating in the White House was an unabashed curiosity which would have not been tolerated in someone less youthfully candid.

"He's not saying a lot," Basinger answered. "You know how he is." That was an honest enough report of the situation, wasn't it? He'd gone over five or six items with the President. They'd discussed some bills which were coming over from the Hill and the political trade-offs in signing or vetoing. They'd talked about some requests for appearances and then he'd got to the matter which had been in the forefront of his mind since morning.

"Sir," Basinger remembered he'd said, "I guess you know you broke a lot of china walking out of the press conference that way. I've been getting calls all afternoon wanting to know what happened."

"I don't think I need to explain," the President said. "I watched a tape of the conference, and I think it's pretty clear what happened. I just got damned sick and tired of the probing and prodding, especially when Frye got started. I can't even describe what it is about him that sets me so much on edge, but, damn, he's irritating."

"I had the conference tape run for me too, and I have to say he doesn't come off very well. He looks so disreputable and has that abrasive manner. Some of the calls I've been getting have a sympathetic tone to them, and I'd say we owe that to Frye."

The President didn't answer, and so Basinger went on with what he'd really come in to say about Frye. "I got a couple of calls from press corps people who happened to be around Frye after you walked out. In the hearing of a number of reporters, he apparently declared you to be a liar and said if they wanted evidence they should just keep reading the *Post*."

"Goddam!" The President slammed his fist down on his desk and then got up and began pacing. "Goddam, goddam," he muttered.

"Sir, if there is anything . . ."

"No, no. He can't have anything. I know he can't."

"If there is anything, just any small thing he could take out of context and blow up, any little thing at all, it'd be better if we handled it first and put the right spin on it."

At that, the President seemed to relax somewhat. "Dale, you're a good man, but you worry too much. I know Frye hasn't got anything, so we'll just leave it at that tonight."

"One other thing is Ewing, sir. What with the log and now all this business about psychiatrists, a lot of people are very anxious to talk to him. His secretary says he hasn't been in all week. The press people I've talked to say they can't reach him anyplace else either. I wonder if having him out of sight is the right thing at this point, or if it looks suspicious."

"You remember our discussion this morning, Dale, our talk about executive privilege? Well, I really meant what I said. If that log hadn't leaked, nobody'd care where Malcolm was right now, nobody at all. Damned if I'm going to explain or ask him to explain. Some things are going to stay confidential around here."

So, Basinger thought, looking at the three men around the conference table, it was true enough to say that the President really hadn't said much. Not nearly enough, as far as he was concerned. Where in the hell was Ewing? That bothered him, and so had the President's response to being told Frye had called him a liar.

Well, none of that could show through. He'd seen back during the campaign how important it was for him to seem calm and positive, no matter what disaster was impending. So many staffers took their cues from him, and if their spirits were low, the press was sure to pick it up, and it wasn't long then before the stories started about how demoralized the Jenner staff was. From there it was just a matter of time until the campaign was labeled a losing one or the administration was perceived to be in deep trouble.

And so he adopted what he hoped was a cheerful tone. "Let's go downstairs and grab a sandwich. I'll even put it on my tab."

As the four of them walked through the small reception room outside his office, Joanie, his secretary, called out to him, "Did you get back to Marie?"

He put Joanie off with a wave of his hand, feeling guilty that he hadn't called his wife, but realizing he had probably forgot deliberately. She'd want him to come home for dinner, and it was easier not to call her, he thought, than it was to call and try to explain why he couldn't make it. Unless you were there, unless you were living it, how could you understand how important it was to spend your evening cheerleading the troops? It had been two days, he thought guiltily, since he'd seen his children. They had been asleep last night when he had got home, and they weren't awake when he left this morning.

He put the thoughts of his family aside as he and the other three took the hall elevator to the basement level, walked past the Situation Room, and down a few stairs to the White House Mess. The room they entered was decorated in a nautical scheme, with wood paneling, a brass marine clock on the wall, paintings of ships—all befitting an operation run by the Navy. Basinger had always thought it was appropriate, too, that the room had no windows. It was a little like being in a submarine, though a high-class submarine to be sure. The reason for the lack of windows, of course, was that the mess was in a subterranean section of the White House which extended out under the South Lawn.

The four arranged themselves around a corner table, and then Hank Davis leaned forward. "Dale, the press conference this afternoon looked terrible. The President knows that, doesn't he?"

"C'mon, Hank," Gersten interposed. "Your *weltschmerz* is showing. It wasn't that bad."

Basinger reflected that Davis and Gersten were falling into their usual sad-guy, glad-guy roles. Though maybe they weren't roles. Davis, a tall horse-faced man in his late forties, really did seem always to see the dark side of life. Gersten really was an irrepressible optimist.

"You know what you are?" Gersten was saying good-naturedly to Davis, "You're our court doomster. Other administrations had their court jesters, but we get you. Or at least we've got you until you succumb to terminal pessimism."

Press Secretary Mark Westfield ignored the interchange. "Dale, do you think the Old Man did see a shrink? That's what Frye must have meant when he called him a liar."

"There's nothing to worry about," said Basinger, indirectly relaying the message the President had given him.

"I know that's the line to take, upbeat, confident, like there's no reason we should feel any other way, but I want to tell you, it's getting harder and harder. They're screaming out there in the pressroom. Especially they're screaming because they can't find Ewing. I gotta give them something."

"No, what you've got to do is exactly what the Man wants you to do, and that's say nothing for right now."

"Well, I just think he's wrong. And I also think he'll figure that out pretty soon. But how long will it take him? Shit, do you remember 'domestic propaganda'?"

Basinger's mind flashed back to that awful time during the presidential campaign when an interviewer had asked Jenner a hypothetical question about using troops to aid our NATO allies. Jenner had responded that he thought it would be very difficult to get the support of the American people for sending American troops anywhere in the world without first conducting an intense campaign of "domestic propaganda." The statement brought numerous denunciations, but it had been days before Jenner had finally been willing to concede that perhaps his choice of words had not been the best.

"How could I forget 'domestic propaganda'?" Basinger said, choosing his words carefully. He didn't want Westfield to find in them any support for his contention that the President's approach to the present difficulty was wrong. He was relieved when the approach of a mess steward prevented his having to say anything more.

"Would you like to order?" the red-jacketed steward asked.

"Hey, Danny, how are you?" Gersten said to him. Unlike most of the White House staff, Gersten know all the mess stewards by first name, and he went out of his way to be friendly to them, even visiting them when they were working in the kitchen behind the mess. His gestures had not gone unrewarded, Basinger had noted. More than once, he had seen his young aide leaving the mess in the morning with a packet of fresh-baked sweet rolls in hand.

Instead of answering Gersten's greeting, the steward was staring hard at his order pad.

"Hey, Dan, is everything O.K.?"

"I dunno, I dunno, Mr. Gersten." But then the steward seemed to gather himself up. He looked at Gersten and declared with some fervor, "Is gonna be O.K. I been prayin' and is gonna be O.K."

After he'd taken their order and gone back to the kitchen, Basinger asked Gersten what he supposed the steward's trouble was.

"Maybe he's just worried about the Old Man. Some of the people who take care of him and press his clothes and fix his food get involved with him in a very personal way. I can't see that the press conference should get Danny so upset, but maybe it's that. Or maybe," he suggested, eyeing Hank Davis, "maybe it's just that the whim-whams are catching."

Later, after they had finished and Basinger was back up in his office alone, he went through his pink telephone slips and noted that Marie had called again. It really wasn't fair to her, he thought. His hours had been so bad this week, he'd hardly seen her, much less talked to her, and it wasn't going to get any better. And so he tried to think of a treat for her, a reward for long-suffering.

He pressed a buzzer on his desk and when Joanie appeared in the doorway, he gave her instructions for tomorrow morning to call over to the social secretary in the First Lady's Office in the White House's East Wing. "You tell Pamela," he instructed, "that I want the Basingers on the list for the Japanese state dinner. And tell her I'd appreciate it if she'd see that Marie had a good dinner partner."

He packed up his briefcase, something he always did before going home, no matter how late the hour. Ever since he'd been working in the White House, such a sense of urgency had possessed him, such a sense of how much there was to do and how little time there was to do it. And so he always went home with a full briefcase, on the chance that he might be able to snatch a moment here or there to do some reading.

He could not find one report he'd particularly wanted to get to, a report on the Indian situation in Montana. After looking for it a minute or two, he remembered he'd given it to Gersten to read. Well, maybe Gersten was still in his office, and he could get it from him before going home.

He walked up the stairs to the West Wing's second floor and saw, as soon as he had stepped out of the stairwell, that Gersten's office was closed and dark. The report had been classified, so there was no sense getting into Gersten's office in the hope of finding it lying on his desk. The White House guards made nightly rounds and locked up any classified materials they found on desk tops. They also left pointed notes behind to let the careless know their carelessness had been observed.

He was about to go back downstairs when he noticed a light was on down the hall in Ewing's office. Probably just the cleaning crew, he thought, but he walked down to check anyway. If there was one person he'd like to talk to right now, it was Ewing.

When he opened the door and looked in, he was surprised to see Danny, the mess steward, standing over Malcolm's desk. Danny was equally surprised to see him.

"Mr. Basinger, sir," he said, visibly startled.

"What're you doing, Danny?"

"Well, sir, we're missin' some coffee cups in the mess, and I'm checkin' all the offices to find 'em. None here, I guess." He turned out the lights and came out the door.

It seemed a plausible enough answer, so Basinger let the matter drop, said good night to Danny, and left. It wasn't until he was downstairs, walking out the basement door to the West Wing, that it occurred to him to wonder why in the world Danny was conducting the search personally. Couldn't the cleaning crew have kept an eye out for the missing cups?

He got into the waiting limousine, snapped on the reading light, opened his briefcase, and began to read, putting the matter out of his mind as the car drove through the darkened city toward Virginia.

Chapter 8

ALL NIGHT long, Rudy had tossed and turned. Try as he might, he could not quit going over and over the press conference. What did Frye know? Did he have some evidence that Ewing was the President's psychiatrist? Or that Jenner had seen a psychiatrist back in Montana? And if he did have evidence, how in the hell had he got it?

Finally, shortly before dawn, he gave up and got up. He pulled on an old pair of jeans, put on a heavy wool shirt, and made his way quietly downstairs. He unlocked the front door, went down the iron stairs outside, and headed for the corner. He had to admit he felt foolish. He wasn't even sure Frye's story—whatever it was—would be out this morning, though it did seem probable what with the way he was shooting off his mouth yesterday.

Still, no reasonable human being should be so anxious to get his newspaper that he would get up while it was still dark and walk down to the corner where the delivery truck threw out the newsboy's daily bundle. But if he was not entirely reasonable when it came to news, he took some comfort that neither were most of the people he knew in Washington. If they weren't watching the news shows, they were reading the newspapers or the news magazines, or they were anxiously tuning in to one of the city's news stations.

But the obsession with the news wasn't even the most embarrassing part. By doing what he was doing, he was really testifying to the *Post*'s supremacy, and it galled him to think he was so anxious to read another publication's story. The damned *Post*, it did dominate the town, especially since Watergate. When he had tried before to analyze why that was, he had concluded it wasn't just that the *Post*'s reporters were bright, clever, and hyperambitious, but also that the newspaper was in the forefront of defining what the news was. Whenever there was a tradition that certain information should not be reported, the *Post* was usually the first to violate it. Was the wife of a high-ranking diplomat given to making racial slurs? Interview her and print them. Was one of our most important allies being funded by the CIA? Get proof and print it. Was the United States developing a new and deadly weapons system? Find out the details and print them. Why should one newspaper have so powerful a voice in selecting what the nation would be indignant about? The question nagged at him. But, hell, he was probably just jealous. After all, he was up this morning because he was worried they'd already figured out what he was still puzzling about.

When he reached the corner, he pulled a newspaper

out from the plastic-wrapped pile and put in a note for the newsboy saying he had picked up his paper. As he stood under the street lamp and unfolded the *Post,* the first thing he noted was that Frye had graduated into the lead story today. And then the headline itself began to sink in. "Jenner Visited Psychiatrist Regularly," it said. "Although President Zern Jenner denied in a press conference yesterday that he had ever been under psychiatric treatment," the story began, "the *Post* has learned that for a period immediately following his unsuccessful 1962 bid for the Senate, he made twice weekly visits to a psychiatrist's office."

The source, Dodman saw, as he read on, was apparently one Rita Walton, a receptionist who had worked for a Great Falls psychiatrist named Dorothy Brewer. In late 1962 and early 1963, according to Walton, Jenner had visited Brewer's office twice a week. The receptionist apparently did not know exactly what Jenner's visits were about, but the story went on to suggest that they were related to the emotional trauma of losing a second try for a Senate seat. There were extensive quotes from the autobiography Jenner had published during his presidential campaign. It was called *The Man from Montana,* and excerpted from it was Jenner's own description of how disappointed and depressed he had been at the time. "I had lost my enthusiasm for life," the man who was now President had written.

> The simplest tasks, which I had done almost automatically before, now seemed to require great effort. And the larger chores, especially decisions like what cattle to buy and what ranch hands to hire, those were simply impossible, partly because they forced me to project into a future which I did not want to visualize, a future which had in it no goal I wanted to achieve, no object I

could strive for. I began to withdraw into myself, shutting out even my family and closest friends, all of whom, despite their best efforts to lighten my load, reminded me just by their presence of my failure. I felt as though I had some great wound and that I needed to tend to it off by myself somewhere. I began to sleep more than I ever had before, but even when I was awake, I did not feel rested.

Frye also quoted at length Jenner's description of how he came through this period:

One day I was checking fences—or at least that was what I had said I was going to do. I really wanted simply to be by myself without getting my family worried and upset about my behavior. And so I had said that I was going to check fences, and I was riding along the fence line, though I was paying very little attention to whether the wire was sound or not.

It was almost as though the motion of the horse and the passing of the fence posts one after another had a hypnotic effect. I was overcome by the sensation of being outside myself, of watching myself, and what I saw was a very foolish human being who somehow thought his lot was special, who thought that no one else had ever suffered disappointment or setback. It was all over in an instant, but in that instant I realized that I had to commit myself to the future, because that was the only way I could find happiness in my life. Like every man who ever lived, I had to invest my life with meaning in order to make it meaningful. That sounds very simple now, but I cannot tell you what a revelation it was to me at that period of my life.

At the end of the excerpt from Jenner's autobiography, Frye had appended, "It was during this period that Walton claims Jenner was making twice weekly visits to Great Falls psychiatrist Dorothy Brewer." The implication was clear. Not only had Jenner lied in his press conference, he had skirted the truth in *The Man from Montana*, romanticizing his recovery, omitting to note that he had sought medical help.

Dodman folded the paper, put it under his arm, and walked back toward his house, a number of thoughts racing through his head. "A woman shrink," he kept thinking irrelevantly. "Jenner saw a woman shrink." And then, "He lied. That tears it. That means he's dead in the next election." And then, "Ewing. How does he fit into all this?" And then, "Frye. That bastard. How did he find this Walton woman?"

Back in the living room where she was waiting when Rudy returned with the paper, Nancy had her own theories about Frye. "I think he started with the log and just kept pushing and pushing on what was there. Like 'Woodstein' did with Watergate, just pushing and pushing. When he saw the log and Ewing in there all the time, the idea of Jenner and a psychiatrist probably surfaced with him. And even when it was clear Ewing couldn't have been Jenner's psychiatrist back in the days when the campaign rumors had Jenner seeing a shrink, Frye probably went ahead and tracked down every psychiatrist who'd been practicing in the area at that time."

"Hell, that was done during the campaign, but none of the shrinks that were run down would say a word."

"Right, but Frye wouldn't stop there," she countered. "He'd track down everybody who'd ever worked for one of those shrinks, people who wouldn't be hung up on the doctor-patient relationship and confidentiality. The craziest thing about it to me is how it started with Ewing and now all this other stuff is unwinding. And Ewing's still a mystery."

"Well, the pressure's sure going to be building to make his role clear. Unless the White House can show that this Walton woman is a liar or prove some other way that Jenner's never been treated by a psychiatrist, there's going to be an increasing amount of suspicion that Ewing's treating him now."

"It's bad enough for Jenner to have lied about the past—I mean it's devastating. It could even threaten his chances to get his party's nomination—but it's totally unthinkable that a psychiatrist could be treating him now."

"Not unthinkable at all, Nance. Everybody's going to start thinking it unless the White House makes clear exactly what it is Ewing and the President are doing in the one P.M. meetings."

The telephone rang, startling both Dodmans.

"Who in the world?" asked Nancy.

"Hell, it's only a little past six," Dodman noted, getting up to answer it.

"Hi, Rudy?" said a half-familiar voice when he answered.

It took him a minute to identify the caller as Washington attorney Mark Sunler. "Sure, Mark, how're you doing." If he hadn't been a reporter, he might have pointed out the hour, but he had learned early on not to do anything like that, anything that might discourage anybody who might have information from calling him anytime.

"Well, I tell you," Sunler said, "I'm just sitting here mad. That s.o.b. Frye's got himself another victim, it looks like. A real big one this time. That little son of a bitch."

The bitterness in Sunler's voice brought back to Dodman the time when he had been covering the Hill for *Newstime* and Sunler had been the chief staffer for then Senator Daniels. Nicholas Frye had been covering an ethics committee investigation into alleged payoffs to members of Congress by the automobile industry. It was widely known that the committee was looking into the affairs of Daniels, who was up for reelection, and in October, just a month before the election, Frye had written a front-page story in which "informed sources" were quoted as saying that the committee had found considerable evidence of wrongdoing on Daniels' part. "That story came out on the same day, the same goddam day, that we got word from the committee that the senator was going to be cleared," Dodman remembered Sunler telling him. "It was pure bullshit, that story, but do you think we could get that word around? The *Post* ran the story about the committee clearing the senator a few days later, on page three, I think it was, but do you think they ever wrote anything about they'd made a mistake? And how many voters, do you suppose, only knew about the first story, the one that said the senator was a crook. That little son of a bitch lost us the election."

At the time, Dodman had seen that Frye's error might well cost Daniels his Senate seat, and in an article on the upcoming elections for *Newstime*, he had included a lengthy section on the *Post*'s mistake and the unfair advantage it gave Daniels' opponent. The magazine's New York editors had cut the section considerably, but it had still been clear to Sunler that Dodman had tried to right the wrong the *Post* had perpetrated. Since then, Sunler had called him whenever he thought he had useful information to convey.

"You know, I ran across the little son of a bitch twice yesterday," Sunler was saying, "both times in the Hay-Adams. I had a client there for lunch and then met some others for drinks later. And both times I saw him, he sorta had his head tucked down like he wasn't too anxious to be recognized, and you know how that isn't like him. He usually struts around like the cock of the walk. Anyway, the second time I saw him, I was by myself, waiting for those fellows, and Frye didn't see me, he was so busy trying to fade into the woodwork, so I decided just for the hell of it to follow him. If Frye's sneaking around, sure as hell he can't be up to any good. Well, I never did find out what he was doing, but I did follow him up to the fourth floor, and whatever he's doing, he's doing it in 417. I just thought I'd pass it along and see if it'd do you any good, old buddy. God, I hate that little son of a bitch."

Dodman thanked the lawyer for calling, hung up, and told Nancy what Sunler had called to report.

"Well, if Frye was a sixty-year-old congressman," she said, "you'd figure he had an out-of-town cutie pie stashed away in 417. But that's hardly his style."

"Whatever's going on just about has to be tied in with the log and the psychiatrist. Frye's obviously not spending time on anything else."

"What are you going to do? Just go over to the Hay-Adams and knock on the door of 417?"

"I don't see any reason to be more subtle about it, and besides I don't have time for subtlety. I've got to write today, and before I can do that I've got to come up with something new on this story. Damned if I'll just do a rehash of Frye's piece."

He went upstairs, dressed, and came back down to find Nancy reading the editorial page and shaking her head.

"According to Morris and Latvala," she said, "Ewing leaked the log. Can you imagine that?"

"Ewing! What could possibly have led them to conclude that?"

"Let's see," Nancy said, looking over the column. "Basically it's because the log makes Ewing look more influential than he's generally known to be. Uh, oh, here's the real reason. Allen Crawford told them Ewing leaked the log."

"He said that? On the record?"

"No, no. Listen. 'Those who believe the log to be representative of the way Zern Jenner spends his time are revising upward their assessment of Ewing's influence in this administration. But many Washington insiders are not believers. Any schedule of the President's which does not show him huddling frequently with his crafty political operative, Allen Crawford, these insiders say, cannot be representative.' Ergo! Crawford's the source."

"Morris and Latvala are so full of crap."

"What is it Jack calls them?"

"Instead of 'B. Morris and Andy Latvala,' he always says 'More B.S. and lots of it.' But you know, there might be just a kernel of truth in what they're saying."

"Ah, c'mon."

"Well, it's a small one, I admit, but whoever leaked the log probably did do it for his own benefit."

"Or for her own benefit."

"Or her own benefit, right. Do you have somebody in mind or are you just correcting my sexist grammar?"

"Just your grammar. I can't think of any woman in this administration who'd have access to the log except Gretchen Burrows, and you know she'd never do it."

Rudy agreed, then leaned over and kissed her on top of the head. "See you tonight. Kiss Mac for me."

"Have a good day, and if you do find out anything, call me."

"You're getting as bad as Jack," he noted good-humoredly as he headed out the door, "always wanting to know what I'm up to."

As he left, Nancy was pounding on the arm of the sofa,

crying out in mock despair, "And I try so hard to be my own person."

Dodman walked over to the Eastern Market metro stop and took the escalator down. As he waited for a train, he reflected that he had one of the easiest commutes in the city. It was only a short subway ride to Farragut West, the metro stop closest to the White House. He and Nancy had just stumbled into their good luck, really. When they'd been looking for a house, metro hadn't yet opened. They'd bought their restored row house on Capitol Hill just because they loved old houses and because Capitol Hill prices weren't quite as far out of line as Georgetown's or Old Town's in Alexandria. When metro had opened, they'd realized their fortune at being close to a station, and Dodman never failed, as he took the short subway ride to work, to thank whatever benevolent god it was who watched over reporters.

He got off at Farragut West and walked the few short blocks to the corner of 16th and H where the Hay-Adams was located. Though not really old by Lafayette Square standards, it was a charming place. It had been built in the twenties, but it was thought of as older, partly because it had been constructed on the site where John Hay and Henry Adams had once had their homes, and over the years the hotel's management had skillfully nurtured the impression that somehow the hotel itself was a historic landmark.

Dodman felt awkward as he entered the small, wood-paneled lobby and made his way through a group of people and suitcases crowded in front of the door. It was unlikely that anyone would ask him his business if he matter-of-factly took the elevator to the fourth floor. Hotels didn't operate like that anymore, not even the ones that cultivated the aura of tradition. Still, he felt uncomfortable, and during the short elevator ride up, when he thought again of the possibility—unlikely as it was—that Frye was using the Hay-Adams as a trysting place, his discomfort increased. What if Frye himself were in 417?

Much to his relief, his knock on the elaborate wood door was answered almost immediately by a short, somewhat overweight, middle-aged woman. Although it was still early, her unnaturally blonde, laquer-sprayed hair had been carefully backcombed, and she was dressed with similar precision in a rose-colored pantsuit and shoes which matched the suit's color exactly. Like her suit, the shoes looked stiff and new, and they were, Dodman thought, glancing at them a second time, just about the most unusual shoes he'd ever seen. They should have been white. They were lace-up orthopedic shoes, the kind he'd seen on nurses. Where had she found them in rose? Was it possible to get orthopedic shoes dyed to match?

"Mrs. Walton?" he said, when he had managed to take his eyes away from the shoes. The picture the *Post* had run with its morning story had obviously been several years old, but Rita Walton hadn't changed her hair style, and though she had aged, her face, with its close-set eyes and round cheeks, was easily recognizable.

She nodded an acknowledgment and smiled in what struck him as an unexpectedly friendly way. He was, after all, a perfect stranger.

"What can I do for you?" she asked.

Dodman identified himself.

"*Newstime?*" she said excitedly. "I've read your magazine. Come in. Come in."

It had been a while since Dodman had encountered a reaction like that. Many of the politicians he interviewed had a real antipathy toward the press, and even when they and others in Washington wanted publicity—as

96

they usually did, since it was lifeblood to a politician—part of the game was that they had to appear not to want it.

But Rita Walton was clearly not sophisticated in Washington ways, Dodman thought, following her into the hotel room. The obvious approach seemed to be to play to her desire for attention. "*Newstime,* of course, is very interested in what you have to say about President Jenner and his visits to the psychiatrist's office," he began, when they had sat down.

"I just knew you would be. I told Mr. Frye that I thought I should have a press conference today so I could talk to reporters, but he wants me just to stay here. I mean this is a nice room, but when he told me he'd pay my way to Washington, I didn't plan on spending my time in my room. I'm the kind of person who likes people, Mr. Dodgeman. Isn't that what you said your name was?"

"Dodman," he corrected.

"Well, Mr. Dodgeman," she went on, "I've always been one to say people need people. I've always believed that. And I think I should be talking to as many people as I can. You know since my Charlie died—it's been fifteen years ago, now—and since we never had any kids, I've always thought the good Lord meant me to take all the love and caring I've got stored up inside and just use it on the whole world. But I can't do that if I stay in my room, now can I?"

"When was it you worked for Dr. Brewer?" Dodman asked, trying to get the interview on track.

"Now that Dr. Brewer, she's one who just never understood about people. She was always talking about being orderly and efficient. You just can't believe, Mr. Dodgeman, how upset she would get over just little things, like if I would get the patients' records filed wrong. She just doesn't have the feeling about people needing people. That's the thing that's important, not where pieces of paper get put away."

"Did you yourself actually see Zern Jenner when he came for his appointments?" Dodman asked patiently.

"Sometimes I did. But he usually came late in the afternoon on Tuesdays and Thursdays, and lots of time I had to leave early because I was on a bowling team, you know, and they played a lot of their games Tuesday and Thursday afternoons. That was another thing that used to make Dorothy Brewer mad, but how could I be in the bowling league if I didn't bowl with my team? I want to tell you, it was a real relief to me that I didn't work for that woman any longer than I did."

"How long was that?"

"Well, exactly how long it was sort of escapes me right now, but it was less than a year, I remember that. I remember, because I told myself that every year I worked for that woman was probably a year off my life, she made me so nervous. And I was glad I didn't work for her a whole year."

"How many times, then, did you actually see Zern Jenner in Dr. Brewer's office?"

Well, like I said, I'd see him come in whenever it was a Tuesday or Thursday and my team didn't have a game to bowl."

"But did they bowl pretty regularly on Tuesday and Thursday afternoons?"

Suddenly Walton seemed to get the drift of the questions. "How many times I saw him doesn't matter much, Mr. Dodgeman," she said indignantly. "I saw him enough to know that the fellow who was seeing Dr. Brewer is the same fellow who is now the President. And I kept the appointment book. That's the important thing. I know he came in every Tuesday and Thursday afternoon whether I was there or not, because I scheduled him in." She smiled triumphantly, her feeling of victory seeming to dissipate her indignation.

"Do you have the appointment book?"

"Now why would I have that?" she asked sweetly. "When I left Dorothy Brewer's office, I sure didn't want to take any reminders with me."

"Was there anyone else who might have seen Zern Jenner on those Tuesdays and Thursdays?"

"Now, Mr. Frye wanted to know that too, and I've thought and thought about it. There's Dr. Brewer, and then there's one other person I can think of. He had an Indian kind of name, like Timberwolf, I think it was. John Timberwolf. He was the janitor for that little building in the afternoons. I think maybe he had another job too. He was just a young man with a wife and a lot of children and not enough money. He might have seen Zern Jenner coming into Dr. Brewer's office for his appointments."

Dodman asked a few more questions, but he didn't really listen to the answers. Instead, he was thinking about the story Rita Walton had told. It was possible that she was lying, of course, making up this story in order to put herself in the limelight. But it wasn't probable. Even Rita Walton was smart enough to figure that she'd get caught in a lie that big. But maybe she didn't care about being caught. Maybe she wanted the attention so much she didn't care about the consequences. That was possible, and locating John Timberwolf, if he existed, was one way to find out.

He got away from Walton with a promise that he'd return—and bring a photographer with him. A photographer with color in his camera, he thought to himself, as he took one last look at the shoes. He walked the blocks to the *Newstime* offices in record time, and as soon as he got to the desk, he called down to the library.

He was happy to hear Francine's voice at the other end of the line. She was an excellent researcher, and if anybody could locate Timberwolf, it was she. He suggested to her that she start with Great Falls, Montana, city directories for 1962 and 1963.

It was almost noon when she called back. "O.K., here's what I've got," she began. "No Timberwolf listed in Great Falls for the years you asked or five years on either side."

So it was possible Walton *had* made the whole thing up, he thought. But Timberwolf? Why would she have made up a name like Timberwolf for him to confirm? Why not something like Smith or Jones, something that would have taken days to check out? Or why give a name at all? Why not just pass out some vague hints that would take forever to run down?

Francine was going on. "But there is a Timberlake, John Timberlake listed. He's about the right age and has five children. I've tracked him down at the University of Montana where he's now an associate professor of anthropology. Do you want the phone number?"

That figures, thought Dodman. That crazy woman would be incapable of getting a name straight. The only thing she was capable of doing was destroying Zern Jenner. "Damn," he said aloud.

"Now what kind of thing is that to say," Francine asked indignantly, "after I worked my ass off for you the last couple of hours."

"Ah, hell, Francine, it hasn't got anything to do with you. You're terrific as always, and I appreciate it. So what's that phone number?"

Dr. Timberlake was easy enough to reach, but it was hard to get him to talk once he was on the line. Yes, he had done some janitorial work in the small building where Dr. Brewer had her office, and yes, it was during 1962 and 1963. But he wasn't the least interested, he firmly explained, in saying who might or might not have been going in and out of Dr. Brewer's office.

"I understand why you might not want to be quoted," Dodman said. "But there are other ways we can talk. We can put our conversation off-the-record, if you want, so that it's just between you and me."

"That's exactly what that other smooth bastard said," Timberlake burst out. "And now it's all over the news. Not my name, of course, or anything about me. But I know that reporter—what's his name? Frye?—wouldn't have written anything Rita Walton told him without my backing up the story. And I sure as hell didn't know I was doing that. He didn't even mention her. The way he asked the question, it was like he was doing some kind of innocuous biography of Jenner, and he said he'd heard I'd seen him a few times and what was he like and so on. Even at that I didn't want to say anything until he said it would be 'off-the-record.' And then all I said was, yes, I'd seen Jenner coming and going pretty regularly over about a six-month period, and he was always friendly and cordial. And then this morning on the news there's this damn story about Jenner and the psychiatrist."

"Listen," Timberlake went on, "I'm not a stupid man, and I know I'm responsible for that story. I know this Walton woman, and no reporter would stake his reputation on her alone. I was suckered into backing her up, and I'm not going to be suckered again, so don't give me this 'off-the-record' crap." After a moment he added, considerably less heatedly, "And I hope you understand that I don't want to be quoted on anything I just said, and I don't want to see my name in any of those Jenner stories."

Some reporters refused to let subjects they interviewed put things off-the-record after they had said them, but Dodman had always felt that novices, at any rate, should be allowed a second thought or two. Instead of challenging Timberlake, he simply asked him why he didn't want to be a part of the Jenner story. "Off-the-record, of course," he added.

"The way I look at it," Timberlake said, "if somebody sees a psychiatrist, it's entirely his or her own business."

"But what if that person is the President? Then don't you think the public has a right to know?"

"Maybe so, if it were happening now, but we're talking about a long time ago. What do you think, Dodman, do you think you ought to be held responsible for what you were doing nearly twenty years ago?"

Twenty years ago, Dodman had been twelve, and he couldn't remember anything really scandalous he'd done. Still, Timberlake's question hit home. Twenty years ago, he'd been an entirely different person. There'd been the same name, but beyond that, when he thought back to that twelve-year-old kid in Prairie Village, it was hard to feel any sense of identification. It was like thinking about someone else, not like thinking about yourself. "But I'm not the President," he said, standing his ground with Timberlake.

"But you're human aren't you? And aren't we all? Aren't we all vulnerable and liable to weakness and error?"

Dodman continued to argue, but he left Timberlake unconvinced. Well, that was all right, he told himself, as he hung up. He'd got what he needed—confirmation of the Walton story. And besides he wasn't sure Timberlake was wrong. Was it anybody's business if Jenner saw a psychiatrist almost twenty years ago? But, of course, the President had lied about it. That made it everybody's business, didn't it? And what about Malcolm Ewing?

He picked up the phone, got information, and put through a call to Dorothy Brewer's office. He was not in the least surprised when an answering service informed him that Dr. Brewer was unavailable and offered to connect him with another doctor who was taking her calls.

As he hung up, he realized he really shouldn't put off writing any longer. It was past one o'clock, and his deadline was getting near. Besides, he was into this far enough now, so that he'd have his own story to write. He wouldn't have merely to rehash Frye's. He made one more call, this one to get a photographer over to the Hay-Adams. He didn't see any need to talk to Rita Walton again, but Jack would want pictures. As he waited on the line, he looked at the butt-filled ashtray in front of him and thought to himself that he'd been smoking too much. Maybe that was why he felt bone-weary and it was only the middle of the day.

Chapter 9

THE THOMAS JEFFERSON reading room was not as spectacular as the main reading room at the Library of Congress, but Nancy Dodman found it a cozier place, an easier place to concentrate. And there were apparently a number of people who agreed with her. The Regulars, she called them, the people who day after day came in and took the same place at the same one of the long tables. Whenever a newcomer to the reading room un-wittingly took one of the Regulars' places, Nancy was always amused to watch the newcomer's confusion in the face of the icy indignation which the other readers directed at him.

She was trying to ignore the hunger pangs which told her lunch was overdue. The one really unattractive spot in the library was its depressing basement cafeteria, and so she usually tried putting off going there as long as possible. But she was about to give up. She was getting too hungry to concentrate on the book in front of her, and she found herself instead reading the Jefferson quotations that were inscribed on the walls and watching people come in and go out.

At first she didn't recognize Kitty Crawford. Every time she had seen her before, Kitty had been perfectly groomed. Her makeup was always carefully done, her hair expertly styled. Obviously careful about her diet, she was fashionably thin. And so the disheveled woman coming out of the genealogical reading room was at first unfamiliar. She was gaunt-looking, with no makeup, and her hair was carelessly pulled back in a bun. She had on a pair of too-loose, wrinkled slacks.

As soon as she realized it was Kitty, Nancy waved to catch her eye. The older woman looked confused at first, but then came over.

"How are you, Nancy," she said sitting down on the edge of a chair.

Nancy murmured pleasantries, concealing her shock at the way Kitty looked.

"It's so good to see you," Kitty said, nervously swinging one of her legs back and forth. "Have you had lunch?"

Nancy wasn't eager to get caught up in an extended conversation. She had so few hours at the library each day, and she hated to spend any of them socializing, but she could think of no way to refuse the other woman's offer without seeming rude. "No I haven't. Why don't we go down together?"

As they rode down in the elevator, Nancy recalled the first time she had met Kitty. The President had been spending a few summer weeks at his Montana ranch, and many of the press and White House people who traveled with him had brought their families along. There was a seemingly endless round of parties, and at the second or third one, she'd found herself in a corner with Kitty. They had talked the entire evening. Kitty had confessed how much she hated "circulating," coming up with clever things to say to each new face encountered. And Nancy had confessed that she'd never been able to see the point to it either. Later when she'd mentioned the conversation to Rudy, he'd told her the gossip going around in the press plane. The President had ordered Crawford to bring his wife along on this trip because he'd heard some of the stories about Crawford's playing around. The Secret Service men, the President had been told, had even started a pool on the number of women Crawford would try to get into bed between the time Air Force One left Andrews Air Force Base and the time it returned.

Nancy's sympathies were aroused, and when Kitty Crawford cornered her at the next party and the next, she was patient and friendly, though she really didn't feel the two of them had much in common. Kitty was probably twenty years older, her children were grown, and her outside interests were limited to the volunteer efforts—the charity balls and benefits—to which so many political wives devoted themselves.

The two women went through the library's cafeteria line and found a table. Kitty ignored her salad and began talking rapidly about how she'd decided to trace her ancestry. One of her foremothers, she had already confirmed, had been a missionary and one of the first women to cross the Continental Divide.

Nancy was interested. Finding out more about a woman like that was a project on which she could have happily spent time. But when she looked closely at Kitty, she suspected that the genealogy was more a distraction for her, more a coverup for what was really important. The older woman seemed fragile, brittle, held together by the thinnest of threads, and there were tears in her eyes.

"Kitty, what is it? What's wrong?"

Kitty was silent for a moment. "There's hardly anything right," she said finally. "I'd thought the genealogy might help, but it only makes it worse. I keep comparing my life with Eliza Manser's. You know, she died when she was only forty-two, but the church she and her husband started kept going. And think how worthwhile she must have felt every day of her life to be. I feel, I don't know, maybe ashamed is the right word."

"Ashamed! Why should you feel that way?" Nancy tried to lighten the mood. "You know there's just not much call for female missionaries to ride horseback to Oregon these days."

"It's not the life I don't have that troubles me. It's the one I do have. It's the shame and pretense I go through every day. You know about Allen. Everybody in town knows about Allen. Except they all pretend not to know around me. And I pretend not to know."

Nancy didn't know what to say. Kitty was right, of course, and she herself was one of those who made a show around Kitty of being unaware of the women Allen was sleeping with.

"I should leave him," Kitty went on. "My pride should make me leave him. But you know what? Without him, I'm not anybody. Do you think I'd ever be invited any place if I left him? That anybody'd ever call me to do anything? Not a chance. And the worst part is, I care about that. What kind of person does that make me? I don't want to be a nobody so much that I keep pretending, even when everybody must think I'm an utter fool." Tears began running down her face.

"Kitty, that's not true. You have friends."

"No, I don't think so. This is a funny town. You really

don't have friends here unless you have power. Or at least people have to think you have power. If I had friends, do you think there'd be this silence about Allen? If I had friends, the first time he went to a party without me and left with another woman, there'd be a mention of it somewhere. You know, just enough of a hint in the newspaper so that he wouldn't feel free to do it again. And again."

"It's not because you don't have friends that reporters don't mention those things. It's more like an unwritten rule that a man's sex life—and a woman's too, I guess— is nobody's business. Unless someone does something really spectacular to make it everybody's business, like jump into the Tidal Basin or something."

"But is that fair?" asked Kitty leaning forward. "Is that really fair? Look what they're doing to the President right now. What does the fact that a man saw a psychiatrist almost twenty years ago have to do with anything? I'd say that whether a man can keep his pants zipped or not tells a lot more about his character." She leaned over, picked up her large purse, and fished through it. "Listen to me. I *sound* like a rejected woman. I don't even like myself this way." She took a wadded-up Kleenex from her purse. "He's such a fool too," she said, wiping her eyes. "He thinks those women are interested in him. He doesn't know that without the White House they wouldn't look at him twice."

Nancy again found herself unsure how to respond. She had never understood either why the press, so eager after private details about public figures, generally regarded sexual behavior off-limits. From some of the things she'd heard from Rudy about the reporters themselves, she'd wondered from time to time if it was a kind of gentleman's agreement between the press and the politicians. Something like: you don't tell my wife and I won't tell the world about you.

If she were Kitty, she knew what she'd do. It was hard to imagine leaving Rudy, but she would if she found out he was sleeping with another woman. There was a basic standard of honesty that had to be met in a relationship, if it was to have any meaning at all. But she wasn't Kitty, and she understood the older woman's dilemma. What could she do without Crawford? Who would she be? And yet was any kind of identity worth having when it required so much humiliation?

"Kitty, would you like to come by the house for awhile? It's not too long a walk."

"No, no. I'm going home." She wiped her eyes again with the much-used Kleenex. "I'll be fine. I don't know why these things are bothering me so much." She attempted a smile. "It's not as though it's a new situation."

The two women parted, and Nancy rode the elevator back up to the reading room. She was too distracted to study now, so she decided to give up and go home. She gathered up her books, took the elevator down again, and went out through the revolving doors into the cloudy autumn afternoon.

IT WAS after ten P.M. when he finished writing. As he usually did on Thursdays, Rudy had come home in the early afternoon and shut himself up in the spare bedroom he called his study. Nancy had brought him coffee and sandwiches around dinner time, but she hadn't stayed to talk, and so, aside from a phone call to Sarah to make sure nothing new had come out at the daily briefings, he'd been writing—and rewriting and rewriting— for almost eight hours.

Still, he wasn't happy with the result. The problem was trying to write the story according to his own inclinations and still satisfy the editors in New York. It was their business to sell magazines, so if what he wrote didn't strike them as having enough zip, they'd hype it until he couldn't recognize it. Therefore, he generally tried to put in enough zip so that they wouldn't make changes too major—and usually that was enough to make him slightly dissatisfied with his work.

He looked at his lead: "Zern Jenner is now facing the worst crisis of his presidency, not because of any action he has undertaken during his tenure in office, but because of events which occurred almost two decades ago." It read well enough, he decided. It would more accurately reflect his current feelings if he wrote it to question whether events from twenty years ago ought to be causing such a crisis, but that would never get by. He smiled to himself, remembering the comment of one of his White House colleagues, a reporter from another of the news weeklies, who had complained that when New York finished with what he had written it looked like a "chicken that had been hit by a Mack truck."

Oh, hell, it was fine, he thought. It was as good as he could do. He picked up his story and headed downstairs. "I'll be back," he yelled out to Nancy as he took his coat off the hall rack. She'd know he was taking his story in.

Twenty minutes later, he walked into the *Newstime* offices to find Jack Sasser and Sarah Hoff sitting in the glass-partitioned area where Sasser worked.

"Jack's trying to cheer me up," Sarah said, when she saw him. "I was downstairs and walked through the art department and you know what they've got hanging up on the wall? A cover with Boyston's picture on it, and the banner reads, 'The New President.' I know they've had them for every Vice President. I know they have to make them up just in case. But Boyston. God, I can't even stand to think of that."

"Because you love Jenner more or because you love Boyston less?" asked Dodman.

"I don't want to see Boyston President."

"Sometimes," said Sasser, "it does happen that a man

110

totally unsuited to power nonetheless achieves it in a democracy. I think Boyston's one."

"But how does that happen?" Sarah asked. "Can't people *see* what he is?"

"Well, the ones who do are usually scared to say so. Or they let him buy them."

"Buy? Who's he bought?" Rudy asked.

"Oh, I was just thinking back to Boyston's gubernatorial race and some of the stories that came out of it."

"Oh, yeah, wasn't there something about a newspaper editor?" Rudy asked.

"Right," said Jack. "He'd gone after Boyston hard, when Boyston was in the state legislature. Several really stinging editorials about Boyston's arrogance, about how his only motivation was self-interest. But then the paper was strangely quiet during the governor's race. Finally, somebody found out that Boyston had picked up the entire tab for the editor's kids to go to college."

"So now he's Vice President," Sarah said.

Sasser shook his head slowly from side to side. "Nobody ever said it was a merit system. Not all the time anyway."

"Have you heard Basinger's story?" Rudy asked Sarah. "His story about Boyston?"

"I don't think so."

"Dale told Jack and me, off-the-record, of course, that Boyston called him one night at home, and the man was ranting and raving. Basinger said a stream of profanity came over the phone, but he couldn't understand the point of it. Boyston was mad as hell about something, but he was so mad, he couldn't even get across the idea of what he was mad about. And whatever it was, he seems to have forgotten about it by the next day, because he never said another word to Dale."

"That is not the kind of man you want to have in control of the football," Sarah said, using the White House slang for the little black bag that was always near the President and that contained the SAC codes, the information necessary to launch a nuclear attack.

"That is not the kind of man you even want to have close to the football," Rudy said.

"Well, this is not talk to raise your spirits, is it?" Sasser said, looking at Sarah and leaning back in his chair. He glanced at Rudy, "I've been trying to cheer up this gorgeous young woman with my standard lecture on how life imitates art."

"Rudy," she said, "did you know that in the sixties there was a movie called *"The President's Analyst?"*

"Not a very good movie," said Jack. "A heavy-handed satire, and it was never clear whether LBJ was the target or whether it was psychiatry in general they were aiming at."

"But it was about a President who had a shrink," Sarah said to Rudy.

"Do you think that now about Jenner and Ewing?" Dodman asked her.

"I don't know. But it looks bad, that's for sure. A President with a record of psychiatric treatment whose close adviser is a psychiatrist. And that close adviser sees him for an hour every day and nobody'll say why. How'd you write it?" she asked, nodding toward the file of papers he was holding.

"I said something about the spotlight falling on Ewing now." He looked through the pages he was holding. "Here it is: 'Before Zern Jenner can hope to put this crisis behind him, he not only needs to explain why he lied about past visits to Dr. Brewer, he needs to clarify the role presently being played by his aide, Dr. Malcolm Ewing.'"

He laid the story down on Sasser's desk. "You know Nancy was saying this morning how strangely this whole thing is unraveling. It all started with the log and questions about why Ewing was in the Oval Office every day, and we still don't know about that, but we've found out a hell of a lot else. We've found out things that happened almost twenty years ago."

"It's really not so strange if you compare it with Watergate," Sasser said. "It's still a mystery, if you think about it, why they wanted to get into Democratic headquarters and tap Larry O'Brien's phone. If they wanted information on the McGovern campaign, they should have tapped McGovern's office. No one's ever explained why they zeroed in on O'Brien. We found out other things. We found out about Nixon's tapes and his taxes. But I'm still not sure we know why those guys broke in."

"All of which proves what the entire country has always suspected," said Sarah. "Washington is not a rational place."

"And sometimes I think we're part of the problem," said Dodman. "All of us, I mean. The newspapers, the magazines, the networks. When all of us zero in on a story like this, each of us looking for his own angle, it grows and expands and develops so many parts and facets it's no wonder we lose sight of whatever event catalyzed the whole thing."

"But all those parts and facets are important," Sarah said. "I mean the American people deserve to know if the man they've elected President has been treated by a psychiatrist. And especially they deserve to know if he's lied about it."

Dodman put out his cigarette in a Cinzano ashtray Jack had on his desk. "Sure they do," he said without much conviction. "Sure they do." Then he picked up his coat and announced he was going home.

"I'll walk out with you," Sarah volunteered.

Neither of them said anything during the elevator ride down, but when they got out to the street, Sarah spoke.

"You do think what we're doing is important, don't you? You do think these Jenner stories are necessary?"

"Ah, hell, Sarah, ask me in the morning. Right now I'm beat, and when I get tired, I get down. You know what a damned roller coaster this business can be. One minute you're up, convinced that you're saving the Republic, and the next minute you're convinced that what you're writing is crap. Tomorrow morning I'll be sure again that it's the public's right to know what Zern Jenner was doing twenty years ago. It's partly trying to write the damned story so New York will like it that gets me. To make them happy, you've always got to push things a little, to make them about five percent larger than life. And when I get through doing that, I always wonder if I shouldn't have tried for five percent smaller." He paused for a moment. "Right now I feel a little like this is Salem and we're helping run this year's witch hunt."

"Oh, Rudy, don't say that."

She sounded genuinely distressed, and he looked down at her, surprised at how emotionally she had reacted to what he had said. He hadn't meant to upset her. "You want to go get a drink?" he asked.

"Sure," she answered, putting her hand through his arm.

They walked over to H Street where the Demonstration was located. It was a restaurant which, despite the elegant black-and-white canopy over its entryway, had a loose and low-key atmosphere—especially compared to other gathering spots in the vicinity of the White House, such as Sans Souci or the Metropolitan Club. Consequently, the Demonstration had become a favorite hangout of the Washington press corps, and even though the price of its drinks had gone up recently, it was crowded. Rudy managed to get them a table, and when they sat down, Sarah ordered a Scotch. He ordered a double.

114

"Tell me more about the briefings today," he said, trying to get back to business as usual.

"Well, this morning, Westfield used the old squeeze play. It must have been 11:30 before he started, and then the wires tried to end the briefing about quarter to twelve. I know it's not the wire services' fault that so many newspapers have to be fed by noon, but it makes me so mad, the way it plays right into Westfield's hands. Anyway, there was so much griping this morning that he took a couple more questions, but he wouldn't confirm or deny the *Post* story, like I told you earlier, and he wouldn't say anything about Ewing. It was the same this afternoon. 'No comment' whenever the *Post* story came up, and a lot of crap about executive confidentiality when anybody asked about Ewing.

"Markham was really funny," she went on, mentioning a wire service reporter whom they were both fond of. "When Westfield kept refusing to answer questions, Markham said, just loud enough for everybody to hear, 'If somebody doesn't tell me something pretty soon, I'm going to start writing lies.'"

"Any new ideas floating around the pressroom about who might have leaked the log?"

"Not really. Everybody's having a lot of fun with Morris and Latvala's suggestion that Ewing did it. If that isn't them at their worst, passing on gossip and not really investigating it, not even thinking it through. It's so ridiculous to think Ewing would have leaked the log, given the headaches it means for him. Markham suggested that if Ewing did put the log out, he ought to go into the *Guiness Book of World Records* for—how did he put it?—'the largest wound ever inflicted upon himself by a human being.'"

Dodman laughed, drank his Scotch, and ordered another. "About the only sensible thing in the Morris and

Latvala column was the idea that whoever leaked the log sure as hell didn't do it for the fun of it. He expected to get something out of it. So who stands to gain?"

"Boyston, maybe? I don't know, maybe he'd like to get Jenner in trouble."

"Yeah, but could he have known how much trouble the log would get the President in? I doubt he'd have known the stuff about Jenner's past that's come out. I suppose it's possible—just possible—he suspected Ewing might be treating the President, but if he did, there are more direct ways he could have put that out, ways that wouldn't also have spread the embarrassing news that he's hardly ever in the Oval Office."

"But just how embarrassing is it for him to have that known? My impression is that his hard-core followers won't be turned off to find out he's cut out of the action. Instead they'll be indignant . . ."

"And they'll be writing letters, I bet. Why don't you see if you can get some sort of breakdown from the press office tomorrow on how much of the mail the White House is getting has a pro-Boyston twist to it?"

"And I'll call the Vice President's office too."

The waitress brought Dodman a second drink, and Sarah looked around the restaurant. There were a few new posters up, she noticed, a Joan Baez she hadn't seen before and an Eldridge Cleaver she didn't think she had. Practically every face she could remember from the sixties was memorialized somewhere on the Demonstration's walls.

"Have you heard of anybody who's even seen Ewing since this whole thing started?" Dodman asked.

"Nope. He's not answering at home or returning calls at the office. Somebody told me a couple of the guys had even set up a watch for him at the southwest gate, but they haven't seen him coming or going."

"You suppose he's out of town?"

"Could be. But where would he go? And why?"

"Let's war-game it out a little," said Dodman, sipping his drink. He was thinking to himself that he should slow down. Two doubles was more Scotch than he usually consumed in a month. "If there were some innocent reason for Ewing being gone, we'd know about it, right? I mean if it were something like he was in Montana helping settle the Whitefeather claims. But we don't know, so suppose it's not innocent. Suppose you're Zern Jenner and it's true Ewing's your shrink. Would you want him talking to the press?"

"Of course not."

"And what's the best way to keep that from happening?"

"Well, next to putting out a contract on him, sending him out of town, I guess."

"But where? That's the sixty-four-dollar question."

"There's practically no place he can be that we can't get to him."

Dodman was silent for a minute. "Sure there is!" he said suddenly. "Sure there is! Camp David. I'll bet Jenner sent him to Camp David."

"Where Nixon sent Dean," Sarah said, drawing on the Watergate trivia she remembered, though it seemed now it had been an age ago that that had all happened.

"Camp David. Of course. Nobody can get to him there without clearance from the White House. Why didn't I think of it sooner? Hey, we're a hell of a team." He reached across the table and put his hand over hers. It was a gesture of enthusiasm, but as soon as she looked up at him, it quickly became something else. Dodman thought to himself that the Scotch was to blame, but whatever it was, he knew he was crossing over into a territory where he hadn't been before. "You're beautiful," he said.

The catch in his voice told her it was more than a

117

flippant compliment he was offering. "So are you," she said. "Come home with me, Rudy."

"Ah, Sarah, I want to. I want to. But there's Nancy and Mac."

"Shhh. This doesn't have anything to do with them."

"Yes, it does," he said pulling his hand away. "Damn it, I want to come home with you in the worst way. But there really is a sense—hell, I don't even know how to say it—but if I go home with you that really is an act of deceit. It's nothing I could ever tell Nancy without destroying our marriage."

"So why do you worry about telling her? It's not like she loses anything by what we do." She could feel tears coming on.

"I guess the bottom line is that I can't stand the idea of Nancy sleeping with someone else. I don't know what I could 'lose' if she did, but there's something. And it's got to cut both ways."

"You should have been a Jesuit," she said. "No, I don't mean chastity," she added, catching his quizzical glance. "I just mean you'd be perfect worrying about how many orders of angels there are and how many deadly sins. You're too . . . too . . . *mental*," she said finally, unable to think of a better word. "That's not what life's about. Rudy, in forty or fifty years, we're going to be dead. Let's take what there is now."

"You know," he said reflectively, "I can remember back when I first met Jack. One night we had a couple of beers together, and he said you could tell a lot about a man—I guess he was talking about politicians particularly—by whether he cheated on his wife. His theory was that any man willing to be deceitful in what was probably the closest relationship of his life was likely to be deceitful when it came to his work too."

"If Jack said that, then I think he was being goddamned self-righteous. And you can't tell me he's never

118

slept with anyone besides Anne. And what about you," she said, anger in her voice now. "You can't tell me you've never slept with anyone besides Nancy."

"Not since we've been married."

"Not even during the campaign?"

"No, not even then, though I admit it sounds unlikely."

"The thing about a campaign is that nobody's ever expected home," she said as much to herself as to him.

They were both silent, each aware the other was thinking that Nancy was indeed expecting him home.

"Let's go," Sarah said, standing up abruptly. She walked quickly out of the Demonstration, leaving him behind to settle the bill. He caught up with her outside.

"I'm taking you home," he said. "It's past midnight and you shouldn't be on the street alone."

"I can take care of myself. What are you all of a sudden? My male protector?"

"Well, if that bothers you, don't think of it as a male-female thing. Just think of it as a buddy system. After midnight you should only walk the streets of Washington with a buddy."

They walked to the metro stop in silence, took the short ride to DuPont Circle, and then walked the two blocks to the building her apartment was in.

"I appreciate your concern," she said icily, putting her key into the outside door.

"Sarah, I'm sorry," he said, putting his hand on her shoulder.

She turned, and then she was in his arms, crying.

"I'm sorry, I'm sorry," he kept repeating. And then he was kissing her, tenderly at first, and then with greater insistence.

"Rudy, come home with me," she whispered in his ear.

"Yes, Sarah. Oh, yes."

She unlocked the outside door to the apartment building, and they started up the wide, dimly lit staircase. Halfway up, he stopped her and kissed her again. He was running his hand down the length of her tawny hair, when he felt her body go tense.

"Rudy, there's somebody up there," she whispered.

"What?"

"At the top of the stairs, there's somebody standing up there. Not coming down or going up, just standing there."

He didn't say anything.

"Rudy?" she said finally.

"Ah, hell, Sarah," he said quietly. "Just hell!" He stepped back, took her face in his hands, and looked at her intently for a moment. Then he told her to stay where she was, and he walked up to the second-floor landing.

The woman he found waiting up there outside Sarah's door regarded him coolly.

"Can I help you with something?" he offered, not knowing what else to say.

"I'm just waiting for someone," she answered.

Dodman turned and motioned for Sarah to come on up.

"Wendy?" she said when she had arrived at the top of the stairs. "Wendy Greene? What are you doing here?"

"I didn't know where else to go. I stayed with a friend last night, and he even found me there."

"Who found you? What are you talking about?"

"I'm sorry. Of course, you don't know. It's that fellow from the *Post*, Frye's his name. He kept calling, along with everybody else, and then when I quit answering the phone, he started following me. Yesterday he was waiting for me outside work, waiting with his questions about Malcolm. He followed me home so I packed a suitcase and went to stay with a friend, but he followed me there too and he was waiting outside this morning. I lost him by acting as though I were going into my studio, but then not going there. I've sort of been wandering all day. I went to a late movie tonight, but I don't have enough money with me for a hotel room, or any clothes, so I don't know what to do now. I remembered where you lived and thought I'd see if you have an extra bed. One of the fellows who lives downstairs let me in when I said I knew you, and I've been waiting since. Will you put me up?"

Sarah looked at Rudy, trying to read his face. It was regret she saw there, wasn't it? "Sure I will," she said finally.

The two women went into the apartment. Dodman went back down the wide wooden steps, out the door, and headed back toward the DuPont Circle metro stop. He walked rapidly, trying to break the tight bands of frustration he could feel across his chest and shoulders. He found himself halfway hoping he'd encounter a mugger—or someone—anyone—he could kick and hit and lash out at.

Chapter 10

THE PRESIDENT of the United States turned on the lamp beside his bed. Although it had been years since he'd been unable to sleep, he'd not forgot the lesson he'd learned long ago about insomnia: the best remedy was to ignore it, to act as though you didn't want to be asleep. Then, sometimes, sleep would come, but if you pursued it, if you lay there in the dark and tried with every cell and nerve ending to sleep, it never came.

As he swung himself out of bed, intending to get a book, his glance fell on his wife Mary, lying asleep on her back in the other twin bed. He remembered asking her once how she could possibly sleep on her back, and so quietly too, and she had smiled and told him that she lay on her back because sleeping with her face in the pillow might cause wrinkles.

Well, that was typical of Mary. Whatever the pundits said about his tenacity and self-control, they were nothing compared to hers. She truly had a will of steel, and there never yet had been any difficulty too big for her.

But because she was so strong, so certain of herself, she wasn't the kind of woman you could easily turn to with your problems. Just talking about problems seemed self-indulgent to her. If you had some difficulty, you identified it and overcame it. You didn't examine it or "wallow" in it, as she put it. Tonight at dinner, she'd wanted him to deny the Frye story. "Zern, why don't you just tell them it's untrue, tell them that wretched woman is lying."

"Mary, some things just aren't easy," he had said. "It's a complex matter."

"I don't see what's so complicated about standing up and saying the story isn't true." When he didn't answer, it seemed to puzzle her at first, then to make her angry. "Zern, you didn't see that psychiatrist, did you? I remember you were in Great Falls a lot on business that year. You weren't going to a psychiatrist, were you?"

"Mary, look, I'm not sure . . ."

"And if you did see her, why did you deny it at the press conference?"

"Mary, damn it, just listen a minute. O.K., I did see Dr. Brewer. After I lost that Senate race to Clarke, I felt like I had to talk things out with somebody. I felt like I'd let you down and myself down and everybody down. I had to talk, but I didn't want to burden you with how I felt or anybody else who was close to me. I'd burdened you enough already. So I went to see her a couple of times a week for about six months."

"I . . . I just don't understand. We've talked about all that psychiatric nonsense before, and you've agreed with me about it. People can take care of their own lives. They don't need analysts to do it for them."

"I wasn't looking for someone to run my life or tell me how to solve my problems. I needed to talk, that was all, to talk to somebody I wasn't personally involved with."

"But why did you deny it at the press conference? It didn't solve anything. It made everything worse." She paused for a moment. "All right, I can understand why you might have been embarrassed about it, but you've got to come out now and admit you saw that psychiatrist, and you've got to do it quickly. All three networks tonight mentioned Malcolm Ewing and his psychiatric training, and they'll mention it tomorrow night and the next and the next. If you're not forthright and direct about the past, pretty soon the whole country's going to think there's something devious going on right now."

"Mary, I don't think . . ."

"It's not to think about, it's to do! This is just like that 'domestic propaganda' nonsense during the campaign. You were wrong to say that, but you wouldn't admit it, and you're wrong now, but you won't say so. This time your stubbornness is going to cost you the presidency."

She had slammed from the room, and they hadn't spoken since. Yet despite the quarrel, despite the tension between them, there she was, sleeping as though nothing were troubling her, nothing at all.

Walking to the bookcase, he suddenly had a picture in his mind of Mary, standing in front of the fireplace in the living room of their Montana ranch house. "So you lost again," she was saying, standing there trim and neat in a wool shirt and exquisitely tailored riding pants. "That just means you'll have to run again, that's all." Funny, he thought, the tricks the mind plays, picking out that one particular scene from the past now. He tried to remember what had led up to Mary's making that fireplace declaration and what had followed it, but he couldn't bring the surrounding events into as sharp a focus.

He did remember, though, that she simply could not

understand his pain and humiliation. He still wasn't sure why losing had been such agony for him, but he had begun to suspect, during the hours he had spent talking to Dorothy Brewer, that part of it was simply that his life had prepared him to win. As the eldest son, as an outstanding student, he had learned to expect praise, honor, and accolade, not defeat. He hadn't been prepared to lose, especially not the second time when it looked as though loss might be a pattern for him. And he still wasn't a good loser. He still expected success.

He looked through the bookcase, but his mind kept wandering. It was interesting, he thought, that he still valued success so highly, even now that he had experienced it and knew how it differed from the fantasies about it. In the fantasies, the successful person had hundreds wanting to be his friend and the problem was to sort the true from the false friends. Well, in real life there was also the falling away of old friends. Not anybody he had been terribly close to—he was not the kind of man who had ever cultivated very close friends—but men he'd known and liked for a long time. He remembered Bob Murain and how he and Bob had grown up together, played football together, and dated the same girls. But Bob had ceased to be his friend the moment he'd become a senator. Whenever their paths would cross, he could see Bob asking himself, "Why you and not me? I'm as good a man as you are; why should you be the senator?"

Myth to the contrary, not everybody loved a winner. He and Dale Basinger had been able to see that when they looked at the statistics showing which age groups tended to give him most support. Almost always it was voters younger than he and older than he to whom he most appealed. Those his own age were not so supportive, almost as though they wished to deny any worldly success greater than their own to one of their own.

He could feel the same thing at work in congressmen and senators and Cabinet members, in the commentators and columnists of his generation. "What's so special about you?" he read in their eyes, time after time. Perhaps, he thought, that was why he'd come to depend so much on Dale Basinger and Malcolm Ewing. Younger than he, they seemed not to envy or resent him. Perhaps they, unlike his peers, hadn't yet had to give up the dream that they might one day be sitting behind the desk in the Oval Office.

He picked up a volume of Sandburg's biography of Lincoln and leafed through it. Whom had Lincoln confided in, he wondered. Lincoln had had a Mary too, he remembered, a very different Mary from his own, a far less formidable and far more vulnerable woman. She couldn't have been a confidante. Mary Lincoln had been too insecure and fragile a personality to make her a source of solace and counsel. He put down Sandburg, picked up Churchill's *Their Finest Hour*, and turned to the familiar first page. What a feat, he thought, to be able to write with such order and clarity about the chaos of war. Churchill had used writing and painting as therapy, he remembered reading once, therapy to combat the moods of depression which had sometimes threatened, usually when he was out of office. And Lincoln suffered severe depressions. Was it he—or had it been Churchill—who had described the dark cloud that descended from time to time as "the black dog"?

He picked up Sandburg again and took it and the Churchill volume back to his bed. As he arranged the pillows so that he could read comfortably, it occurred to him again how strange a mechanism the mind is. How odd it was that now, of all times, his hand should have fallen on books by and about men who, had they lived in the last quarter of the twentieth century, might easily have been prospects for the psychiatrist's couch.

Chapter 11

AT FIRST Dodman thought it was the alarm clock, but when the noise persisted even after he had pushed in the clock's button, he realized the telephone was ringing. As he stumbled down the hallway to answer it, he wished for at least the hundredth time that he and Nancy had had the upstairs extension put in the bedroom.

"Hullo," he said.

"Mr. Dodman? Would you hold one moment, please, for Mr. Crawford?"

He recognized the voice of one of the White House operators. "Sure," he said, looking at his wrist to see what time it was. But his watch was lying on the bedside table. "Uh, ma'am," he said, trying to catch the operator before she connected Crawford. "What time is it please?"

"It's six forty-five," she said pleasantly.

Whatever Crawford wanted must be pretty important, Dodman thought. He was notorious for being unavailable in the mornings, for being too hung over to make the White House morning staff meeting. Dodman rubbed his own throbbing head, and for the first time felt some small measure of sympathy for Allen Crawford.

"Dodman?" Crawford came on the line. "I just wanna know where the hell you get off using your wife to try to find out things about me."

Dodman was immediately and thoroughly irritated. "Listen, I don't know what you're talking about."

"You know what I'm talking about, setting your wife to trip Kitty into discussing our personal life. Well, I want you to know, Dodman, that I'm going to your bureau chief and your editor on this one, and you damn well better not try to print one word of it. This is the goddamnedest violation of journalistic ethics I ever heard of."

A loud click told Dodman that Crawford had hung up. He stood looking at the receiver for a moment, stupefied with sleep, the hangover, and the shock of Crawford's sudden attack. Then he slowly hung up the phone and walked back to the bedroom.

"Nance, Nance, wake up. I've got to talk to you."

"Where were you last night?" she asked as soon as she was awake.

"Let's talk about that later. Right now I need to know about Kitty Crawford."

She looked at him, and he could tell she was considering whether to let him temporarily off the hook or not. Finally she relented and told him about her encounter with Kitty at the Library of Congress. "I didn't want to bother you with it yesterday while you were writing," she concluded. "And then you were so late last night."

"I don't think it's that important anyway. She didn't

tell you anything about Crawford that isn't common knowledge."

"Except how upset she is. I don't think anyone realized that. Maybe I should call her later this morning."

"Don't do that. You'd really set off Crawford's paranoia. Just let it alone."

"Rudy, where were you last night?" she asked after a moment's silence.

"I took Sarah home," he said, reaching over and touching her face with his fingertips.

She said nothing and turned her head away.

"There wasn't anything, Nance," he said, thinking that that wasn't quite true. "There won't be anything."

When she still didn't answer, he decided to leave her alone for awhile. He shaved and dressed, being as quiet as he could so he wouldn't wake Mac, and then he went back to her bedside.

"Look, Nance, I've gotta call Sarah. There are some things she needs to get on first thing. Don't be this way. Hey, you know I love you. Just you."

She still didn't answer, and he went down the hall and dialed Sarah's number. When she came on the line, he asked her with matchless objectivity, he thought, to get together with Francine in the research department and see if the two of them couldn't come up with a way of confirming whether Ewing was at Camp David. "Francine can pull together all the dope on the place, and the two of you can put your minds to it," he told her.

Sarah's voice at the other end of the line was also objective and even. He remembered that Wendy Greene was staying with her so that she probably had an audience too. Just as well, he thought.

Back in the bedroom, Nancy's eyes were shut, but he knew she wasn't really asleep. He was sure she had monitored carefully every word of his phone call to Sarah. He went around to her side of the bed, leaned over, and kissed her. When she opened her eyes, he could tell she had been crying.

"Hey, I'm sorry," he said.

"Rudy, you just know how it has to be with us. It won't work any other way."

"I know. I know," he said, kneeling down and putting his arm around her. But he realized as he kissed her that keeping things the way they had to be wasn't as simple as he had thought.

SITTING AT her desk in the *Newstime* office, eating a doughnut and waiting for Francine to come up from the research department, Sarah decided to do some more phoning. Her first call, the one she had just made to the Vice President's office, had produced some interesting information: Boyston was getting hundreds of letters from citizens who were indignant that Jenner wasn't consulting him more. Far from embarrassing the Vice President, the log was stirring up his supporters, a fact that deserved some thinking about.

Sarah wasn't at all sure that the other calls she had in mind would be as productive, but she went ahead and dialed Jerry Gersten's office. She and Jerry had an easy affection for one another, based partly on the fact that both of them enjoyed hinting to their friends that the relationship went far beyond that.

"Gersten here," he said, answering his own phone.

"Hi, Jerry. It's Sarah. What's happening?"

"You probably know as much about that as I do," he said, sounding distracted.

"C'mon, that's hard to believe," she said, surprised at his curtness and seeming inattention. "Like I'll bet you know where I could get hold of Malcolm Ewing."

"Nope. Sorry. I don't know who can help you with that question."

"Basinger knows, doesn't he?"

He didn't answer her question directly. "I think you'd be surprised at all the people there are trying to figure out where Malcolm is."

"What's that mean, Jerry?"

"That's it, Sarah. No more for now. I'll talk to you later."

She made a few notes on the conversation and concluded it had raised more questions than it answered. So who did know where Malcolm was? And what was going on over there in the West Wing anyway that had Gersten acting so unlike himself?

She dialed the number of the White House advance office. The advance men, who traveled ahead of the President, seeing to the million details which made a presidential trip go smoothly, were incredibly good sources of information, though it was usually hard to pry out of them what they knew. Sarah was pleased when Steve Bravo, head of the advance office came on the phone.

"Hiya, Steve. Listen, you advanced anybody up to Camp David lately?"

He laughed. "What're you fishing for, Sarah, my love?"

"I just thought you might know who's up at Camp David."

"No, not me. The President himself could be up there, and I wouldn't know it. The procedure for getting him up there is so standard, the advance office isn't even involved in it."

"I figured it was a stupid question, but I thought it might lead you to say something brilliant."

"Well, of course you'd think that. But I'm saving 'brilliant' for my book. Listen, little lady, maybe one of these days, I'll hire you for my ghost writer."

"It's a deal," she said, signaling Francine, who had walked up to her desk with a thick folder, to sit down.

When Sarah hung up the phone, Francine put the folder on her desk.

"There's a lot here," Francine said, "but I don't know how useful it's going to be."

"Let's look through it," Sarah said, picking up the folder, "and see what inspires us."

Francine pulled her chair around so they could both read the information sheets. They skimmed through the brief history of Camp David—known as Shangri-la during FDR's time, renamed by Eisenhower, modernized by Nixon—and set it aside by mutual consent. They lingered longer over the map that was next in the pile.

" 'Aspen.' That's where the President stays, isn't it?" said Sarah, pointing to a blacked-in shape in the map's lower right-hand corner. "And 'Laurel,' what's that?" she asked, moving her finger upward.

"Laurel's one of the places Nixon built. It's a big conference center. There's an office for the President in it too, and mess facilities."

"If Ewing's up there, is that where he'd stay?"

"No, people don't stay in Laurel, as I understand it, though he'd probably have his meals there."

"So where would he stay?"

"In one of these other cabins, like 'Walnut,' or 'Holly,' or 'Dogwood,' or 'Birch.' "

Sarah was silent a moment. "Nobody's ever in any of those cabins though, unless it's somebody the White House sends up, right?"

"Basically."

"So if we could confirm that *somebody's* staying up there, we'd have some support for the idea that Ewing's there, wouldn't we? There's nobody else I can think of the White House would have up there right now."

"True."

"So how can we do that?"

Both women studied the map.

"I wonder," Francine said, "if there's any pattern to where this administration puts its guests. I mean it might be easier to confirm if just one of those cabins is occupied or not than it would be to have to check all of them out. Is there one place, do you suppose, where they usually put visitors?"

"Let's look through the clips and see what we can find out." She handed half the newspaper and magazine clippings from the folder to Francine and began to look through the other half herself.

"It's 'Birch'," Francine said, after a few minutes. "Here's Boyston staying at 'Birch' and here's Basinger and his wife. It looks like 'Birch' is the cabin they use first, then they fill up the others."

"Same thing here. It's 'Birch,' all right. If Ewing's up there, that's where he'd be. But now that we know that, what'll we do? Who's in charge of Camp David anyway? Who'd be likely to know if 'Birch' is occupied?"

"It's run by the Navy, so the military office, I guess."

"I've got a phone number for them here someplace," Sarah said rummaging through her desk. "And I've got an idea." She found the number, dialed, and waited for an answer.

"This is Joanie in Mr. Basinger's office," she said to the voice that answered. "A cold? Oh, yes, I do have a little sore throat. Nothing serious. It's this crazy weather, hot and then cold. You never know what to expect.

"Anyway, the President has invited Mr. and Mrs. Basinger to use Camp David this weekend, and Mr. Basinger asked me to call and tell you they'd like to stay in 'Birch'." She paused, listening to the voice on the other end of the line. "Well, would you mind if I called you back instead? I've got a couple of errands to run, but I'll be back in about ten minutes, and I'll give you a call."

She hung up the phone and looked at Francine. "They have to check with the officer in charge of Camp David.

Pray they aren't too efficient about getting the information and calling Basinger's office with it."

Both women waited anxiously for ten minutes to pass, then Sarah dialed the military office again. "Hi, this is Joanie calling back." She listened for a moment. "O.K., well, thanks. I'll get back to you."

She smiled triumphantly as she hung up the phone. "Mr. and Mrs. Basinger can't stay in 'Birch' because it's occupied."

"Fantastic," Francine said.

"If we could just be sure by whom it's occupied," said Sarah. "Ah, hell, it's worth a try." She turned to the phone again and dialed 456-1414, the White House switchboard. "Would you please connect me with 'Birch' cabin at Camp David, please?" She listened for a minute and then said, "I'd like to speak to whomever's staying there." She listened again, and then whispered to Francine, "She wants a name." Francine shrugged her shoulders. "I'd like to speak to Malcolm Ewing, please," Sarah said finally into the phone. She looked disgusted with the operator's response and put the phone back in its cradle. "She offered to connect me with his office."

"Well, anyway, we know somebody's staying there."

"Yeah, I'd better tell Rudy."

She reached him at the White House press office.

"So, somebody's up there, but you can't be sure it's Ewing," he said, when she finished telling him what she'd learned.

"That's it."

"And you don't think you can use this sudden skill you've developed of passing yourself off as a White House employee to find out if it's Malcolm?"

"No. For one thing, I don't think many people know where Ewing is, so whom would I call? I talked to Gersten this morning—it was a most peculiar conversation—and he left the impression that even Basinger might not be able to locate Ewing right now."

"What's Wendy Greene have to say?"

"She doesn't know where he is. She says she hasn't seen him since last weekend."

"Did he tell her he was leaving? Did he take a suitcase?"

"I asked her if he'd told her he'd be gone, and she started crying."

"So what'd you do? Let her off the hook?"

"No, At least not then. When she calmed down, I asked a couple more questions, but all she'd say was that she just couldn't talk about it."

"So then you let her off the hook."

"Well, more or less, I suppose so. But if I kept pushing, I was afraid she'd leave. As it is, she's going to stay tonight, anyway."

"You're getting soft."

"Listen, you wouldn't have pushed her any harder. I know you wouldn't."

"But Frye would. You suppose that's how come he's ahead of us on this story, because we're both soft?"

"Something like nice guys finish last, you mean?"

"No, but maybe nice journalism does."

"Well, it's not just us. He beat everybody out on the psychiatrist in Great Falls."

"But he had the log to get him started. I'd still like to know how he got that."

"Christ, I almost forgot. The Vice President's office. I talked to them this morning, and do you know they're getting mostly favorable mail off the publication of the Oval Office log? They're hearing from all those crazy followers of Boyston's who think that if Jenner isn't going to have Boyston in the Oval Office more, then maybe they ought to consider putting him in there permanently."

"I suppose Boyston knows that crowd well enough so that he could have predicted their reaction. But how could he have leaked to Frye? The two of them can't stand each other, especially Frye can't stand Boyston. I gotta believe that if Boyston tried to leak something to Frye, Frye would find a way to make that a part of the story. He's always hated Boyston."

"But maybe for a story this big . . ."

"I dunno. It just doesn't fit. Anyway, the important thing right now is Ewing. That's the big story, the possibility that Jenner has been under psychiatric treatment since he's been President."

"We might be ahead on this one. I don't think anybody else in the press corps knows there's somebody up at Camp David."

"But now we've gotta figure out if it's Ewing. Maybe I should drive up there."

"But you can't get in."

"No, but I can hang around outside tomorrow and maybe tonight ask some questions in that little town close by. What's the name of it?"

"Thurmont." She paused for a moment, then asked, "Hey, do you want some company?"

"You'd better stay here in case something comes up," he answered quickly.

"Nothing's going to happen tomorrow. It's Saturday. If you don't want me to go with you, just say so, damn it!"

"You'd better stay here, Sarah."

And although he said it gently, she slammed down her receiver with vigor. Francine tried very hard to act as though she hadn't noticed.

"Is HE still on the phone?" Jerry Gersten asked.

"He was off for a minute, but then got on again." Joanie was sitting at her desk in the small room just outside Dale Basinger's office. "He's got so many calls backed up, he'll probably be on all day."

"So if I want to talk to him, I better wait here." Gersten leaned against the doorjamb.

"That's probably best."

Gersten wandered over to the love seat across from Joanie's desk, sat down, and surveyed the small room, noting that some new pictures had been hung. A black-and-white blowup showed Jenner with a crowd of schoolchildren, and next to it was an enlarged color print of the President waving to a friendly crowd just before a speech he had given at the University of North Carolina. Both pictures captured the President at his best, smiling warmly, but with just a hint of reserve, just enough to convey the sense that he was special, apart from other men. You could count on the White House's own photo operation, Gersten thought with amused satisfaction, always to show their man in the best light.

"He's off," Joanie said.

Gersten knocked at the heavy wooden door and then walked in to find Basinger sitting at the huge bookcase-desk combination, which H. R. Haldeman had designed and had specially installed when he worked in this office. Basinger was holding the phone receiver in his hand, obviously ready to make another call.

"I need just a few minutes," said Gersten.

"Make it quick."

"O.K., look, last night I got halfway home and remembered I hadn't read that Indian report you gave me. And I figured you might want it first thing this morning, so I turned around and came back to get it so I could read it before I went to bed. I was coming out of my office when I noticed the lights were on down the hall in Malcolm's office, so I walked down there, and you know who was in there?"

"Danny."

"How'd you know?"

"Never mind. So what'd you do?"

"Well, I asked him what he was doing, and he gave me some story about looking for coffee cups. I let it go then, but when I started thinking back on it, he didn't act like a man who was looking for coffee cups. There was something—I don't know—frantic, almost, about his manner. Maybe I'm making too much of it, but it's been nagging at me all morning, and I thought I should tell you."

"Do you know what time it was when you found him in Malcolm's office?"

"About 10:15."

"O.K., I'll check into it." Basinger swung back around to face his desk, dismissing Gersten. As soon as his young aide shut the door behind him, he dialed Joanie and told her he wanted to see Bill Talbot, the head of the White House police force.

It was only a short while until there was a knock at the door. Basinger admitted the stocky, balding Talbot, and told him about his and Gersten's encounters with Danny. "It may be nothing at all," Basinger said, "but I can't see the mess getting so compulsive about coffee cups that he'd be in there twice in one evening. And the second time, the time Gersten saw him, was almost a half hour after I found him in there."

Chief Talbot promised to investigate and report back with the details.

Chapter 12

SARAH DECIDED she needed a walk. Her head was starting to go in circles from assimilating the new information she had gathered, and her spirits were low. Why in the world had she asked Rudy if she could go with him? Maybe she was a closet masochist, she decided.

But angry and resentful as she felt, she wondered if she shouldn't go over to the press office where Rudy was. The abrupt termination of their conversation had left up in the air exactly when he was planning to leave for Camp David. If it was before the afternoon briefing, she should be at the White House to cover it for the magazine. So maybe she would walk over that way, wander around Lafayette Square, breathe some fresh air, and then see if there was anything Rudy needed her for.

That made sense, didn't it? She wasn't looking for more rejection, was she?

Jack Sasser was standing in front of the bank of elevators as she approached. "Isn't it a little early for the White House's junior correspondent to be heading for lunch?" he asked, smiling and looking at his watch.

"Well, Jack, you know how it is. I've gotta have enough time, if I'm going to get in all three martinis so I can gouge the nation's taxpayers properly."

They rode the elevator down. "Where are you headed, Jack?" Sarah asked as they got off.

"Embarrassing you should ask," he said. "I've got an appointment at Sans Souci at 12:30, but I thought I'd start out early, walk around a bit, absorb some of the autumn beauty of this fair city. Now, you don't need to spread that around," he added, looking down at her. "I wouldn't want anyone to think I'm mellowing in my old age."

"Don't worry. I promise not to start any vicious rumors." They walked south, and between companionable silences, she filled him in on what she'd learned during the morning, and he offered some suggestions. The real story was Ewing, he said. That's where she and Rudy ought to concentrate. But if they did have time to work on who leaked the daily log, they ought to try to get in touch with Gretchen Burrows. "I don't know if she'll talk, but she's the one who keeps track of Oval Office visitors, and she'd know everybody who had access to the log," he said.

When they reached Lafayette Square, she asked him if he wanted to sit in the sunshine a minute.

"I know just the bench for this time of day," he answered.

When they sat down, Sarah closed her eyes and leaned her head back so that the sun streamed onto her face. "This is one of my favorite spots in the city," she said.

"Your favorite, mmm? Why's that?"

"Oh, the atmosphere, I guess. All the marvelous old buildings and the White House across the street."

"I like the atmosphere too, but for me that's the people—the bums and the bagwomen and the White House aides all mixing together. Those marvelous old buildings strike me as a little phony. They're just facades, most of them. Inside, they've been completely gutted and rebuilt. Hell, for that matter, the White House itself is just a facade."

"The White House!" Sarah said, raising her head and opening her eyes.

"Sure. During the Truman years, they completely gutted it and rebuilt it. It was a sin the way they went about it. Instead of trying to save the interior, they just dug it out and threw it away. I remember you could go over to Fort Meyer and buy the old bricks from inside, great old handmade things, for about a quarter."

"Why'd they do that instead of restoring it?"

"Just the way they did things in those days. It was about the same time they decided to raze the old southwest section of the city. Hardly any attempt was made to save what was old and charming down there. Instead they tore it up and built a new city."

Sarah looked around. Jack was right about the people in the park. They were a colorful mix. On the bench closest to them, a young man with long blond hair, who was either exhausted or doped up, was nodding. A neatly dressed little girl of about four was watching him curiously, ignoring her mother, who was signaling from across the way for the child to come back to her. "What's going on over there?" Sarah asked, pointing to a street corner.

"Looks like demonstrators. Sure, see the masks? It's the Chileans protesting against Pinochet. They've been out here almost every day recently."

"And they're protesting the usual."

"Yes. Repression, Pinochet's secret police, and so on. Here comes the bill of particulars now."

A man in a white cardboard mask was walking quickly through the park, pressing leaflets on all who would take them. Sarah looked at the one he handed her. "2500 Political Prisoners Missing," it was headlined. She started to read the text, but quickly gave up. "These things are impossible," she said. "All this fiery indignation, grating against long, Latinate words, and the weirdest syntax." She started to shake her head "no" when another man, this one unmasked, came up and tried to give her a sheet of paper, but when she noticed that the one he was handing out had a different headline, she changed her mind.

"Looks like one out of every three prisoners disappears," she said, showing Jack the newest leaflet. "Five Thousand Political Opponents in Jail," this one read.

"No, we've got two different groups going," said Jack, reading the handout. "This one's from students against Marcos." He looked around. "That's their sound truck." He pointed to the other end of the square.

She looked to where he pointed and saw a van with loudspeakers mounted on top. A number of people, all wearing white shirts, milled about the truck. "What does either of these groups hope to gain by demonstrating here? I'd think they'd be more effective, if they'd make a show in Santiago or Manila."

"And more likely to get thrown in jail. Besides, both groups are convinced that pressure from Washington can force the changes they want in their countries."

"I know we've been leaning pretty heavily on Pinochet, but we seem to be proceeding a lot more gently with Marcos. How come, do you suppose?"

"He supports us, for one thing, and he's about the last Asian leader we've got. Hell, we've been kicked out of

Thailand and Vietnam. We've pulled out of Taiwan and Korea, and a lot of Japanese want us out of Japan. If we want to maintain any sort of American presence in the Pacific, we need the Philippines. And so, we're nice to Marcos."

The loudspeakers on both sound trucks were going now, making conversation difficult. Sarah listened for a minute, as the demonstrators shouted their slogans at the White House, then she turned to see Jack smiling broadly. "Why are you so happy?" she shouted.

"I like the noise of democracy," he shouted back. "President Buchanan said that once, and I just understood what he meant."

She leaned over, kissed him on the cheek, and then stood up, stuffing the leaflets she had been holding into her coat pocket. "I'm heading back to work," she mouthed, pointing at the White House.

"I'd better get going too," he shouted, motioning at his watch.

The District police on hand for the demonstration watched Sarah closely as she crossed Pennsylvania Avenue, and the White House guards were even more careful than usual in scrutinizing the press pass she handed them. Whatever else they achieved, she thought, the demonstrators certainly managed to get security tightened up around the White House.

She entered the pressroom to find it almost deserted. Hoping that Rudy was still around, she went downstairs, but it too was practically empty. She asked one straggler if he'd seen Dodman, and he told her he thought Rudy had gone to lunch.

At the *Newstime* cubicle, a message in red ink caught her eye. "*Sarah—call Scarlet,*" it screamed, "*urgent! 530-5655.*" She looked at the note in puzzlement. She knew somebody named Scarlet, but who was it? Then she remembered Jane Minnick. Scarlet was the code name Crazy Jane had said she was going to use. Sarah dialed the phone number, thinking she should ignore this nonsense, but curious too, in a morbid sort of way, about the latest turns Jane's paranoia had taken.

Someone picked up the phone at the other end, but said nothing.

"Jane?" said Sarah into the silence. But still there was nothing.

"Scarlet?" she tried.

"Sarah, is that you?"

"Jane, what are you doing. This is crazy."

"They're following me, Sarah. They think I did it."

"C'mon now, I haven't heard anybody say anything like that. Where are you anyway."

"In my apartment. I'm afraid to leave. I haven't been out of here for two days."

"Look, that's silly. And it's not healthy. You get out of there and come on over here right now. I'll be waiting for you."

She hung up the phone before Jane could object. She didn't feel like arguing, and besides she sometimes suspected that Jane's eccentricities—if that wasn't too mild a word—were attention-getting devices. It wouldn't help her to break the pattern she was in to continue to cajole her, to pay attention to her for acting strangely.

But for nearly two hours, Sarah worried that her tactic hadn't worked. Rudy came and went, returning from lunch to say he was going home to gather together some things to drive up to Camp David. And, yes, would Sarah please cover the afternoon briefing. Other reporters began to drift in, but there was no Jane. Sarah moved around, picking up one theory after another about why Jenner had lied, about where Ewing really was. But still there was no Jane.

She wandered over to look at a yellowed picture hanging on the wall. It showed Woodrow Wilson with the press corps of sixty or sixty-five years ago, a small group of men in straw hats and high collars. She peered at the faces of the reporters with the President and tried to understand their expressions. Did any of them ever wonder about the mental health of the proud and enigmatic Wilson? It was then she felt the tap on her shoulder.

"Let's go someplace where I can talk to you," Jane said plaintively. Her glasses were even more askew than usual, and she looked as though she had dressed in the dark, Sarah thought. That skirt had never been meant to go with that blouse; in fact, maybe there wasn't any blouse in the entire world that skirt could go with.

When they had found a quiet corner downstairs, Sarah decided to be direct. "Look, Jane, I know that you and a couple of the others have acquired a kind of reputation over the last few years, and I think maybe you've even started enjoying it a little, the jokes about the 'pressroom zanies,' the attention. But you just have to pull yourself together. If you act crazy long enough, pretty soon you won't know how to act any other way." As soon as the words were out, she wondered about what she had said. It sounded like the warnings her grandmother used to give her about not twisting up her face when she cried or it might get stuck that way. Nevertheless, in some part of herself, she believed that about emotions. If you let yourself act as though you were out of control, pretty soon you would be.

"Sarah, I'm not acting this time," Jane was saying.

"Jane, nobody's following you. Nobody thinks you leaked the Oval Office log. The story would have had your name on it then, not Frye's."

"I gave the log to Frye."

"You what?"

"I gave it to him."

"But why would you do that? And *how* could you? Where would you get the log?"

"Why? Well, I guess I wanted to impress him. All of you look down on me and make fun of the stories I do. 'Puff pieces' you call them. Frye's never said anything to me, but it's always seemed like he was the worst, the one who thought the least of what I do. You know, he's always uncovering and exposing, and I just don't do that. I don't know. I just wanted him to see that I could come up with heavy stuff too."

What Jane was saying struck a familiar note. There was something about Frye—a condescending manner—that made you want to prove to him you could do as well as he. Sarah had felt what Jane was describing, though, of course, she had never done anything about it. And Jane couldn't have either, she told herself. "Where'd you get the log?" she asked, trying to keep the doubt out of her voice.

"I can't tell you that. It wouldn't be fair." Jane began to pick at her skirt. "But I shouldn't have taken it. I shouldn't have. And I shouldn't have given it to Frye. When I think of everything that's happened . . . I didn't want to hurt anybody." She was crying now.

Sarah shifted around so that she was between Jane and the other people in the room. "Maybe it's just because you feel guilty that you think you're being followed," she offered, her mind racing, trying to think where Jane could have obtained the log. Could she be telling the truth?

"It could be, I guess. I don't know."

"You've got to get your mind off it. Isn't there something else you're working on? Something you can lose yourself in and put all this other stuff aside?" She put her arm around Jane's shoulder, trying to quiet her.

"There isn't anything, anything at all now. I can't go on with the Boystons . . ." She broke off suddenly, brushed Sarah's arm away, and ran from the room.

Sarah watched her go, stunned by what she had said.

Had Jane been doing a piece on the Boystons? Was that it? And had the Vice President given her the log? But then why would she feel guilty? And could you tell what was real and what was imaginary with Jane? She thought about going after her, but a female voice was announcing over the P.A. system that the afternoon briefing was about to start. She was sure Westfield wouldn't have anything to say, but if he did and she wasn't there—well, it just wasn't worth risking. She could get hold of Jane later, she decided, joining a group heading up the stairs. She stopped by a small green room off the upstairs corridor, bought a chocolate bar from a vending machine, and then entered the pressroom. She was too late to get a chair, so she staked out an area near the wall. The stenographer who would transcribe the briefing was in place, a signal corpsman was adjusting the controls for the P.A. system, but Westfield hadn't yet appeared.

Sarah looked around at the reporters crowded into the room for the briefing and considered what a motley crew they were. There were young and hungry ones, like Ron Schaeffer of the *New York Times*, and the old and tired ones, like Al Goldman, who worked for a chain of western radio stations and who had never yet been known to ask a single question at a press conference. Westfield himself entered the pressroom at that moment, moved behind the podium, and fiddled with the microphones until they suited him. Looking warily out at the assembled reporters, he began the briefing with a series of announcements. He talked about bills Congress had sent to the White House and about legislation still pending on the Hill. He talked about a meeting the President had had that morning with the southern governors, who were in town for a conference. There was fidgeting and whispering among the reporters, who were bored by Westfield's announcements; all they really wanted was for him to talk about Malcolm Ewing, for him to tell them when the President planned to explain how his denial of having ever been under psychiatric care fit with the evidence he had seen a psychiatrist. When the press secretary began to talk about the upcoming visit of the Japanese Prime Minister, a few of the reporters perked up a little and took careful notes, but most of the room was waiting, just waiting for the opportunity to jump on Westfield with their questions. Finally, they got their chance.

"Mark, when will the President be commenting on yesterday's story in the *Post?*" one of the network reporters asked.

"I couldn't say."

"But it's been a day and a half now since the charge was made that the President saw a psychiatrist. It's been two days since he denied that he ever had. Don't you think it's about time the American people had an explanation?"

"Since when do you represent the American people, Pete?" It was clear that Westfield regretted the comment almost as soon as he uttered it. He shut his eyes and shook his head, as though to clear it of tension and frustration. "Uh, look," he said into the microphone, "it's been a long day, tempers are frayed, mine just like yours, and that was an undeserved crack. The answer to your question, Pete, is that the President hasn't yet decided on a timetable for responding to the *Post* story."

The network reporter nodded curtly. He would accept the press secretary's apology only for the sake of politeness and getting on with the briefing. Probably there was nothing Westfield could have done to mollify him truly or to lower significantly the level of hostility in the room. Most of the reporters understood that Westfield didn't know the answers to the questions they had pressed him with the last two days. He was a spokesman for the Jenner administration, not a tactician, not one of the men in close. He was a mouth, not a mind, as some of the reporters put it, but even knowing that, they became angry when he was unresponsive. Because he was the only daily contact point they had with the White House, he bore the brunt of their frustration.

"How long do you think it'll be, Mark," a reporter up front was asking, "before we have an explanation of why Malcolm Ewing's in the Oval Office for an hour every day?"

"The President explained at Wednesday's press conference that he had no intention of ever talking about the meetings set out in the portion of the daily log that the *Post* printed. As he said at that time, he considers that there is a need for confidentiality about such meetings."

There was general confusion as several reporters began shouting at once, each of them trying to say that the game had changed since the President's press conference, that now there was an overwhelming reason why the President should explain what was happening in the Oval Office. Westfield silenced the outcry by calling on the woman reporter who was standing over to the side in front of Sarah. Yvonne Garrity was her name, and she had a reputation for never asking anything to the point. Several administration's worth of press secretaries had learned to call on her when they needed a respite from a hostile line of questioning.

"Is it true, Mr. Westfield," she drawled, "that Malcolm Ewing was once made an honorary member of the Whitefeather tribe?"

The question seemed incongruous, coming as it did out of the past, out of a time when other connections of Ewing's, ones which had nothing to do with his psychiatric training, had had importance. Several reporters laughed, but Westfield responded seriously. "Malcolm Ewing did work on the Whitefeather reservation," he said, "but whether he was made a member of the tribe, I'm not sure."

"Well, could you find that out for me?"

"I'll give it a try, Yvonne."

Sarah tucked the half-eaten chocolate bar into her purse and decided to ask a question. Standing as she did, right behind Yvonne Garrity, she managed to catch Westfield's eye right away. "Mark, I wonder if you could tell me how the daily log is kept? I mean who makes entries in it and who has access to it?"

A look of indecision passed over Westfield's face, a look Sarah interpreted as meaning he knew the answer to the question, but wasn't sure if he should give it. Westfield wasn't really tough enough for the press secretary's job, Sarah thought. Or duplicitous enough.

"C'mon, Mark, answer the lady's question," a reporter up in front said. "We've got you down for two hundred thirty-three 'no comments' already this week. Five more and you break the all-time record."

"I don't need you to tell me how to do my job," Westfield shot back. But despite his snappishness, he apparently decided that there was no harm in answering Sarah's question. Or at least the possibility of harm was not sufficiently great to warrant his giving another unresponsive answer.

"Gretchen Burrows keeps the log," Westfield said. "Since she sits right outside the Oval Office and sees everyone coming and going, it's natural for her to make the entries. As to the question of 'access,' I suppose you could say that all those presidential aides who spend time in the anteroom where Gretchen works have that. Tom Lester, the President's civilian aide, for example, certainly has access."

"But what about high administration officials," Sarah

asked, casually, she hoped. "Does the Vice President see the log, for example?"

"Well, sure, I suppose the Vice President could see the log if he had some reason to. It's not that closely held. It's not even a big deal, generally. Until last Tuesday, hardly anybody'd heard of it."

If Westfield had been trying for a laugh, he probably would not have got it, given the strained relations between him and the press corps. But the almost plaintive note in his voice made it clear he wasn't playing for laughs, and so there were a few chuckles here and there.

More questions followed, but none of them produced any newsworthy information. Then one of the reporters closed the press conference, calling from the back of the room, "Thank you, Mark." Some grumbling ensued. There were a few moans from reporters who felt that if they could only ask one more question . . . if they could only get a coherent string of questions going instead of having everybody take off in different directions . . . if they could only, somehow, get the press corps to act in concert instead of in competition with one another. And meanwhile Westfield slipped from the room.

Sarah took the chocolate bar from her purse and headed for the back corridor where she checked the handout bins and tried to make a plan for the rest of the day. There were three people she wanted to talk to, Gretchen Burrows, Jane Minnick, and Wendy Greene. Three women, none of whom was powerful herself, but each of whom might well be able to tell her about those who were. Was it because they were women, she wondered idly, as she finished her candy bar and looked through the day's handouts, that they were satellites instead of being at the center? But that wasn't true of Wendy Greene, she decided. Wendy was a person in her own right, a person who in another context, say at an art show, would be at the center herself. And Jane, well, her neuroses weren't sex-linked. The vulnerability which made it easy for people to use her wasn't a particularly female weakness. Gretchen Burrows, now, might well be another case. Sarah didn't know her well enough to say for sure, but what she did know seemed to indicate that Burrows fit a familiar Washington stereotype: the office wife, the woman who loyally serves until one day she wakes up middle-aged and finds that her life is totally defined by the man for whom she works. And by then it's too late for her to choose another path.

There was nothing she needed in the handout bins, Sarah concluded, putting back a press release about the First Lady. Who cared if Mary Jenner was speaking to the Senate wives? She went downstairs and dialed Jane Minnick's number. When there was no answer, she dialed the White House switchboard and asked to be connected with Gretchen Burrows. "Miss Burrows? This is Sarah Hoff with *Newstime* magazine," she said when the operator connected her. "Is there a time this evening or this weekend when we could sit down and chat for a few minutes?"

"I'm sorry, I never give interviews."

"I wasn't thinking of anything so formal as that. I just need some background information."

"No, I'm sorry. I'm very busy."

There was a click, and the dial tone told Sarah she had hung up. She found a listing in the D. C. phone book for a "G. Burrows" at 4000 Massachusetts Avenue, an address almost at the Maryland line. It was in a section of highrise apartments, Sarah thought. Well, she'd go out there tonight and try to see G. Burrows, try to see if maybe she couldn't be persuaded to talk if she were confronted personally.

As she tucked her notebook into her purse, a wave of nausea swept over her. She put her head down on the desk for a minute and realized that her total intake of food for the day had been a doughnut and a chocolate bar. She'd O.D.'d on junk food, that's what was wrong. Before she did anything else, she resolved, she was going to get something decent to eat.

Chapter 13

A PINGING noise caused Dale Basinger to look over at the locator on his desk. It was a television screen with four numbers glowing in green on its dark face, and the information beside the second number, which represented the First Lady, had just changed. She had been out of the White House, and now she had returned, so the monitor had sounded and listed new information beside her name. "Arrived residence, 5:03 P.M.," it read. Number one, the President, was shown to be in the Oval Office. Number three, the Jenner's married daughter, was at home in Sacramento, California, the machine said. Number four, the Vice President, was en route to Detroit.

Basinger had never bothered to find out exactly how

the Secret Service agents protecting the four people listed on the machine fed information into it, but he thought they probably called it into a central location. The locator was just one of the many feats of communication he had come to accept as routine since he had begun to work at the White House. Like being able to pick up the phone and have the White House operators connect you with anybody, anytime, anyplace, in a matter of minutes. Like asking the White House communications agency to play back for you on the office television last night's news shows. Like being able to listen to the Super Bowl aboard Air Force One, as they had done when the President had flown to Australia last year.

But, damn it, the best communications in the world weren't any good if you were dealing with unresponsive people. Why hadn't he heard from Chief Talbot? He ought to have something to report by now on the mess steward in Ewing's office.

He punched the intercom button. "Joanie, get me Chief Talbot on the phone."

"Mr. Basinger," she reported back a few minutes later, "his secretary says he's not in."

"I don't care where he is, damn it, I want to talk to him."

Within a few minutes, Joanie announced that the chief was on line three.

"Chief? What's the status of that problem you and I discussed earlier?"

"It's taken care of, Mr. Basinger."

"Taken care of? What's that mean?"

"Just that, sir. It's been taken care of."

Basinger felt his irritation mounting. "So it's been taken care of, has it? Well by whom, Chief? And how?"

"Look, Mr. Basinger, my instructions don't cover that. I'm just to report to you that the matter has been handled."

"And whom are you taking your orders from these days, Chief? You know, I had the impression there for awhile that you took them from me."

"Now look, Mr. Basinger, I don't want to get caught up in the middle of this thing. I no more started asking for the mess steward you talked to me about than Joe Carnahan was calling me."

Carnahan, Basinger thought to himself. Now that was a puzzle. What was the head of the White House Secret Service detail doing with his finger in the pie?

"Anyway," Chief Talbot was going on, "Carnahan gave me to understand that the matter was taken care of, and that I ought to tell you that and keep out of it."

"And you took his word on that?"

"Well, not *his* word exactly. He didn't precisely say so, but he left the definite impression that he was conveying a message."

"From whom?"

"From the President, sir."

"The President?"

"Yes sir, that's what he gave me to understand."

Basinger hung up, trying to assimilate what he had just heard. How could the President be involved with Danny, the mess steward? There must be some mistake. He swiveled his chair around so that he could look out the west windows facing the Executive Office Building. It was dark now, and the interplay of shadow and light on the old building gave it an even more fantastic air than it had in the daytime. He sat quietly for a few minutes, seeming to study the old building, and then he suddenly made up his mind. He got up from his chair, walked out of his office, through the anteroom and down the hallway toward the Oval Office. The hallway door was shut, and a Secret Service agent was sitting outside it. The agent would let him use that door if he wanted, but determined as he was to speak to the President, he saw no reason to chance breaking into the middle of something. He walked into the anteroom in which Gretchen Burrows had her office. "What's he doing?" he asked her. "Is anybody with him?"

"No, he's alone. Signing mail and pictures."

When Basinger entered the Oval Office through the door from the anteroom, the first thing he noticed was how dark it was. Only the President's desk lamp was on, creating a strange effect in the large room. The President seemed apart from everything around him, cut off in the pool of light.

The President looked up. "Yes, Dale?" he said, breaking the strangeness.

"Sir, you and I need to talk."

"Sure, Dale, c'mon in. Would you like a drink?"

"No, sir."

"Then what can I do for you?"

"Well, I suppose I should begin by saying that I don't expect to know everything that's going on around here. A lot has happened this last week which I don't understand, and I wish I did, but I accept the idea that I don't need to know everything. But now something's come up that I have a firsthand involvement with, and it has me worried. It's about Danny, the mess steward."

The President said nothing, just looked at him and nodded as though to encourage him to go on.

"You do know about the situation I asked Chief Talbot to investigate?"

Again the President nodded.

"And do you know that Chief Talbot was discouraged from investigating by Joe Carnahan?"

"Yes, Dale, I do."

Basinger had been sure, so sure, that there'd been a mistake. "Well, I guess that's all I need. I was afraid that the whole thing might have seemed so trivial—you know, mess stewards looking for coffee cups, that

doesn't sound like much. I thought maybe with everything else you have to think about, that it might not have
seemed important, that it might have slipped between
the cracks somehow." He got up to leave, feeling terribly awkward.

"Dale, just a minute," the President said. He gestured
to a wall switch. "Turn on some lights would you? I've
let it get too dark in here. Then come back and sit down.
There are some things I think it's time you knew."

SARAH COULD not find the key to the outside door to her
apartment building. It was on the same ring as her car
key, so she knew she'd had it only minutes before when
she'd parked her car, but the keys weren't in either of
her coat pockets. They had to be in her purse, she concluded. She hadn't been thinking, and she'd probably
just dropped them in, and now no amount of groping
through the large leather bag seemed sufficient to re-
trieve them. Finally, she set the bag down on the top
step and removed items from it, one at a time, until the
elusive key ring appeared. All in all, she thought, putting the various items she had removed back into her
purse, it was a fitting end to a lousy day.

She let herself in, walked up the wide stairs, and
knocked at the door of her apartment. In a minute or
two, it opened a crack and Wendy looked out. Then the
door closed again so that Wendy could take off the chain.

"What's that delicious smell?" Sarah asked as she entered the apartment. "Is it sausage?"

"Yes. I hope you don't mind. I didn't want to go to the
grocery store and you had some eggs and sausage."

"I don't mind, as long as you'll give me a bite or two."
It did smell good, and she never had managed to get
anything decent to eat.

"Sure, there's plenty," said Wendy, running back to

the kitchen. "And everything's going to be burned, if I don't take care of it."

Sarah put her key ring carefully into her coat pocket and felt the wad of paper there that she'd stuffed into her pocket earlier that day when she'd been in Lafayette Square with Jack. Before she hung her coat on the brass halltree, she pulled the paper out, thinking it would give her something to talk to Wendy about. She didn't want to start asking her about Ewing right away, but it was hard to think what else to say. Maybe they could talk about the demonstrators at the White House. They were demonstrating about the Philippines, after all, and Wendy knew something about the Philippines.

In the kitchen, Wendy was dishing up eggs. "How was your day?" she asked, as she set a plate on the table.

"Long, long, long," Sarah answered. "Do you know Gretchen Burrows?"

"I've heard of her. I know she's the President's secretary."

"Well, I wanted to talk to her, so I went out to the apartment building where she lives to wait for her. I talked the security guard into letting me wait in the lobby, but when she showed up after almost an hour and a half, she scurried into the elevator and wouldn't say a word to me. The guard watched the whole thing and was really irritated. Said I had misled him into thinking Miss Burrows was expecting me, and what right did I have, and on and on. Anyway, if I try to catch her there again, I'll have to wait outside."

"Why won't she talk to you?" Wendy asked as she sat down.

"I guess she figures the things I want to know aren't any of my business."

There was an awkward silence with the questions Sarah wanted to ask, and the answers Wendy didn't want to give, hanging in the air between the two women. Hoping to end the awkwardness, Sarah put down her fork and smoothed out the wadded-up paper she had laid on the table. "Did you know there was an anti-Marcos demonstration in Lafayette Square today?"

"No, I didn't. I haven't had the radio or TV on. What was it about?"

"Well, here," said Sarah, glancing over the leaflet, "here it says Marcos is a 'ruthless dictator' who established martial law in his country simply in order to maintain himself in power. . . . He and Mrs. Marcos have 'enriched themselves while their countrymen have starved.' . . . It talks about a 'Philippine Gulag' and says thousands of Filipinos have been jailed for political reasons . . . and some of them tortured."

"It sounds a little extreme, but I have heard Malcolm say there's a lot of discontent in the Philippines right now. In the universities and in the church, especially."

"Does Malcolm know Marcos?"

"He's met him a few times, but doesn't really know him. He says, though, that Marcos is an impressive fellow, very articulate, very persuasive. And Imelda, his wife, well, Malcolm says she's one of the most fascinating women he's ever met."

"How so?"

"She's gorgeous for one thing, but I think what's really fascinating about her is that she's impossible to figure out. On the one hand, she seems absolutely determined to better the lot of the Filipinos, and they love her for it. But she also spends huge amounts of money on herself and showers her jet-set friends with gifts. Some say what she really wants is to be President of the Philippines herself someday, and what she's doing is laying the groundwork."

"That's one way for it to end up."

"For what to end up?" asked Wendy, puzzled.

"Oh, I was just thinking out loud. Earlier tonight I realized that none of the three people I wanted to talk to for the story I'm working on are powerful themselves, and it also happened that all of them are women. Now in some cases those two facts—being behind the scenes and being female—don't have anything to do with each other. But sometimes they do. And when you take a bright and aggressive woman like Imelda Marcos must be and put her behind the scenes, it's bound to happen once in awhile that a woman like that will use her position to gain upfront power."

"I take it I'm one of the people you wanted to talk to tonight," Wendy said, pouring both of them more coffee. She made the observation with a good-humored smile.

"That's right. And I also decided right away that you weren't behind the scenes for anybody, that you were at the center of your own life."

"Thanks for that. I can't tell you how hard it is to keep it that way. Not being married helps, I think, though there are times when it seems almost silly not to marry Malcolm. We could hardly be more settled and comfortable with each other."

"Marriage certainly has never tempted me. But then I've never felt settled and comfortable with anyone. I've never even wanted to feel that way."

"I suppose it sounds a little dull, but it's a nice feeling really. It goes along with having another person you can absolutely be yourself with, someone you can tell everything to."

"And they tell everything to you?"

Wendy looked down for a moment and then stood and went to the stove. She picked up a spatula and began to scrape at the egg stuck to the bottom of the cast-iron skillet. After a moment she spoke. "I don't know where he is, Sarah," she said. "But I don't think I need to know. When I was talking about being close and comfortable and telling the other person everything, I didn't mean things like what Malcolm does at work or where he goes for the President. I meant things like how he feels about himself and how I feel about myself and what each of us is worried about. It's being able to talk about those things that makes a relationship close. I've never wanted him to tell me the details of his job. If I fill my head up with what he's doing, then there's less and less room for the things important to me. I suppose if he were digging ditches that wouldn't be the case. The details of a job like that wouldn't overshadow the details of my own work. But the things Malcolm does are so fascinating, so compelling. If I get caught up in them, I just know that the mental energy I need for my own work won't be there."

"You make it sound like politics is a kind of quicksand. If you step too close, you'll get pulled under."

"A quicksand," Wendy said thoughtfully. "That's not a bad comparison, except it's a seductive quicksand." She looked up. "Is that a mixed metaphor? I don't know. Anyway, it's like those sirens in the *Odyssey*, who lured sailors to destruction with their singing. If politics is a quicksand, I have a feeling that being pulled under is an experience some people love." She finished scraping out the pan, squirted some soap and ran hot water into it. When she had finished drying it, she sat back down at the oak table and sipped at her coffee.

"But how can you stand not knowing where he is?" Sarah asked.

"It's hard, but at least he wrote me a note."

Sarah looked up abruptly.

"Oh, hell, I suppose I shouldn't have said that." She sat her cup of coffee down. "This really is impossible, my staying here and trying to keep secrets from you. I'm terrible at secrets." She looked at Sarah. "So I suppose it's a good thing I don't know much."

Sarah was silent.

"It was a nothing note, really. Just a few scribbles on a piece of paper. I found it on the kitchen table last Sunday when I got home from getting the groceries. The note just said he had to leave and he'd be back as soon as he could. Those were just about the exact words. 'Have to leave. Back as soon as possible. Maybe a week, ten days. Love, M.'"

Sarah, still saying nothing, carried her plate and cup to the sink, rinsed them, and put them in the dishwasher.

Wendy watched her, worried. "I shouldn't have told you. I know I shouldn't. You won't put it in the magazine, will you?"

"No, I won't put it in the magazine." She turned and looked at Wendy. "But I have to tell you, I'll use it, if I can, to find out more."

"Does it have to be that way?"

"There's no other way it can be. I can't quit knowing it, can I? And I can't quit using what I know to uncover this whole thing." Wendy was upset, Sarah could tell that. But what else was there to say? She had to be honest, didn't she?

Later that night, as she undressed, she tried to decide what was the most important thing she had learned from Wendy. Probably, she concluded, it was that Malcolm had left last Sunday. That would have been two days before the story about the Oval Office log came out, three days before there was any talk at all about psychiatrists.

She hung the wool challis skirt she had been wearing in the wardrobe, and reconsidered the Camp David thesis she and Rudy had developed. Why would the President send Ewing up there before the psychiatrist story broke? The President couldn't have known—could he?—that suspicions would develop about Ewing being his own personal psychiatrist. So why would he have sent him off on Sunday?

As she got into bed, she resolved to sleep on it, to quit turning it over and over in her mind and let what Wendy had told her lie quietly. Maybe then her subconscious would come up with the answers that were eluding her. Just before she fell asleep she remembered Jane Minnick. She never had got hold of her, that poor crazy woman. She worried about Jane briefly and drowsily resolved to locate her tomorrow.

Chapter 14

ZERN JENNER drank his orange juice, real orange juice just squeezed in the small kitchen off the dining room in the White House family quarters. He savored the sweet taste and pulpy texture, realizing as he did that he was merely delaying the inevitable. He had to keep in touch with what was being said on the networks and in the newspapers across the country. He had to read the daily news summary, which, as usual, was lying atop the newspapers stacked by his place at the table. But it was becoming increasingly painful to find out what was being said about him.

The butler brought him an egg poached just as he liked it, and when Jenner had finished it and the one piece of dry toast he had requested, he moved the plate aside and lay the news summary directly in front of him. "News and Comment," it was headed in large blue letters, and then in smaller print, "The President's Daily News Summary." Below that was the date, Saturday, November 17, and then there were several subject headings. It was under "The Presidency," Jenner knew, that most of the bad news awaited.

"Jenner Still Silent on White House Psychiatrist," the first entry read. Both wires and two of the networks, the President saw, had carried stories pointing out that he had still not given a public explanation of Ewing's role in the White House—and they had all, apparently, described Malcolm as a psychiatrist, surely implying to readers and viewers he was the White House's psychiatrist-in-residence.

The second entry was similar in tone. "White House: 'No Comment' on President's Psychiatric History." Jenner rubbed his forehead and considered his alternatives, as the butler removed his breakfast plate from the table. He could try to explain why he hadn't talked about his appointments with Dr. Brewer before. He could explain it as a sin of omission which had seemed less and less important with each passing year. But how could he explain having directly denied in his news conference that he'd ever seen a psychiatrist? He couldn't explain it. Not right now. And even if he tried, it would only focus the spotlight more brightly on Malcolm, on those hours his young friend had spent in the Oval Office and on what he was doing now. Jenner knew he couldn't answer questions about those things. That was a certainty. And so thinking about alternatives was pointless, he concluded for the hundredth time, because there really weren't any. The only choice he had for now was to sit tight and keep his mouth shut.

He looked up to see Mary coming into the room.

"Good morning," he said, unable to keep the surprise out of his voice. She never joined him for breakfast.

"Good morning," she said, looking polished and perfect, even though she was wearing casual clothes, a plaid cotton blouse, and dark slacks. As he helped her with her chair, she looked up at him and smiled.

The butler fussed and bustled until a place had been set for the First Lady and her breakfast order taken. As soon as he had left the room, Mary Jenner leaned over to her husband, and in a teasing tone asked, "Are you never going to let Matthew use the Williamsburg blue tablecloth? It really does suit the room better, you know."

He smiled at her, warmed by her good humor. "It's good to have you here," he said.

She looked down at her plate, seeming slightly embarrassed. "Well, I thought we should talk," she said. And then she rushed into the details of Monday's state dinner for the Japanese. "I really haven't consulted with you like I usually do," she said. "I even decided on the final guest list. I hope that's all right. It just didn't seem right to bother you with those things right now. And besides . . ."

"Mary, why are you really here this morning?"

It was a moment before she answered, and when she did, she chose her words carefully. "I spent most of yesterday thinking," she said. "I woke up early yesterday morning, even before you were awake, and I looked over and saw your bedlamp was on and you'd fallen asleep reading Sandburg. And I knew you must have got up in the night to get a book and you hadn't been able to sleep.

"Well, I started trying to think how I could help you. But, you see, I didn't know what the problem was. I kept ending up back at the press conference of yours, and I

167

kept asking myself, why would you lie about seeing that psychiatrist?" She put her hand over his. "I know how your mind works, how you always weigh an answer before you give it, and you'd have known that getting caught in a lie would be far worse than the consequences of telling the truth to Nicholas Frye, especially since you saw Dr. Brewer so long ago. So why would you have lied, when you'd have been aware of how devastating it could be? And the only thing I could think was that you didn't want the press to turn their attention to Malcolm, and that would have happened, if you'd said you'd ever seen a psychiatrist. All of them would have started asking, 'This Ewing who's on your staff, he's a psychiatrist isn't he?' "

"They've started asking that anyway," the President interjected.

"Yes, but that's because the Dr. Brewer story came out despite your denial."

"But why would I have wanted to keep attention away from Malcolm?" Jenner asked noncommittally.

"Because—oh, Zern, you have been talking to him, haven't you. He has been helping you."

"You think that?"

"Of course," she said, slightly puzzled at his response. "It makes sense. You said that when you saw Dr. Brewer it was because you needed someone to talk to, and I know you must need someone now. I'm still not a very good listener. I know that, and I'm going to try harder."

He patted her hand and didn't say anything. Her logic was impeccable, he thought, but it had still led her to the wrong conclusion. Over the past three years, he had spent many hours talking to Malcolm, but not like a patient talks to a doctor. More like a father talks with a grown son, or an older friend to a younger one. Malcolm's being a psychiatrist had nothing to do with it—

did it? It had never even occurred to him before that perhaps Malcolm was so easy to talk to because he had been trained to listen. But that wasn't the point. "Mary, Malcolm isn't my psychiatrist."

She looked relieved and then mystified. "But then, why? Why the lie? Why is all this happening?"

"It's all happening because the damned log was leaked," he said. That was the truth, though it sidestepped what she was really asking. "It's because of the log that we've got the nation's press wondering about my sanity," he said, pointing at the news summary entries he'd been reading. As he glanced down, he noticed an entry farther down the page which he hadn't seen before. "Boyston Says President Will 'Own Up' to Psychiatric Treatment," it read.

"That bastard," Jenner said, leafing through the news summary to the page which had the Boyston story. "Listen to this, Mary. 'In response to a question put to him at a Birmingham, Michigan, news conference, Vice President Robert Boyston said he expected President Zern Jenner would shortly "own up" to having been treated by a psychiatrist in the early 1960s.' "

"Have you talked to him since this whole thing started?"

"No, I haven't. In fact, I've been avoiding him. I have a suspicion he may have been the one who leaked the daily log in the first place."

"The Vice President?"

"There's no love lost between us. Never has been. He knows and I know that he's Vice President simply because he was the only choice possible for that crazy convention we had in Los Angeles. I've never trusted him, never wanted him in close, and he's resented that. I think he's the kind who would be vindictive enough to leak the daily log if he thought it'd make me look bad.

And besides, he's had the opportunity. A month ago, just to keep him busy, I asked him to be in charge of a study of how efficiently my time is scheduled. He's been looking at the log regularly since then."

"So he probably did it."

"The only reason I have to doubt it is that Nicholas Frye came out with the story. Boyston hates him, and the feeling's mutual, I understand. I just can't imagine Boyston would have given Frye a story."

"What are you going to do?"

"Nothing. Nothing at all for right now. Do you know since that log was printed there's been mailbag after mailbag coming into the White House full of letters supporting the Vice President, asking me why I'm not making greater use of him? It's hardly the time to dress him down and chance having him go public. Like so much else about this damned situation, there's nothing for me to do right now. Just sit and wait."

"Do you sometimes wish things had turned out differently?"

"How do you mean?"

"Oh, that you'd stayed in the Senate, maybe. None of this would have happened then."

"It's not like you, looking back, thinking how things might have been."

"I know. I know it's pointless trying to rewrite the past, but yesterday and last night, all the 'what-ifs' kept coming to mind no matter how hard I tried not thinking about them."

"Funny," he said, "that's not happening to me, and I'm supposed to be the worrier in the family. But maybe it's not happening just because it's so clear to me that I wouldn't have missed a day of these last three years no matter how it all turns out. Even when I'm wondering if this job can really be done successfully in the twentieth century, I'm glad to have had the chance to try."

"But can you stand it if you lose it, if you have to give it all up?"

"Yes. There's not a doubt in my mind about that, even when I remember how devastating it was to lose that Senate race to Clarke. I think I was thrown so badly then because it made me doubt the concept I had of myself. A man can lose once—most men in politics have at sometime or other. Hell, there's even a saying about it. 'You run the first time to get noticed and the second time to win.' But when I lost twice, I had to question whether I had the stuff to be a leader or not."

"Did you know William Proxmire lost three times before he ever won?"

"Three races for governor, wasn't it, before he won his Senate seat?"

"I think so. I don't know that I ever learned the details, but I heard about his losing three times years ago, and it always stuck with me."

"Probably because you saw how hard on me just losing twice was."

"Probably," she said, looking into his eyes.

"Losing the presidency would be painful, maybe more painful than anything that's ever happened to me, but it wouldn't undo me like losing that race to Clarke. You know, when I ran against him, I didn't keep anything in reserve, any emotional or physical energy. I poured it all into that race and when it was over, I didn't have anything to fall back on.

"Well, I know how to pace myself now. And I know who I am and what I am, and I know there have been other men, some of them great, who've held this office and had to give it up. Gerald Ford, Lyndon Johnson, Harry Truman, they'd all have liked to live in this house longer, but it didn't work out that way for them and they left with grace, and I can do that."

"Truman?"

"Sure. He announced he wouldn't seek another term less than three weeks after Estes Kefauver beat him in the New Hampshire primary."

"Why does the system work that way? It seems to require that the man we elect President be—oh, what are the words—chewed up by the office, I guess is what I mean."

"I don't know, though I've thought about it often enough. I've wondered if it doesn't have to do with the mood that prevails in democracy. A kind of resentment at being subordinated to anyone. Giving anyone precedence over anyone else runs counter to the idea of equality, counter to what we're told about everybody being equal from the time we're old enough to think about such things. So when we're forced in a democracy to choose leaders, our first impulse, maybe, is to humiliate them, to make them pay for their elevation."

"But that's awful."

"Not really. Not when you consider the alternatives to democracy. Besides, a President can fight it. He can hold his head up and be proud and do what he thinks is right. The office almost demands he do that, that he try to make the presidency stronger, because every day he can see how the country would be better served should he succeed."

"So you are going to fight."

"Yes," he said, nodding his head, "as soon as I can."

Despite his brave words, he looked troubled and tired, and she didn't have the heart to keep questioning him. But why, she wondered, why did he have to wait? If Malcolm wasn't his psychiatrist—and he said he wasn't, and of course she believed him—then what possible reason could he have to put off denying it?

Chapter 15

NANCY DODMAN was getting Mac down from his high chair when the telephone rang. She quickly took off his bib, made a swipe at his face with a wet paper towel, and then tried to clean her own hands. "Little boy, your stickiness is catching," she said to him as she picked up the phone.

"Nancy, where's Rudy?" she heard a female voice ask.

"Who is this?" she demanded.

"It's Kitty, Nancy, Kitty Crawford. Please tell me where Rudy is."

Nancy thought quickly. "Kitty, I can't tell you. Allen's trying to reach him too, do you know that? He called twice yesterday. Anyway, I'm sorry I can't tell you where he is, but can I help you? What is it you need?"

"Oh, Nancy," the older woman sobbed. "Allen is like

a wild man, he's so upset. He's convinced Rudy's avoiding him, and he thinks it's because Rudy's written what I told you and it's going to be in *Newstime* next week."

"Kitty, that's not true. You can tell Allen it's not true. You didn't tell me anything that Rudy could write anyway."

"I know that. But Allen thinks I told you about the time the police . . . but he told them he was just taking her home . . . and he didn't even know what she was high on, anyway."

If Kitty hadn't been sobbing so hysterically, Nancy would have tried to find out what she was talking about, but she couldn't possibly poke and probe with questions right now. "Kitty, listen, why don't you just get away from him for awhile? The magazine will be out Monday, and then he'll see there's nothing and it'll be all right."

"If I left, I don't know that he'd ever let me come back."

Nancy restrained herself from suggesting that such a circumstance could only be to Kitty's benefit. "I'll ask Rudy to call Allen, but I really do think it'd be good for you to get away from him for awhile. Go shopping or something."

Kitty seemed to hear only the promise to get Rudy to call. "Oh, please, do have him call. Please."

When she had hung up, Nancy went in search of Mac. She found him in the living room drawing designs on the glass coffee table with his still sticky hands. Ordinarily she would have put an end to his design-making, but today wasn't ordinary. She felt depressed, lethargic. Things hadn't been right since Thursday night when Rudy had been out so late, when he'd been with Sarah. She supposed that most of the strain between her and Rudy now was her fault, but the idea of Sarah and him together—it caused her an actual physical discomfort. It was like something was stuck in her chest, preventing her from breathing deeply. It was simply impossible for her to respond to Rudy in the usual way. When he'd come home yesterday to pack up a few things to go up to Camp David, she knew she'd been cold and stand-offish. She'd helped him find things, answered his questions, even kissed him. But there was a part of her—most of her, in fact—holding back.

Mac abandoned his design-making on the glass table, retrieved a shoe box full of building blocks from the corner, and set about constructing something he called a "barage." Probably a garage, Nancy thought, or maybe a bridge. She looked around the room, at the contemporary furniture and the original prints which she and Rudy had chosen together. She loved the room. The contrast of the old wood moldings and window casings with the glass and chrome never ceased to delight her. And she knew Rudy loved the room too. It was like Mac. Not nearly so important, of course, but still a part of both of them. They had a good marriage, they really did, and she knew she shouldn't let one incident like Thursday night's disrupt it. But there was that tightness in her chest, that feeling of betrayal and anger.

She walked over to the record cabinet, pulled out Beethoven's *Sixth*, and put it on the turntable. She shut her eyes, listening to the green, happy notes of the "Pastoral." She could feel the tensions inside her ease, and she knew that she could make things be right. What she and Rudy had was good, so good it deserved some working at, some sacrifice. And what was her sacrifice, anyway? A little of her pride, that was all.

She thought of Kitty Crawford, and she tried to imagine what it must be like to be married to a man like Allen. But she couldn't project herself into the situation. She herself would never have chosen a man like that. Not ever. Of course, she knew many good women who were married to men she couldn't imagine choosing.

She opened her eyes. Mac was carefully stacking up his blocks, playing quietly, and she continued to consider the matter. Swaying slightly to the gentle notes of the "Pastoral's" second movement, she concluded that she'd never met anyone besides Rudy whom she could possibly be married to. She went over a mental list of every man she knew in the least well and concluded there was none of them she could live with. Sleep with, yes, but live with? That was different.

She made up her mind and placed two phone calls, the first to a friend nearby with whom she sometimes exchanged baby-sitting. As soon as she had Mac taken care of for the rest of the weekend, she called Hertz and arranged to rent a car. It was expensive, but she wasn't in a mood to worry much about money.

By two P.M., she had deposited Mac safely with her friend, and she was on the road in a rented Ford, heading for Thurmont, Maryland, where Rudy was staying. She followed Interstate 270 to Route 15, and then, less than an hour and a half after she left Washington, she saw the turnoff to Thurmont. The town was small enough so that the motel where Rudy was staying was impossible to miss. The Cozy Motel, it was called. When he had told her the name, she had laughed in spite of being angry with him. It was the Cozy Motel and Restaurant, actually, and she could not help but note, as she pulled into the parking lot, that at some stage in the establishment's history, the management had suffered a fit of creativity and erected a water wheel and covered bridge outside the entrance.

She was about to park and go into the office when she spotted Rudy, carrying some things—she couldn't tell what—and putting them into the Dodman family Volvo. She pulled the rented Ford into the next parking lot, leaned over to the passenger side, and rolled down the window.

176

"Hi there, mister. You wanna ride in a good car?"

At the sound of her voice, he whirled around. "Nancy! What're you doing here?"

His surprise at seeing her was so complete that she had to smile. "Should I have called first?"

"No, no, not at all. But why are you here?"

"Aren't you glad to see me?"

"Of course I am." He leaned into the window, put his hand on the back of her head, pulled her to him, and kissed her. "Of course I'm glad to see you." He looked around. "But where's Mac? And where'd you get the car? And why *are* you here?"

"Mac's with Donna, the car's rented, and I just thought you might like some company."

"I'm afraid I don't have much excitement to offer you," he said. "I've been sitting in a parking area down the road from Camp David all day, and I'm heading back now. I just came down to call into the magazine and get coffee and sandwiches."

"That doesn't sound so bad. We can even take my car. It has a heater."

"You got yourself a deal." He transferred the sack and thermos he had just put into the Volvo over to the Ford and then got in himself. "I nearly froze this morning in that Volvo. We're going to have to buy a new car."

"Or we could just get the heater fixed," she offered, starting up the Ford. She drove back to Route 15 and followed the signs to Catoctin National Park. When they reached the Visitor's Center, she followed Rudy's directions and turned right. They passed several paved parking areas, from which trails took off to various points of interest, before Rudy instructed her to turn in at the next one.

"Why? Is that Camp David?" she asked.

"No. It's called 'Hog Rock Parking.' It's where I've been waiting. Camp David's a little farther up."

"Then let's go on up and come back. I've never seen it."

A few minutes later, he pointed out the fences to her. They were shining through the trees, double and sometimes triple chain-link fences, topped by rolls of barbed wire.

"Looks friendly," she commented.

"Inside you really don't notice all the security."

"Shall I turn here?" she asked, seeing a road to the right with a discreet Camp David sign on it.

"No, go on up a little. There are Navy guys down that road a way, and we don't want to attract any more attention to ourselves than we have to."

A few minutes later, they were back at Hog Rock Parking, sharing tuna sandwiches and coffee. "What exactly are we waiting for?" Nancy asked between bites.

"We're waiting for any sort of vehicle to come out of there that might have somebody in it besides Camp David personnel. A limousine is probably what we're looking for."

"But how do you know they'll come this way?"

"This is the shortest way to the highway, to Thurmont, and to Washington. It's the way most of the traffic comes out of Camp David. I must've spent three hours asking questions around Thurmont last night, and that's the one useful piece of information I picked up. It's amazing that Camp David can be so close, and nobody in that little town really has any idea about what's going on up here."

"Turn on the heater for awhile, would you?" she asked, gathering up the sandwich wrappers and stuffing them into a brown paper sack.

"Wastes gas," he said, smiling at her. "Why don't you just come closer and I'll keep you warm."

She slid over next to him. "This is like the old days, high school and parking and all that. God, my nose is cold." She burrowed her face into his chest.

178

"Mmmm. Your hair smells good." he said, and when she lifted up her face, he kissed her.

"Ah, hell, Nance," he said, holding her. "I'm sorry I screwed things up Thursday night."

She couldn't resist. "As long as you didn't screw Sarah."

"You're terrible," he said, smiling. "No, I didn't screw Sarah, but I . . ."

"No, don't," she said, putting her finger on his lips. "I've been fighting green demons all day, and you'll just bring them back. But be careful, Rudy. We have something very special, but it's very fragile too. I thought this morning about spending my life with anybody but you, and I couldn't imagine it. We are so lucky." She put her face against his chest. "What if I'd ended up married to someone like Allen Crawford?" She shuddered, and then went on to tell him about her phone call from Kitty.

"You were right not to tell Kitty where I was," he said when she was through. "Crawford's been calling for me all over town—and probably calling *about* me all over town, making sure anybody who'll listen hears how irresponsible I am. Well, I'm not gonna talk to him and have him chew me out again. He's such a bastard. I don't know why the President puts up with him. And I don't know why Kitty does either."

"It's a complicated thing for her. She's never prepared herself for any sort of life without him, and so she has to stay with him, or at least she thinks she does. By the way, when she called, she was talking about some incident involving Crawford and the police and a woman high on something. Do you know about it?"

"No, but there's another story I heard parts of. It had to do with Crawford flying overseas and a stewardess in the first class section."

"What'd he do to her?"

"It's more what she did to him."

"Well, what?"

He smiled. "Are you looking for pointers?"

"You're never too old to learn," she answered, unbuttoning his shirt.

"Do you know how cold it is in here? What're you doing?"

She finished with the last button and started on his belt buckle. "Just making damned sure you don't have any scarlet letters embroidered on your chest," she said to him. "Or anywhere else for that matter."

AFTERWARD, HE lit a cigarette and noticed how dark it was getting. "If a car went by now," he said, "I don't think I could tell if it was a jeep or a limo."

"Maybe we should call it a day and go back to the motel."

"You are shameless aren't you?" he said, looking at her out of the corner of his eye. "But that's not such a bad idea, really. Imagine, sex in a bed. Sex without having to worry about the gear shift. Sex with all the amenities."

"C'mon, serious up. Where would Ewing go tonight?"

"I suppose you're right. But then where would he go tomorrow or the next day either?"

"Maybe he'll go to church tomorrow. Are psychiatrists religious?"

"Oh, hell, I don't know. He stamped his cigarette out in the ashtray. "Maybe this whole thing is a bad idea. I can't spend my life waiting at some place called Hog Rock Parking." He started up the car. "Let's come back tomorrow for a few hours and then give it up if nothing happens."

When they arrived back at the Cozy Motel, Rudy unlocked the door to the room and went in, while Nancy got her overnight case from the trunk of the Ford. As she came into the room, he was watching the end of the weekly Washington news show, "McBride *et al.*" The regulars on the show were offering summary views of the events of the past week, and they were in surprising agreement. "The next polls, I'm convinced, are going to show a drastic reversal in this President's popularity," one of the more liberal reporters said while the others on the show, liberals and conservatives alike, nodded in agreement. "And it's difficult, really, to see what Jenner can do to remedy the situation. He can tell the truth, I suppose, but the fact he hasn't done that already makes me think that the truth is likely to be as ugly as the various rumors that are circulating about the President."

"Sometimes I wonder why anybody'd want to be President," Nancy commented, as the end credits for "McBride *et al*" began to roll.

"What I'm not sure about is if anybody *can* be President," said Rudy. "What'd happen to a Jefferson or Lincoln if they held offices today? They had flaws in their personal lives just like everybody else, but somehow the nation's appetite to know about the flaws wasn't so voracious as it is now."

"The modern media weren't there to feed the monster either."

He nodded in assent. "With the kind of microscope we put a President under now, it's almost impossible for him to look heroic in the way Presidents used to. But, on the other hand, I don't see what choice we have. I don't think we should be in the business of withholding information we uncover. It certainly shouldn't be our business to try to make the President or any other politician look good."

"Not all your colleagues agree with you," said Nancy, watching the television. Vyra Mumford's weekly program was beginning, and Mrs. Mumford's smiling head was delivering an encomium about Robert Boyston, Vice President of the United States and guest for the program.

"I've never been able to understand how the guests on that program can keep from looking embarrassed, she spreads it on so thick," said Rudy. He punched a couple of pillows into a backrest for himself and lay down on the bed.

"I suppose that unassuming modesty is a demeanor you learn after you've been introduced by a few thousand sycophants," Nancy observed. "We don't have to watch this, do we?" She started to change the channel.

"Wait! Wait! What's he saying?"

"I've never observed any sign of instability at all in the President," Robert Boyston said. "I'm sure that the people of the United States understand that seeing a psychiatrist is not necessarily a sign of instability."

"He didn't clear that with the White House," said Rudy from the bed. "He's not expressing the slightest doubt about whether Jenner saw a shrink. The way he's talking, you'd think it was just last week."

"Maybe it was," Nancy reminded him.

"Have you ever seen a psychiatrist, Mr. Vice President?" Vyra Mumford was asking.

"Me?" Boyston responded. He rubbed the side of his face in what Nancy took to be an effort to keep himself from smiling. Then he gave up and laughed. "No, of course not."

"How sanctimonious can you get?" Nancy commented. "I can't stand any more of this. I'm going to go take a shower."

As she passed by the bed, Rudy grabbed her skirt and gave an exaggerated leer. "Hurry back, lady."

Nancy stopped still, dropped the few things she was carrying, and jumped onto the bed, on top of Rudy. "Enough of this easy talk," she said in his ear, lowering her voice to a mock growl. "Take off your clothes, you gorgeous man."

He laughed. And then he stopped laughing.

Chapter 16

THE NEXT morning, they were back at Hog Rock Parking early, before nine A.M. It was snowing gently.

Nancy took a sip of coffee from the thermos lid. "How long are we going to stay here?" They had checked out of the motel, and she was beginning to think about getting back to Washington.

"Noon. No later. Then we're going to write this whole thing off as a bad idea." He turned on the engine and ran the windshield wipers and the heater for a few minutes. "I'm going to move the car closer to the road. At this point, I don't really believe anybody's coming out of Camp David, but if they do, I'd hate to miss them because we can't see the damned road."

She watched him as he maneuvered the car, taking

pleasure in his hands, in his face, in the way he moved. "I love you," she said.

He turned off the ignition and looked at her. "And I love you."

They settled into a companionable silence, with him slouching behind the steering wheel, watching the road, and her reading an old paperback she had brought along. It was about a President and his mistress and a murder. The hero had just met the love of his life. You knew she was that because she was freckled and appealing rather than beautiful. So why, Nancy wondered, couldn't the love of anyone's life be the beauty? She had just come to the part where a roomful of Washington types were sitting around smoking pot, and she was wondering why she'd never been to a pot party in Washington, when she felt Rudy straighten up in the driver's seat. He'd seen something.

"That's it," he said, starting the engine.

"But that's not a limousine," she said, looking down the road and spotting a tan car just before it disappeared from sight.

He swung the Ford out into the road. "It's not your long black luxury car, but it is what the White House calls a limousine these days."

They followed the car down the wooded roadway. "Do you think they'll spot us?" Nancy asked.

"I don't think we need to worry about it. I can't imagine they'd be looking for a tail. But I'll be careful."

As the car ahead made its way toward Thurmont, Rudy kept the rented Ford a considerable distance behind. At the Visitor's Center, however, the limousine stopped before turning left, and the Dodmans pulled close enough so that Nancy could see a head in the backseat.

"Ewing doesn't have very long hair, does he?"

"Not the last time I saw him."

"I didn't think so. I don't know, Rudy, it looks to me

like whoever's in that backseat has got quite a lot of hair. Pulled back in a ponytail or something."

"Hell, maybe he's letting it grow. Maybe there aren't any barbers at Camp David. Anyhow, there's no sense calling this show off now."

After exiting from the park, the tan limousine made its way toward Thurmont. When it entered the small town, it turned down a side street and stopped in front of a red brick church.

"Psychiatrists are religious," Rudy commented, as he pulled over to the curb a few lengths behind the tan car.

"I don't think it's Ewing," Nancy said.

They both watched as the driver of the tan car got out and opened the rear door. He reached in to help someone out.

"It's a woman," Nancy exclaimed, as they both watched an attractive female in her mid-fifties get out of the limousine and start toward the church.

"It's that woman from Great Falls, isn't it?" Rudy said, rolling down the car window and leaning out for a better look. "It is! It's that woman shrink."

He threw open the car door and ran toward the church, intercepting the woman just before she entered. Nancy could see the two of them talking, then Rudy headed back to the Ford. "She said she'd talk to me after church," he said, settling in the car and lighting a cigarette. Then he was seized with a burst of energy. He reached over into the back seat and grabbed an attaché case. He threw it open, pulled out a yellow pad, and began scribbling furiously.

Nancy watched awhile before she ventured, "What are you doing?"

"I've got to think what I need to find out from her." He kept writing without looking up.

"I'm going into the church," she said, buttoning her

coat. "If I stay here, I won't be able to keep from asking you questions."

She got out of the car and walked toward the church, putting up the hood on her coat when she saw how fast the snow was coming down. She entered the red brick building—a Presbyterian church she noted from a sign just inside the door—and slipped into a back pew. She could see Dorothy Brewer sitting halfway to the front on the left side. She was an attractive woman, large-boned, dressed in an understated wool suit, her heavy dark hair pulled back in a chignon.

The service started, and Nancy tuned it in and out—mostly out. She didn't think of herself as religious, and it had been a very long time since she had been in a church. Not that she minded churches. She had always found them good places for thinking, and as she had studied ethics over the years, she had come to look on Christianity as a sound an ethical basis as any. It was interesting, she was thinking, that Immanuel Kant, after a lifetime of devoting his magnificent mind to it, had come forth with the Categorical Imperative—and the Categorical Imperative sounded awfully like the Golden Rule, which the young, sandy-haired minister at the front of the church was talking about this morning. She remembered too that Kant had observed how even the foggiest religious beliefs could impart a peace and serenity to those who held them. Maybe that was her trouble, she thought, a little sleepy now. Maybe she'd never learned to value peace and serenity enough.

She was relieved when it was time to stand and sing a hymn. Once she got sleepy, it was very hard for her to keep awake unless she could move around. Really, she decided, the only thing she had against church was that it put her to sleep. It never set the adrenalin running, not in the way that—well, what?—well, that Rudy's job did, for example.

Which brought her back to the familiar dilemma. She could be home today, writing on her dissertation, trying to explain how Hegel had misinterpreted Kant, and instead, here she was, chasing around the Maryland countryside with Rudy, caught up in his work. For some reason, though, today that didn't bother her. Today it seemed as though she had the best of both worlds. Time enough tomorrow for the life of the mind, for Kant and the eighteenth century. For today there was what the world thought important now. There were Presidents and politics and the craziness and disorder of Rudy's life to be savored.

When the service was over, she filed out of the church and saw Rudy waiting. They stood together and watched for Dorothy Brewer, who, when she came through the church door, spotted them immediately. She walked over to where they were standing and nodded briskly to Rudy, her eyes taking in Nancy too. "Let's talk in your car," she said.

Dr. Brewer declined Rudy's offer to let her sit in the front seat, and instead she let herself into the back. Rudy and Nancy got in front, and Rudy began to flip the pages of his yellow tablet, trying to decide quickly where he should start his questioning. "Maybe we should start with why you're at Camp David. Did the President send you there?" he asked.

"Quite the contrary, Mr. Dodman, he invited me. He knew how many phone calls and visits I was likely to get from the press, so he invited me to stay at Camp David for a short while."

Rudy started to ask another question, but Dorothy Brewer put up her hand to stop him. "I don't really want to answer your questions, Mr. Dodman. I do want to talk to you, but I want to say what *I* want to say—not what you want me to say." She smoothed her gray flannel skirt over her knees. "And one other thing. What I'm telling you is just for you, not for your readers. And if I read anything I say in print any place, I'll deny I said it."

Rudy opened his mouth to argue, but seemed to think better of it, and instead nodded his assent.

"What I really want to do is tell you a story. I want you to imagine a boy, a hypothetical boy this is, and I want you to imagine his mother too. She's a strong woman, an ambitious woman, who sees this boy, her firstborn son, as the fulfiller of the dreams she never carried out herself. And she's a good woman. She loves her boy, and so while she does drive him and prod him, she also gives him an abundance of love and affection."

Nancy found herself enthralled by the woman in the back seat, by her strong self-assurance, by what she was saying. She shifted around so that she could observe her more closely as she listened.

"And there's something in this boy that responds to the way his mother brings him up. He begins to think there's nothing he can't do, nothing that is beyond him. And because he's bright and attractive, all his experience reinforces for him the idea he has of himself. In high school and college, he wins good grades and the esteem of his peers. He marries a beautiful and bright young woman and is a success at the vocation he chooses.

"And because he's still ambitious, he looks for new challenges, new ways to prove himself. And so he turns to politics. He decides to run for the United States Senate, and the first time he tries, he loses, but he manages to accept the loss with equanimity. He sees the first race as a learning experience, and he tells himself now that he knows what he's about in this new area he's entered, he can expect success. He tries again and commits himself totally to the contest. He doesn't hold anything back; nevertheless, he loses again, and the experience is devastating, because it forces him to question the whole matter of who he is, of whether he really is the leader of men he thought he was."

"And so he goes to see a shrink," Rudy interjected.

"That's not necessarily the outcome for this man. He's grown up valuing very much the idea of being independent and self-sustaining, and so professional help is really quite a foreign idea to him. But there's no one else he can talk to as he works his way through the crisis. He's not a man who makes close friends, and his wife is a strong and independent woman, not very given to understanding the emotional difficulties of others."

"So then he goes to see the shrink," said Rudy. Nancy looked at him in irritation. Why was he being so rude?

"I wish you wouldn't use that word, Mr. Dodman. I try to tolerate it usually, but especially in this context, it's so totally inappropriate. It implies such an active role for the psychiatrist in the doctor-patient encounter, and with the hypothetical man I'm talking about, the psychiatrist was no more than a listener, no more than an ear. He did need someone to whom he could talk, but it was he who worked his problem through, not the doctor. In fact, the moment in which his loss came into perspective for him didn't even happen when he was in the doctor's office."

"Was he on his ranch? Checking fences maybe?"

"Exactly what he was doing is of no consequence. What is important is that you understand the kind of man we're talking about."

"This man you're describing, he sounds like he'd be O.K. as long as he never loses."

"No, that's not it. He never will like losing, that's certain. But the experience he's had with it, and with the success which followed, would make him able to accept it, were he to lose again. He knows now, he knows in the bone-deep way experience teaches, that losing doesn't have to be final, that success can follow.

"And because he's got some perspective now, he's not likely ever again to commit every spiritual and physical resource he's got to contest. He'll keep enough in reserve to handle losing—or winning. You know, it's not uncommon for political figures to suffer depression when an election's over, even if they've won."

Nancy couldn't restrain herself. "Then you don't think this hypothetical man would ever need a psychiatrist again."

" 'Need a psychiatrist'—that expresses such a complex of ideas. Some people 'need a psychiatrist' because their friends have one, and some people 'need a psychiatrist' to keep them from sticking their heads in an oven. Most of the people I see 'need a psychiatrist' just because they haven't anyone else to talk to. Sometimes I think of myself as a 'confidante-for-hire,' " she said, smiling slightly.

"But if you're asking me whether I think this man will ever want to seek professional help again, the answer's no. As bright and competent as he is, I suspect he's going to find his life filled with challenge. He's going to have to work hard and stretch himself, and that's the best way for him. I don't think he'll have many more losses in his life, but if he does, he'll be able to handle them."

"I guess I'm puzzled about why you're telling me about this hypothetical man," said Rudy. "What good does it do if I can't print any of it?"

"What's there to print, Mr. Dodman?" She adjusted one of the heavy gold earrings she was wearing. "The kind of man I've told you about is familiar to all of us. Especially you, Mr. Dodman, should find this story familiar, as much time as you've spent studying politics. The only thing unusual about my hypothetical man is the two losses so close together. That didn't happen to Lyndon Johnson or FDR, but I imagine, if it had, their reactions wouldn't have been unlike my hypothetical man's."

"So you're trying to say Zern Jenner's no different from other Presidents we've had?"

"I didn't mention the President's name," she answered. She considered for a moment. "I suppose if there is one thing I'd like to see come out of our conversation, it's some realization on your part of exactly what you're doing, you as a representative of the press, I mean. Is it really newsworthy, this hypothetical man's seeing a psychiatrist a very long time ago? Or are you just making it news? Is what you're doing fair, Mr. Dodman? Is it right?"

"Is it right for a man who's President of the United States to lie about his past?" He turned and snuffed out the cigarette he'd been smoking. Nancy could tell he was angry.

Dorothy Brewer reached for the door handle. "I didn't come to argue with you, Mr. Dodman, or even with the hope I'd convince you. But perhaps I've given you something to think about." She got out of the car and walked quickly to the limousine, which was waiting with its motor running. The chauffeur got out and opened the back door for her. Then he got in himself, and the car pulled away.

After a moment, Rudy started the Ford, made a U-turn, and headed back toward the Cozy Motel where the Volvo was still parked. Nancy waited before she said anything. His jaw was clenched so tightly a small muscle near his cheekbone was jumping, and he drove the car angrily. She knew it was best to keep silent awhile.

Finally, when they were nearly to the motel, she spoke. "Rudy, why did she make you so angry? Why were you so rude?"

"Rude! I wasn't rude. You just haven't been around me when I've been interviewing people. I wasn't rude. I was a pussycat."

"But she made you angry."

"That is true. I'm not sure why." He took a deep breath. "Maybe because I've wondered myself from time to time whether this story is worth doing."

"You don't think the story's fair?"

"That's part of it. But even more, it seems . . . I don't know, unreal, somehow."

"But Jenner really *did* see the psychiatrist."

"I know. It's not that part that's unreal. It's the reaction to it. So magnified, so exaggerated. It's like the mouse labored and brought forth a mountain." He permitted himself a small smile. "Well, it's not the first time."

"But why does it happen?"

"That's one of the reasons," he said, pulling into the parking lot and pointing at the car radio. Out of it were coming the sounds of the hourly news. "There just isn't that much going on, not on a Sunday morning, not that's really important, and so to fill up the void, we struggle to make things that aren't so important seem important. Seem urgent and vital and newsworthy."

"But the President lied. That is important."

"Is it? Oh, I suppose it is. But haven't you or I ever lied? And does that make us evil? Besides, think how contrived the circumstances were. A press conference, which isn't really news itself, but an event where everybody hopes news will be made so that we'll have something for the newspapers and magazines and airwaves. And then Frye. He led the President into the lie. It's not like Zern Jenner woke up one morning and said to himself, 'Hmmm, I think I'll lie to the American people today.' "

"But what about Ewing?"

He nodded his head. "That's the one part of the story I don't have doubts about. I don't think Malcolm's the Man's shrink, but there's something . . ."

"No! No!" He was interrupted by Nancy's cry and

by her reaching suddenly for the volume knob on the radio.

"We have no more details," the announcer was saying, *"but we have learned that police were called this morning to the home of presidential adviser Allen Crawford. There they found Mrs. Crawford, dead of an apparently self-inflicted gunshot wound."*

Rudy reached for Nancy. She was sobbing. "It's all right. It's all right," he said, holding her, patting her back.

"No, no, no, it's not. She reached out to me for help. I could have helped her."

"You can't blame yourself. You can't get through life if you blame yourself for every tragedy that happens to someone you know. Christ, if there's anybody who should feel guilty, it's me. She called me, remember? Maybe if I'd talked to her or if I'd called Crawford back, whatever crisis finally pushed her over the edge could have been avoided."

After a few minutes, Nancy was quieter. She sat up, reached into her coat pocket for a tissue, and wiped her eyes. "It really is ironic in a way."

"How's that?" He leaned back on the seat and took a deep breath to try to relax himself.

"Oh, what you said about how the thing with the President has been exaggerated. This thing with Kitty and Allen was just the opposite. Everybody minimized it. Nobody wrote about how he treated her, about what Washington did to their marriage."

"Washington? Do you think it was Washington?" He reached over and brushed a damp tendril of hair back off her cheek.

"Yes. Well, no, I suppose it happens everywhere that men get middle-aged and tired of their wives. And Washington's not the only place where men get powerful along the way to middle age, or where that power attracts other women. But I'd swear it's worse here. I'd swear it is." She wiped her eyes again. "Oh, I don't know, maybe it's no different anyplace else." She looked up at him. "Let's go home."

He kissed her. "Will you be all right? You're going to have to drive by yourself, you know. I'll be right behind in the Volvo."

She nodded her head, and he got out of the car.

As she drove out of Thurmont, it occurred to her that while she did want to go home, she wasn't sure she wanted to go back to Washington, back to where Rudy's work meant his being away from her, off in a different world.

Chapter 17

SARAH WAS standing in a Spring Valley, Maryland, delicatessen trying to decide what to have for lunch. She considered pastrami on rye, then was tempted to buy herself a pint of ice cream, Haagen Dazs ice cream—as far as she was concerned it was the best in the world. She thought of making a lunch of the honey flavor, but then she decided against it, asked for a carton of plain yogurt, and went to the cash register to pay for it. While she waited her turn, she studied the pictures on the delicatessen wall. Two Presidents and a Vice President were up there, several senators, and a Supreme Court Justice or two, and all of the pictures were autographed with inscriptions to the delicatessen owner. Probably most of the politicians on the wall lived in the expensive suburban neighborhood around the delicatessen, probably they patronized the place often, but still, such pictures on a deli wall. It would only happen in Washington.

She got her change and headed out to her BMW. It was beginning to snow now, and she turned on the car engine so the heater would keep her warm while she ate. She tried to feel proud of herself for paying heed to nutrition and calories and all the rest of it, but when she opened the carton, the yogurt depressed her. Ice cream was better, there was no doubt about it. And who wanted to spend the rest of her days eating white jello? That's what the yogurt looked like, no matter how good for you it was.

The radio was on, but she wasn't really listening to it, so the story was almost over before she caught the name Crawford. *"We are told,"* the announcer was saying, *"that Mr. Crawford discovered his wife's body in their bedroom early Sunday morning."*

Sarah willed the announcer to continue, but he went on to other news items, and it was several minutes before the Crawford story was recycled. Sarah listened closely when it came on again, and after she had heard it from beginning to end, she put it together with what she knew about Crawford. She remembered his penchant for younger women, which he hadn't done much to hide over the past few years, and she thought she understood what had happened. Kitty Crawford—she tried to remember her. She had been blonde, hadn't she? An attractive woman, fifties, well dressed. And she had shot herself. A shiver ran down Sarah's spine. She shut her eyes and tried to push the idea of death to the back of her mind. She focused on the present, on her immediate plans.

Before she'd gone into the delicatessen, she had used

the pay phone outside to call "Boyston's boy," the young lawyer who worked for the Vice President. Her morning had been totally fruitless, what with first trying to reach Jane Minnick, who still wasn't answering her phone, and then waiting outside Gretchen Burrows' apartment. After three hours and no sign of the President's secretary, Sarah had resolved to find a more useful way to spend the afternoon. And so she had decided to call "Boyston's boy"—Harold Stark was his real name. If anybody knew about the Vice President's part in leaking the Oval Office log, it would be he, and she had an idea, a strategy in mind, for finding out what he knew.

Their plan to meet would still be on, wouldn't it? She couldn't imagine that the Vice President's office would be too caught up in the suicide of the wife of a presidential aide. Or that they were likely to get too upset about it, even. They were cold-blooded bastards, all of them who worked for Boyston. But then, who was she to talk? Here she was, calculating, considering. And a woman was dead.

She put the yogurt carton back into the brown paper sack, got out of the car, and deposited it in a trash can. She got back in and headed toward the Wesley Heights address Stark had given her. As she drove, she concentrated very deliberately on not thinking about Kitty Crawford. She focused instead on the man she was going to meet. Stark. "Boyston's boy." He hadn't wanted to talk to her. Not until she told him that she had it on good authority that the Oval Office log had been leaked to Jane Minnick by someone in the Vice President's office. That had got his attention—and an invitation for her to come by his house.

She slowed down to check street numbers, and then pulled her car to the curb in front of a light cream brick house. It was in the $275,000 range, she supposed. It didn't seem especially elegant viewed from the street, but Sarah knew the prices of houses in this close-in neighborhood of wide lawns and quiet, tree-lined streets. She got out of her car and walked up the brick sidewalk.

"Boyston's boy"—she had to make a mental effort not to call him that—met her at the door himself. There was no sign of his wife, a lean, attractive woman, whom Sarah remembered seeing once at the Kennedy Center. Stark showed her into a carpeted, book-lined study off the front hallway, and as she sat down on the brown leather sofa, Sarah noted the pictures hung on the wall. Did self-love, she wondered, account for all the two-dimensional icons displayed on Washington walls? Or maybe it was self-pride. Stark had a framed black-and-white of himself with the Vice President, another of himself shaking hands with the Shah of Iran in a receiving line. There were also two oversized, framed Christmas cards bearing the President's and Mrs. Jenner's names and a couple of diplomas scattered in the mix. Stark had gone to Yale, Sarah noted, and then got his law degree at Harvard.

Stark sat himself down in a high-backed chair at a large, heavy table which he apparently used as a desk. He was about thirty-five, thin, sandy-haired, and he drummed his fingers on the table top. "I don't usually see reporters in my home," he began. He managed to seem condescending, though he was obviously nervous. How was it possible, Sarah wondered, for someone who was so obsequious to his boss to be so condescending to others?

"I don't usually see reporters here," he repeated, "but you seemed to be operating off some misinformation."

"You mean about how the Vice President's office leaked the Oval Office log to Jane Minnick?" She had no evidence, but she was sure her theory was correct.

His eyes narrowed, "That did not happen. The last thing anyone in the Vice President's office would want is to embarrass the President."

"My source tells me that's exactly what happened. The log was leaked to Minnick out of the Vice President's office, and she in turn gave it to Nicholas Frye."

"Your source is in error. Now it is true that Miss Minnick was working on a profile of Vice President Boyston, so she had been in our office recently . . ."

"And you don't think someone handed her a copy of the log while she was in there?"

"That didn't happen."

Sarah was quiet a moment, analyzing Stark's response. She decided to take a stab. "As I understand it, however, your office did have copies of the Oval Office log." His answers had implied that, hadn't they? He hadn't ever questioned the basic premise that Minnick *could* have obtained the log from the Vice President's office.

Stark was taken aback, and his eyes shifted nervously before he answered. "Copies of the log? I don't . . . well, perhaps, one could say . . . uh, as a matter of fact, I do believe that the Vice President was working on some sort of efficiency study for the President, and as a part of that, he may well have been studying the Oval Office log. But it's a long way, Miss Hoff, from there to saying there were copies of the log around and that someone leaked one to Miss Minnick."

A long way? Sarah didn't think so. She remembered Jane picking at her skirt and saying she "shouldn't have taken it." Jane had been in the Vice President's office, and the Vice President had the Oval Office log. There was no way Jane could have taken a copy of a confidential document like the log unless someone had meant her to. What had they done, Sarah wondered? Left copies of it lying on a desk? Probably something like that. But why had they done it? That still wasn't quite clear, though she suspected she knew the answer. "Is the Vice President still receiving a lot of mail as a result of the stories about the log?"

"Yes, we are, as a matter of fact." Stark had his old confidence back now. "Oh, it's beginning to taper off a little, and I suspect it will drop off more next week, but we're getting thousands of letters wanting to know why the President is ignoring the Vice President, why he isn't relying on him more. There's a substantial number of Americans who think the Vice President should have greater input into policy decisions . . ." His voice trailed off as he saw the satisfaction in her face. He saw that somehow, though he didn't know quite how, he had told her more than he had meant to.

That had been it, then, she was thinking. They'd wanted to put a little pressure on the President, pressure to give Boyston a more prominent role, probably pressure to make sure he'd be on the ticket for next year's elections. They had probably expected Minnick to go with the leaked Oval Office log in a story of her own. How could they know she'd give it to Frye and he'd dig away at it in a way she never would? They had probably been as surprised as Jenner when psychiatry and psychiatrists became the main issue.

There was one more question she wanted to ask. "Do you know that Kitty Crawford committed suicide?" She saw the shock register on his face. "Sometime last night or this morning, it seems to have happened. Crawford found her this morning."

The shock had been real. The sympathy he reached for now didn't seem so. "How terrible," he said, avoiding eye contact with her. "How terrible that such a tragedy could happen to someone so close to the President."

Suddenly Sarah wanted very much to get away, to get outside and breathe in the open air. She disentangled herself from the meeting with Stark, and then she was outside, unlocking her car, forcing herself to remember all the good men and women she knew in Washington. They weren't all like "Boyston's boy."

She got into the BMW and began to drive, resolving to think objectively about Stark. Why did he upset her so much anyway? Was it the way he pandered to the Vice President? That was probably a large part of it. In his every thought and action, he let himself be totally defined by the man for whom he worked, and that kind of dependence grated. She'd been wrong earlier when she'd thought it was only women who came to rely totally on the men for whom they worked. It happened to men too, and somehow for them it was worse. Society never forced a man to learn the art of graceful dependence, and so the frustrations built, and he took them out on others, treating them in the same condescending and degrading way in which he was treated.

Her hostility toward Stark had lessened now, and she was glad. Indulging her feelings of animosity would be useless—counterproductive, even. It did no more good than worrying about . . . and there they were again, the thoughts of death and dying and Kitty Crawford. She stopped her car at a stop light, and while she was waiting, she looked down at her hands on the steering wheel. Capable hands, she thought, opening up the left one so that she could see her short, unpolished nails. And what would they be like when she was dead? The nails kept growing, didn't they?

A honk from the car behind told her she hadn't noticed the light turn green. "Enough of this morbid stuff," she said aloud to herself as she turned onto Massachusetts Avenue. There were plenty of things she could *do* something about. She was pretty sure now she knew how the Oval Office log had been leaked, and she could test her theory by getting hold of Jane Minnick, running the scenario past her, and watching her reaction.

She also thought she understood why the log had been given to the press. What she needed to figure out was exactly what the leak had revealed. The big question was still Ewing. What was he doing during all those hours in the Oval Office, and where was he now? Why had he gone to Camp David two days before the *Post* even printed the log? "Maybe a week or ten days," he had written in the note he'd left for Wendy. Today it had been a week since he left. For whatever reason he had gone, he had expected to be able to return by now, or in the next few days.

As she turned into the Dupont traffic circle, the significance of that came home to her. If Ewing had left because he didn't want to answer questions about whether he was the President's psychiatrist, he couldn't come back now. The questions were still waiting for him, and he wouldn't have gained anything by disappearing for a week. And he would have know that from the outset. If he had made himself scarce for the reason everyone assumed he had, he'd have known he would have to stay scarce for a very long time.

So either he'd lied to Wendy—which seemed unlikely—or maybe his absence didn't have anything to do with his being a psychiatrist. And since he'd left two days before the *Post* published the log, it could even be that his departure didn't have anything to do with the leak.

She spied a parking place, and while she was waiting for the traffic to subside so that she could back into it, she decided perhaps it was time for her to review all her assumptions about Ewing.

IN HIS Spring Valley home, Harold Stark was waiting for a call on the White House phone, which had been installed in his study when he first started working for the Vice President. He was pacing the floor, trying to will the knots in his stomach to go away when he heard his wife, Jan, come in the front door. She looked into the study as she went down the hallway.

"Hi, you busy?" she asked.

"Yes, I'm busy," he said.

A look of irritation and disappointment came over her tanned face. She wasn't a beautiful woman, but she radiated an air of health and fitness. "You're always busy, aren't you?" she said.

"Now, Jan, don't start on me." His voice was querulous. "Damn it, you don't ever give me any support or sympathy or try to understand the things I'm worrying about."

"One crazy person in the family's enough," she said from the doorway. The words came easily to her, as they had to him. It was clear they had been over this ground many times before. "Hell, you're not married to me," she went on, "you're married to Boyston." She turned and started to walk away and then turned back again. "No, that's not it. You're not his wife, you're that man's slave, his . . ."

The ringing of the phone cut off her sentence. Stark picked up the receiver, and as he did so, turned his back on his wife.

"Yes," he said.

"I can put the Vice President on the line now, Mr. Stark."

"Fine."

In a moment, Boyston's voice came booming into his ear. "What do you want, Harold?"

"Sir, I just talked to a reporter, Sarah Hoff of *Newstime* magazine." He glanced over his shoulder at his wife, who was still in the doorway. She caught his look, shook her head, turned abruptly, and walked away. "She's working on a story, sir, that the leak of the President's daily log came out of your office."

"What!" the Vice President's voice exploded. "Did you give her that idea? How many times do I have to tell you, goddamit, you're not to speak to the press without my authorization."

"Sir, she had the story when she came to me."

"Goddamit, why am I surrounded by incompetents?" the Vice President raged. "I'd fire you for this, Stark, I'd fire your ass in two seconds flat, except there's nobody else in that goddamned office of mine who's any better."

Stark took the phone away from his ear, held it in the air, and let the Vice President rage on. After a few minutes, he put the receiver back to his ear and spoke into the mouthpiece. "Sir, what I called you about is the demonstration."

"Shut it down! Shut it down!" the Vice President shrieked. "Jesus Christ, if the story's out that we leaked the log, the demonstration's the last thing I need."

"Yes, sir, I just wonder whom you think I ought to call. Feelings are running so high now, I'm not sure who on our list is going to be able to turn it off."

"Call every damn one of them. I don't care how you do it, you get it shut down right now. Just do it."

Stark winced as the crash of the Vice President's slamming down his phone came over the line. Then he hung up his own phone and rummaged through the papers on top of his work table until he found the list he wanted. He counted the names on it. There were twenty-three of them in all. He picked up his phone again, and when the White House operator came on the line, he read the names off to her. "As soon as I finish talking to one, get me the next name on the list," he ordered. "I'll wait for the first one," he added impatiently.

In the basement of the Executive Office Building, where the White House switchboard was located, the operator who was on the line to Stark began work on the calls. As she dialed the first number, she covered her mouthpiece with her hand and leaned over to the operator working next to her. "It's him again," she said. "How come is it, you suppose, that some people never do learn to say please?"

Chapter 18

THE ELEVATOR was slow, as usual, but Mary Jenner didn't mind. Its stately pace gave her time to admire the delicate inlay of wood and mirrored glass which decorated the elevator walls. It was a relief to be able to focus on the fine craftmanship and put the thought of Kitty Crawford aside for the moment.

She got off on the ground floor of the mansion, where a Secret Service man was waiting. With him following just a little behind her, she left the foyer housing the elevator, turned left, and walked down the red-carpeted hall toward the East Wing. She had known Kitty Crawford a long time, she reflected, walking through a door held open by the Secret Service man. She'd known her since Allen Crawford had first come to work for Zern, though she had not been terribly close to her. Kitty had seemed so vulnerable, so helpless, somehow, that she'd never felt quite comfortable with her. But maybe if she'd made an effort . . . She shrugged the thought away and turned into the suite of offices where her staff worked. Pamela Whyte, her social secretary, and Dorothy Stein, her press secretary, were both waiting for her. The three women went into the First Lady's office, and the Secret Service man stationed himself outside the door.

"I've prepared a statement for you and the President," Stein offered. "I called Mark Westfield and read it to him, and he O.K.'d it." She paused while the First Lady read through the neatly typed words of regret. "Shall I go with it then?"

Mary Jenner nodded. "We both called Allen and spoke to him as soon as we heard."

"About the state dinner . . . ," Pamela Whyte said tentatively.

"We'll go ahead with it. The President thinks we should. The Japanese are already in Williamsburg, and it's very important to the entire nation that the meeting go well. But let's eliminate the after-dinner dancing. And the entertainment should be—well, not unseemly."

"I think it will be suitable," the social secretary said, explaining that a world-famous cellist was to play.

They discussed other details, other ways of managing the unexpected intrusion of death into the affairs of state. And when they had finished and Mary Jenner was walking back up the red-carpeted hall with the Secret Service agent, she wondered for a moment why it had fallen to her staff to handle these matters. It had to do, she supposed, with woman's traditional role. Somewhere along the line, society had decided that marrying and burying were female responsibilities, and even in the White House, it worked that way. As she walked through the hallways, she glanced at the pictures of former First Ladies which hung on the walls. There was Jacqueline Kennedy, glancing to the side, looking mysterious, ethereal. Lady Bird Johnson, looking straight out from the canvas, seeming gracious and direct. Eleanor Roosevelt—that was Mary Jenner's favorite. The artist had captured her in many poses, symbolic of the active role she had created for herself as First Lady. She was the first President's wife that young Mary Jenner—Mary Wilson it had been then—had become aware of. To a young girl growing up in Pennsylvania, it had seemed that Mrs. Roosevelt was everywhere, doing everything, and all at once.

She wondered how FDR's staff had regarded Eleanor. Zern's staff was generally respectful and helpful to her, but not long ago she'd heard that some of his staffers called the East Wing, where her offices were, the "toy factory." She'd laughed when she'd heard it, though it had hurt all the same. The matters she was concerned with might not appear weighty to West Wing staffers, but they were nonetheless essential. As she stepped into the elevator, she thought of the meeting she had just concluded. Public expressions of sorrow, state dinners, such were the things that consumed her time. They were ceremonial, but wasn't ceremony important? It eased the friction of life, she thought, as the elevator door slid closed. Ceremony was a way of managing life's tragedy.

Slowly she was lifted to the mansion's second floor. When the elevator had come to a stop, Mary Jenner got off and walked out into the central hallway of the family quarters, turned right, and headed toward the West Hall, the area where she and the President usually sat to relax and read or watch television.

Although it was the end of the long east-west corridor running from one end to the other of the White House's second floor, the West Hall didn't seem hall-like. The flowered chintz draperies and slipcovers helped give it a light, cozy feeling, as did the pale gold carpet and the cheerful Impressionist paintings. Centered behind the sofa, in the window overlooking the West Wing, was a huge bouquet of fresh flowers.

The President was sitting in his favorite chair, a telephone on the table beside him, a manila folder open on his lap. The folder was the daily intelligence briefing, Mary Jenner knew, a top secret report that the President received daily. It was apparent, however, that his thoughts were elsewhere. Instead of reading the daily briefing, the President was staring off into space. She went over to him and put her hand on his shoulder.

"You know, I only made the situation worse, really," he said without looking up.

She knew he was talking about the Crawfords.

"I probably shouldn't have brought him to the White House. I should have put him in an agency, maybe, or on a commission," he said.

"That wouldn't have changed him."

"No, not his basic problems. It wouldn't have changed those, but I think that being in the White House exaggerated those problems. It's self-doubt, basically. He started doubting whether his life was worthwhile, and so he started drinking to anesthetize the doubts and seeing young women to convince himself the doubts were groundless."

"But he did that before the White House."

"Yes, but being here increased the opportunities. Maybe if I hadn't brought him here, he'd have finally been forced to face himself instead of hiding from himself. And maybe Kitty'd still be alive."

"You can't know that, Zern. You can't torture yourself with that idea."

"No, I know." He looked up at her. "Really, what I was sitting here thinking is how this place is like a magnifying glass, how it exaggerates whatever faults a man has. Or maybe it's more like a wedge. It can find the tiniest crack in a man's personality and force it open."

"You know the thing I'm finding hardest?" she said. "Not hating Robert Boyston, that's the hardest thing. I find myself thinking about him and tensing up all over." She crossed her arms and shuddered. Then she caught his quizzical expression. "I know," she said, "I know it's not like me."

"Nobody ever told us the job was going to be easy," he said.

"But somehow I thought it would be fair."

"I remember something John Kennedy said once . . ."

"I know. He said that life isn't fair. But if you keep pushing and if you're persistent, in the long run, you can make it a little fairer. I just know you can."

When she looked down at him, he could see tears in her eyes. And although she was obviously attempting to hold them back, one ran down her cheek. He reached up and wiped it away. "We're going to have to toughen you up, Mary Jenner. You've been through enough of this to know the first rule of politics is don't get mad and don't get upset."

"Just get even. Right?" She tried to smile. "I've just never felt quite like this. Somehow it's always been so easy for me before to set my emotions aside. I don't know why I can't do it this time."

"Do you suppose it has to do with getting older? You know, when we were young and I was losing all those damned elections in Montana, I think you always told yourself that there'd be another election, and what we wanted was to win those, not to get emotionally hamstrung by ones in the past. But now, well, it's a different thing, now."

"Now there might not be any more elections."

"That's right. I think we'll come through this O.K., but we might not. There's that possibility too, and we both need to be able to acknowlege it, to be able to think about it without flinching."

She didn't answer. Instead she shut her eyes for several moments. When she opened them, the tears were gone. "Would you like to have dinner early?" she asked.

"HE TRUSTS you, probably more than he trusts anybody. That's why I want you here." Basinger had called Gersten at home and asked him to come to the West Wing. They were seated in front of the fireplace in Basinger's office.

"The poor guy," Gersten said. "I can imagine what he's going through. Is his son going to be O.K.?"

Before Basinger could answer, there was a knock at the door. Basinger opened it to see the mess steward, Danny, accompanied by two Secret Service agents.

"Come in, come in, please, Danny," said Basinger. He motioned for the agents to wait in the reception area.

"Mr. Gersten," Danny said. "Thank you for being here."

"Sure, Dan. No trouble."

"Do you know anything?" the mess steward asked. "Is he all right?"

"Here, Danny, sit down," Basinger said, "I'll tell you where we are." When the steward had seated himself in one of the green chairs near the fireplace, Basinger went on. "We have a report that your son is still at your sister's house in Manila. There are armed agents guarding the house. It looks like they're there to keep him from leaving."

"But he's just a boy. He's just sixteen. Why they want to keep him there? He's not gonna hurt anyone."

"It's not him they're interested in, Dan. It's you."

The mess steward nodded, his misery evident. "For that boy I could do most anything, most anything at all. My Lily died when he was born, you know."

"I know."

"But the thing I couldn't do is give them information like they wanted. I thought maybe I'd find something in Mr. Ewing's office. You know he was in the Philippines for a couple of years once? Anyway, I thought maybe if there was something about my country, he might have it. And that's what they wanted me to look for. Anything about the Philippines."

"But they didn't direct you toward Ewing, did they, Danny?" Basinger asked.

"Oh, no. That was my idea. You know, I was in Mr. Ewing's office two times. You saw me once," he said, nodding at Gersten. "And you saw me, Mr. Basinger. But I couldn't go through his office, I felt so bad. And I couldn't look through anybody else's either." He was leaning forward, his elbows on his knees. "To work for a President is a thing so grand, I never thought it would happen to me. Such a trust and an honor, it is. I couldn't go through the office." He looked up. "But what about my Sergio? What will they do to him?"

"I don't think anything will happen to him," Basinger said. "Marcos doesn't want any big embarrassment, anything that will worsen his public image or make Congress think twice about military aid for the Philippines. We've had our ambassador in Manila file a protest, so now there's no way Marcos can claim to be unaware of the situation."

"I hope Sergio be safe. Some bad things happen in my country sometimes. I hear about people who get tortured with ice, with electric shocks. The voice on the telephone say such things could happen to Sergio if I don't look for information for them."

"No, they can't do that now because they know that we know. Marcos can't say that some underling did things he didn't know about. No, Sergio won't be jailed or tortured. We just have to make sure we get him over here for Thanksgiving, like you'd planned in the first place."

"Thank you, Mr. Basinger." Danny stood. "And thank you, Mr. Gersten."

Gersten stood up, put his arm around Danny's shoulder, and walked him to the door. "Where are you staying, Dan? You're not staying at home, are you?"

"No, sir. They got a cot for me over in the basement at EOB. Mr. Carnahan say that's best."

Gersten closed the door behind Danny, then turned to Basinger. "I suppose there's always been some vulnerability there, having men who are citizens of another country work so close to the President."

Basinger shook his head. "I'm not sure that's true, not with the thorough checks we run on all the President's personal staff, Filipino or not."

"But having a family in the Philippines where they're such easy targets for a guy like Marcos, such a temptation for him . . ."

"Not under normal circumstances," Basinger interrupted. "Under normal circumstances, Marcos wouldn't dare try to set a spy in the White House. The consequences of his being found out would be too serious. He'd alienate every supporter he has in this country. It just wouldn't be worth the risk."

"So what's going on that they'd try to get to Danny now?" Gersten asked. "I just don't get it."

"And right now," Basinger said, poking at the fire in the fireplace, "right now, you don't need to understand."

Gersten shrugged and walked over to one of the windows overlooking West Executive Avenue. He looked out to see Danny and the Secret Service agents crossing the lighted street to the old Executive Office Building. Danny's head was hanging down. "Crawford's wife,

Danny's son," Gersten said under his breath. He turned abruptly. "You know, it's almost like what you need to run this place is a bunch of monastics."

Basinger looked up. "I've thought of that more than once. You know what today is? It's my daughter's birthday. She's nine, and I haven't seen her all day. I left before she got up, and I'll get home after she's in bed. And it's Sunday, for God's sake."

"So why do you do it?"

Basinger put the poker in its stand and considered for a minute. "I don't know," he answered finally. "Maybe because it's just about the hardest damned job a man can take on. I suppose that's its fascination."

Gersten turned back and looked out the window again. West Executive Avenue was nearly empty. Only five or six cars were pulled into the diagonal parking spaces. "Quiet out there," he observed to no one in particular.

IT WAS not really quiet, but from the window in Dale Basinger's office Gersten could not see the guardhouse at the northwest corner of the White House complex. Just out of the line of his vision, a tall, sallow-skinned woman, whose glasses sat crookedly on her face, had been arguing with the guards for several minutes. She spoke to them with intensity, then they turned away from her to confer. While they were talking, she, like Gersten, watched Danny and the two Secret Service agents cross West Executive Avenue. When the guards turned back around, she was close to tears. "I've got to get into the pressroom. Don't you see?" she said. "It's the only safe . . ." She stopped herself, put her hand to her forehead for a moment and then went on in a calmer tone, "I'm working on a story, and I need to get into the press office."

One of the guards signaled to the other, and they

turned their backs on her again. "I don't know," the first guard said. "Her press pass is O.K., and there's nothing that says it's not valid at night."

"But she's weird. Don't you think there's something wrong with her?"

"No more than usual. I know this one. She's always weird. Besides, if she goes into the pressroom, she can't get anyplace else. The guard at the desk outside won't let her."

"O.K., but just to be safe, let's alert him that she's in there."

The first guard handed the woman back her press pass, and she started up the asphalt driveway toward the pressroom entrance.

Chapter 19

SARAH HAD thought of practically nothing else since she got up. While she chose her clothes, while she brushed her teeth (all very quietly so she wouldn't awaken Wendy), while she rode the metro to work, almost nothing else had been on her mind except Malcolm Ewing and where he might be. She did note, as she walked the last few blocks to her office, that flags were decorating the Washington streets. Every quarter block or so, the Stars and Stripes were paired with the Rising Sun of Japan. The sun was out—the last bit of snow from yesterday had melted—and the sunshine and the flags lent a festive air to the city, distracting her momentarily and causing her to remember that she was in the press pool for the Japanese state dinner tonight.

Then her thoughts went back to Malcolm Ewing. If he wasn't at Camp David, where was he? And suppose his absence had nothing to do with his being a psychiatrist—then what was it related to? She knew the questions she was asking were important. The trouble was, she couldn't think of any satisfactory answers.

When she got to her desk, she considered whom she might call. Who could jog her thinking? Gersten was always a good bet, and when she dialed his number, a secretary said he was out. She had better luck when she called Steve Bravo.

"Steve?" she said, when he had come on the line. "This is Sarah. I thought maybe you could give me a little advice."

"Sure, pretty lady, what is it?"

"Well, I'm working on this story, and I've got to locate somebody. All I know is they left Washington sometime in the last few days." It had been more than a week since Ewing had disappeared, but she didn't want Bravo to know that's what she was working on.

"All I can think you can do, Sarah, is check with the airlines and the railways and the buses—and hope he didn't drive."

"Sounds like a big job. And I'll probably have to make up some story to get them to give me the information."

"Why not just tell them you're from the White House, Sweet Sarah. Everybody tells the White House everything."

She felt a momentary panic. Did he know what she'd done on Friday? Did he know about her pretending to be from Basinger's office and calling the military office to find out about Camp David? "Everything, huh?" she said noncommittally.

"Well, more than they tell most folks, that's for sure."

So he didn't know, Sarah thought, relieved. "Well, maybe I just better give up on this thing," she said, more to make conversation than anything else. "I've never been much good at making up stories or dealing with the plane and train people. The last time I flew to California, they scheduled me on a flight that didn't even exist."

"You know, you oughtn't to *pretend* you're from the White House, you ought to get a job over here. If I want to go some place, I just call the travel office, and bango, presto, my tickets are on my desk."

"The travel office?"

"Sure. I don't know how they do it, but it's like some kind of magic. Hey, you wouldn't like a job would you? I bet I can pay you more than you're making now and get you some perks like the travel office besides."

"Listen, I'm not going to forget that offer. Don't you forget you made it now."

"Sarah, dear, that is not the first offer I've made you."

She laughed. "No, but it certainly is the most respectable."

She hung up and sat for a moment, staring off into space. Then she leafed through a directory of White House phone numbers until she had located a listing for the travel office. She dialed the number.

"Good morning. This is the travel office."

"Yes, this is Ginny in Mr. Ewing's office." Well, the big lie had worked once before. Maybe it would work again. Of course, last time, she'd at least known the name of the secretary she was impersonating. She hadn't the slightest idea what Ewing's secretary was named. "I'm calling to confirm Mr. Ewing's arrival time."

"One moment, please."

One moment for what, Sarah wondered. Well, it was a long shot, but Ewing should be coming back soon according to the note he'd left Wendy.

A voice came on the line, a different voice from the

one which had answered. "Could you please tell me again who's calling?"

Sarah's hands suddenly felt clammy, and she could feel her heart beating. "Ginny in Mr. Ewing's office."

"One moment please."

She knew they were probably checking, and they were finding there was no Ginny working for Malcolm Ewing. Quickly, she hung up the phone. Her hands were shaking, though it was silly to be upset she told herself. There was no way they could ever find out who had been trying to call.

She felt a need to talk to someone and dialed the *Newstime* phone at the White House. It rang several times before it was picked up.

"Is Rudy Dodman around anywhere?" she asked the strange voice who answered. And then she waited for what seemed a very long time before Rudy came on the line.

"Hi, I've been wanting to talk to you," he said when he heard her voice. "I had a productive weekend." He told her about his encounter with Dorothy Brewer.

"That fits," she said, filling him in on the note Ewing had left for Wendy Greene. "It doesn't sound like he's just trying to stay out of sight, it sounds very much like he went someplace to do something, something that he knew would only take a week or ten days."

"So now we're back to square one, and the question is still where did he go."

"I tried to find out this morning by calling the White House travel office, but they didn't fall for it."

"You lied about who you were again?"

Lied? She didn't think of it quite that way. Why was Rudy in such a foul mood? "I just told them I was Malcolm's secretary, that's all."

"Well, I don't suppose it matters. I don't suppose it

really does at all. But you know there is a nice irony here. Telling a lie to catch a liar. Like setting a thief to catch a thief, I suppose."

"C'mon, Rudy, what's wrong with you? This doesn't have anything to do with the President's lying. And I don't much like you calling me a liar, either."

"Well, now just think about it for a minute. We've got a President who's got himself into a hell of a mess, and what's he done wrong, really. It doesn't look like he's seeing a shrink now, does it? He saw one once, but that was a long time ago, so what's he done wrong? Well, the answer for now and all time is going to be that he lied to the American people."

"And I'm no better because I lied to the travel office? Is that what you're saying?" She was angry now. "Damn it, Rudy, what's wrong with you?"

'Hell, I don't know. Maybe I'm getting neurotic. Like old Jane. You know she spent the night in the press-room?"

"What on earth for?"

"I don't know. She's not talking much to anybody. Just sitting in the corner, picking at her skirt and looking crazy."

"Put her on the phone, will you? I want to talk to her."

"What?"

"Seriously. Put her on."

After a few moments, she heard Jane's voice.

"Jane? Are you all right? I've been trying to reach you this weekend."

"I came here last night because I'm so scared. You know they arrested somebody for stealing the log?"

Jane was whispering, and Sarah had to struggle to hear her. "Arrested somebody? Who'd they arrest?"

"One of the Filipino mess stewards."

"Jane, how do you know that?"

"I saw them. Last night I saw them. I was waiting at the guardhouse outside the West Wing for the guards to clear me through, and I saw two Secret Service men taking him away. I wanted to come here because I thought it would be safe, and then I saw them."

"Jane, you don't need to worry about being safe. You don't need to be afraid. You're just feeling guilty, and you shouldn't. Boyston's office wanted you to take that log. It was just sitting out someplace, wasn't it?"

"Yes, but I shouldn't have . . ."

So, Sarah thought. Confirmation. They'd left a copy of the log out on a desk, maybe. They probably left Jane alone with it. "Listen, Jane, why don't you get in a cab and come on over here to the *Newstime* offices. Keep me company and I'll keep you company, and maybe you'll feel better."

"I don't know. I think I'll just stay here until the dinner tonight."

"Well, you think about it and quit worrying. Will you put Rudy back on the line?"

Rudy must have gone upstairs, Sarah decided, because she found herself holding the line for several minutes. While she was waiting, she thought of what Jane had told her and tired to sort out the facts from Jane's interpretation of them. It seemed likely she had seen one of the Filipino mess stewards going someplace with a couple of Secret Service agents, and perhaps there was something about the situation which had communicated trouble to Minnick's confused mind.

She mused for a moment on how much there had been in her life lately about the Philippines and Filipinos. She'd never paid any attention to the place at all, and here in the last week it turned out Ewing had been there in the Peace Corps, and there were demonstrations in Lafayette Park, and now the mess steward. She wondered if he really had been arrested. She knew it wouldn't have been for stealing the Oval Office log. That theory was simply the product of Jane's guilt and imagination. But maybe he'd been spying or something.

The thought brought her up short. Spying. That certainly would be a significant breach of security to have one of the mess stewards spying. Whom would he spy for? They were citizens of the Philippines, weren't they? So spying for Marcos maybe? That would be a big enough thing—my God, it would, yes, it would—a big enough thing to account for Ewing's absence and the President's unwillingness to explain. My God, it could be . . ."

"Sarah?" Rudy's voice came on the line.

Her head was whirling so rapidly that it took a conscious effort for her to slow herself down enough to make her idea clear to him.

"It's possible," he said when she had finished explaining. "But where would Ewing go, even if the steward were spying? And what would he be spying about? What's going on in the White House that Marcos would want to know so badly he'd risk sending a spy in there? Listen, why don't you pull everything together you can get out of the research office about the Philippines. What's our exact relationship with them, and who are the important people there now besides Marcos. Does Ewing have any special contact over there from his Peace Corps days? Get everything together and I'll get over there as soon as the arrival ceremony's over."

"You've got to cover the Japanese arrival *now?*"

"Sure. What if the Prime Minister's car should run amuck into the rose garden? Or what if the President decides to ravish his wife in public? And what if *Newstime* isn't there when it happens?"

Sarah was trying to think of an appropriate response

when she realized that Rudy had hung up, and the line was dead.

"REMINDS YOU of Jackson Hole, doesn't it?"

Rudy looked blankly at Timothy Markham. Jackson Hole? What possible resemblance did the South Lawn of the White House, decked out as it was now for the arrival of the Japanese Prime Minister, have to Jackson Hole, Wyoming? But Rudy knew there was probably some method behind Markham's mad question. "Well, now that you mention it, Tim, no, it doesn't."

Markham ignored Dodman's response. "It's got to do with what I call the picture postcard quotient," he said, waving his arms so enthusiastically that the White House press pass hanging around his neck jumped and the chain it hung from jingled. "Now, nobody can really believe in the Grand Tetons. Some clever set designer must have painted them, they're so perfect. And it's the same with this." This time his enthusiastic gesture included the sloping, still-green lawns, the gleaming white mansion, the honor guard of troops with its bright array of flags, the colorful Third Army Fife and Drum Corps. "This can't be real, it's too beautiful."

Dodman smiled and nodded. The fife and drum corps was playing a march. He couldn't for the life of him think of the name of it. Who could tell marches apart anyway? They didn't have any words to them, that was the trouble. But whatever the march was, he liked it, and he found himself tapping his foot in time to it as he looked around.

Down toward the Ellipse was a crowd composed of people connected with the Japanese Embassy and various Washington bureaucrats and their families. It was customary for the White House to give an embassy as many tickets as they could use for an arrival ceremony, and then also to pass tickets out in the agencies and departments around Washington. It was a good way to ensure there would be a crowd—and also to build loyalty in the bureaucracy for the occupant of the White House.

Across from where Dodman was standing, the Cabinet members and their wives were lined up. They were positioned so they would be in the background of any TV shots of the President or the Prime Minister delivering their remarks. Dodman scanned the familiar faces and noted one conspicuous absence—Vice President Boyston was nowhere in sight. But "Boyston's boy" was on hand. On the west stairway going up to the lower balcony of the mansion, many White House staffers were gathered, and near the top Dodman saw Harold Stark standing and fidgeting.

The Army Herald Trumpets, standing in the mansion's south portico, began sounding ruffles and flourishes, and Dodman and the other reporters turned to watch the President and Mrs. Jenner emerge from the White House. The President was wearing a dark gray suit, and Mrs. Jenner had on an orange wool skirt and matching long jacket. They made a handsome couple, Dodman thought, as they stood and waved to onlookers while "Hail to the Chief" was being played.

No sooner had the music ended, than a motorcade moved slowly into sight. The second car in the motorcade stopped directly across from where the Jenners were standing, and the Japanese Prime Minister and his wife got out. They were greeted by the President and Mrs. Jenner, and then, while the wives stood in the background, the two heads of state reviewed the troops. When they had finished, the Prime Minister and his wife and the President and his wife all took their places on a red platform, which had been erected especially for the ceremony.

It was when the President had nearly finished his welcoming remarks that the first noises from the Ellipse drifted up to the South Lawn.

"What's going on?" Tim Markham asked Rudy.

"I can't tell, but they're yelling something. You suppose it's some kind of demonstration?"

"Shhhh. Ah, I can't tell what they're yelling. I thought for a minute there it was 'Boy's Town, Boy's Town.' " He raised his eyebrows and looked at Rudy. "You don't suppose Father Flanagan got tired of Nebraska?"

Out of the corner of his eye, Rudy caught a movement on the stairway up to the balcony, and he looked over to see Harold Stark trying to get down the stairs through the crowd. When he had reached the bottom, he began running toward the southwest gate. Rudy couldn't leave the roped-off press area to follow, but what he had seen told him what the shouting was about.

"They're not yelling 'Boy's Town, Boy's Town,' " he said to Markham. "It's 'Boyston, Boyston,' they're yelling."

"Well, whatever it is, it has sure got the President pissed."

Rudy turned to look at the President, who was now standing listening to Prime Minister Yanaga's remarks. Jenner's eyes glanced over toward the Ellipse from time to time, and whenever they did, the lines of his face hardened perceptibly. As Markham and Dodman watched, the President turned, leaned over, and whispered something to his wife.

"Well, I'm no lipreader," Markham said, "but what do you want to bet that the President of the United States just told the First Lady of the United States that the Vice President of the United States is a son of a bitch."

Dodman couldn't help but smile. "Tim, those may not have been his words, but I have a feeling you got the sentiment exactly."

Dodman waited impatiently for the arrival ceremony

to end, so that he could get down to the Ellipse and find out what was going on. But it was another twenty minutes before the President and the Prime Minister and their entourages went into the White House. Then Dodman made his way to the Ellipse as quickly as he could, but even though he ran much of the distance, by the time he got there, most of those who had been doing the shouting had left. He managed to corner one straggler as he was loading his car.

"Uh, sir. Sir," he called, running up to a stocky, middle-aged man who was putting some large posters into the backend of a brown station wagon.

The man looked up suspiciously.

"I just wonder if you could tell me why you're here today."

The man slammed down the station wagon's rear door. Through the car's back window, Rudy could read one of the posters he had just put in. "Boyston for President," was printed on it in large block letters. "I'm here because I believe in the Vice President," the man said, "if it's any of your damned business."

"You believe in the Vice President?" Dodman asked, out of breath.

"You bet. I thought he should've been our nominee the last time around, but that didn't work out, and I was willing to wait. Or I was willing, anyway, until we found out Jenner'd cut him out of the action."

"Did somebody ask you to come here today?" Rudy asked as the man got into the driver's seat of the station wagon.

The man slammed the door and looked up. "Yeah, they asked me. And then they asked me not to come. But dammit, when you believe in something, you do it." With that he started the car and drove away.

Rudy sat down on a bench to catch his breath. The thought of walking to the *Newstime* offices was just too much, so after a few minutes, he hailed a passing cab. He arrived at the offices to find Sarah reading through several piles of information Francine had pulled from the magazine's files and library. He told her about the morning's demonstrations.

"So somebody's tried to turn them off, huh?" she said. "I wonder if that had anything to do with my conversation with Stark?"

"I wouldn't be surprised. To have your supporters demonstrate for you spontaneously is one thing. But if it's going to look like the end product of a whole chain of deviousness and manipulation, that's quite another."

"And Stark seemed upset, did he?" Sarah assumed an expression of mock sympathy. "The poor baby."

It was almost noon, so they ordered sandwiches sent up. "Don't get mustard on any of those reports," Rudy warned, as they ate.

"It'd liven some of them up a little," Sarah answered.

"You've talked to Jack, haven't you?" he asked.

"Just gave him a quick report."

"Why don't we get him to come over here and let us pick his brain."

"You go get him, and I'll offer him half my sandwich."

Rudy returned in a few minutes with Sasser. "I understand you're offering one half a bologna on whole wheat in exchange for my time," Jack said to Sarah, who'd already started on the second half of her sandwich.

"Make that almost half a bologna," she said.

"Sure, why not." He took the rest of the sandwich from her and pulled up a chair. "So what do you two want to know?"

"Well, you know the theory we're working on," Rudy said. "That there's been a spy for the Philippines in the White House. Does that make any sense? Is that something Marcos would do?"

"It's damned risky, isn't it?" Jack said. "I can't think

of a quicker way to ruin American-Filipino relationships than for us to catch a spy for their country in the White House."

"Is Marcos the kind of guy who'd take a risk like that?" Sarah asked.

Jack thought a moment. "He's a risk-taker all right. But only when the odds are pretty much in his favor."

"I think I need to know more about him," Rudy said. "Is he one of the good guys or one of the bad guys? I just don't have a feel for him yet."

"Depends on your definition," said Jack. "If a good guy is one who's brought a certain amount of stability to his country, then Marcos is a good guy."

"And if a bad guy is someone who's made a farce out of the idea of democratic rule in his country, then Marcos is a bad guy," Sarah observed.

"And if a good guy is someone who opposes Communism, then Marcos is a good guy," Rudy joined in.

"And if a bad guy is someone under whose rule there are some very noticeable violations of human rights, then Marcos is a bad guy," Sarah said.

"All right. All right," said Jack. "You've got the idea."

"So explain why you see him as a risk-taker," Sarah said.

"Look at when he declared martial law in 1972. He ran the risk of alienating American public opinion, but I'm sure as far as he was concerned the potential gain was much greater than the potential loss. He strengthened his position, without a doubt. Under martial law, he's cut down crime in the Philippines, and that's gained him a lot of popular support. He's also arrested most of the Communists' senior guerrilla and political leaders and tried them before martial law tribunals."

"But there's a lot of opposition to him," Sarah said. "You were with me in Lafayette Square and saw the demonstrators."

228

"That's right. In the church and university communities especially, a lot of pressure has built. Some of the more radical religious and intellectual leaders are convinced now that Marcos won't ever fully reinstate democracy in the Philippines."

"And some of those leaders—even ones who aren't so radical—have begun to think of ways of getting rid of Marcos. Or at least that's what I gather," Sarah said, gesturing at the information piled up on her desk. "Here's an article about a priest," she said, picking up a clipping. "Francisco Castillo's his name. He sounds like a sane, stable sort of fellow who's just had enough." She glanced through the article. "He sure doesn't like Imelda Marcos much. He says that thousands of poor people die every year from TB and pneumonia in his country because no medical treatment is available to them. And he says the money Imelda spends to live and travel like a queen ought to go to the poor." Sarah looked up. "He says she took eighty people, including six hairdressers and Christina Ford, to a coronation in Nepal. Six hairdressers? Is that possible?" She answered her own questions by digging through a pile of clippings, pulling out one that had appeared in the *Washington Post,* and holding it up. "I suppose it's even probable when you consider that planes apparently don't cost her anything. When one airline billed her for flights—she owed them six million dollars and they had the nerve to ask her for three—Marcos seized the airline."

"Just like that? He seized it?"

Sarah skimmed through the clipping. "Well, let's see. There were articles in two Manila newspapers about abuses by the airline, but one of those papers is controlled by the woman whom Imelda Marcos chose to be her official biographer and the other by Imelda's younger brother. Marcos's aides said the airline was seized to improve its management and profitability."

Rudy shook his head. "I guess the real question is why the Filipinos put up with that kind of crap."

"I imagine," Jack said, "that if you went to downtown Manila and asked the first ten Filipinos you saw how they felt about martial law, they'd tell you they were glad not to be harassed by criminals. You've got to remember that the reverence we in this country have for concepts like 'due process' isn't universally shared. I'd guess to most Filipinos, our concern for *how* Marcos got rid of the criminals—or how he controls the Communists—would seem eccentric."

"But since we do value democracy and due process, why do we support him?" Rudy asked. "Is it just because he's important to us militarily?" He paused. "I don't mean 'just because.' I can understand that in our own national interest we might need to support regimes that don't always behave the way we want them to."

"He may be a despot, but he's our despot. Is that it?" Sarah asked.

"Up to a point," Jack said. "There's no question that we need those bases we've got in the Philippines if we want to continue to be a Pacific power. Hell, the presence of the Japanese here in town right now underscores that. I'd bet anything Yanaga's going to be talking to Jenner about closing down some American bases in Japan, and that makes Subic Bay Naval Base and Clark Air Base—both in the Philippines—all the more important.

"On the other hand, we pay through the nose for our presence in the Philippines, and that money is important to Marcos. Every once in a while, Congress will get its dander up about one-man rule in the Philippines or human-rights violations, and Marcos goes through all sorts of contortions to calm the good senators and congressmen so that the ever more lucrative agreements he's got for those bases will continue. In 1978, he even let one of his political enemies run for the national assembly in order to soothe some ruffled Senate feathers." Jack paused. "He didn't let the guy out of jail, but he did let him run for office."

Sarah laughed. "Still that was a kind of risk-taking, I suppose. He ran the risk of creating a martyr hero who could have been a real threat to him."

"No question about it. Marcos is a gutsy guy," Jack agreed, "gutsy enough that he'd put a spy in the White House, if he thought there was enough to be gained by doing it."

"But what's to be gained?" asked Rudy. "What seems to be important to him is the general climate of public opinion about him in this country and the way that opinion is reflected in the Congress. And if he wants to know how the President feels about him, I don't think he needs to go so far as a spy to find out."

Jack agreed. "I don't quite see it either." He looked at Sarah. "Maybe you've concluded too much from what Jane said."

"Could be. But you know, crazy as she is, there's been a core of truth to what she's told me, right down the line. She saw something that convinced her one of the stewards was in trouble, and I just can't help but think it's all related. The steward's being Filipino, Ewing's connection with the Philippines, the anti-Marcos demonstrators we saw in the park. I don't know how it's connected, but I think it is.

"The only thing to do, I guess," Rudy said, "is just keep digging and see if we can't get a couple of pieces to fall into place."

There was a silence, and then Jack stood up. "I think I'll go use the phone. I've got a couple of past due favors I'm going to call in. You two keep looking here for the answer."

Both Sarah and Rudy started reading through the pile

of material on her desk. "Did you know more than 300,000 Filipinos now live in the United States?" she asked.

"Mmm," Rudy answered.

She continued to read. "Did you know there are 7,100 islands in the Philippines?" She looked up, but this time he didn't answer at all.

IT WAS early evening before Jack returned. "I have something interesting," he said. "Top Secret interesting."

"You must have cashed in a big chit," Rudy observed.

Jack looked at him out of the corner of his eye and then down at the notepad in his hand. "There is, it seems, a recent CIA report which suggests that the Marcos government is in imminent danger of being toppled."

"Where did you get that?" Rudy blurted out.

Jack studiously ignored him.

"Toppled by whom?" Sarah asked. She was as curious as Rudy about the source of Jack's information, but she knew it was pointless to ask him. "There's nothing here about the Marcos government being in danger." She gestured to the paper they'd been reading.

"Well, the 'who' is a little hazy. Some parts of the army are involved, and you know that priest fellow you were reading about?"

"Castillo?"

"Yes, that's the one. He apparently is one of the main leaders."

"Is it a Communist thing?" Rudy asked.

"Well, Castillo's not Communist, or at least the CIA doesn't think so. But they suspect much of his support is."

"Communist or not," Rudy observed, "this sure could be a sufficient reason for Marcos to want to have a spy in the White House. He could tap into our intelligence network, if he could get access to the President's daily intelligence briefing. He could find out what we know about Castillo and his group."

"Even more important," Jack said, "he could find out about Castillo. The CIA report indicates that Marcos doesn't know yet that he's one of the leaders."

"I'll bet Marcos would also like to find out what our reaction is likely to be," Sarah said. "If fighting broke out, would those 35,000 servicemen we've got at Subic and Clark join in on his side or not. You know, under the guise of protecting Americans."

"But what about Ewing?" Rudy said. "Where does he fit into all this?"

"Could the President have sent him to advise Marcos on how to save his skin?" Sarah asked.

"If the Communists are behind this, we're probably trying to do that, but it doesn't make a lot of sense for the President to send Ewing," Jack said. "Bright and perceptive as Malcolm is, there have got to be twenty guys in the State Department or in one of the security agencies who are more knowledgeable about the Philippines, more attuned to the subtleties of a situation like this."

"Yes, but the President knows Malcolm," Sarah said. "And he trusts him. That counts for a lot. Besides, he did spend that time in the Peace Corps in the Philippines."

"But that was so long ago," said Jack. "I don't see how it's relevant now. On the other hand, there is the coincidence that he was there before and he's missing now. Add that to the steward and the intelligence report, and I agree with you, Sarah, there has to be some connection."

Sarah looked at her watch, then stood up. "Well, I'll keep thinking about it, but right now I've got a state dinner to cover."

"It's almost a week before we can get on the newsstands with this story," Jack said to her. "Be careful what questions you ask."

"I know," she said. "I won't give anything away."

DALE BASINGER was sitting in a chair pulled up to the right side of the President's desk. He had brought with him into the Oval Office a stack of decision papers the President needed to deal with, and now, as they finished each item, he'd remove the paper they had talked about from the pile he had brought in, place it face down on the President's desk, and move on to the next matter. "We need a decision on a presidential mediator to send to deal with the Whitefeather problem," Basinger said.

"I've been putting it off, thinking Malcolm would be able to do it," the President answered.

"I don't think it can be put off any longer. Somebody shot up some of the equipment at one of the mines last night. Nothing too serious, but it shows how tempers are heating up."

"And how we need to get somebody in there to cool them down. Let me see the packet," said the President, reaching across the desk. He looked through the papers Basinger handed him and then gave them back. "Let's go with this fellow at Interior. He looks pretty good."

"Do you think he's heavy enough?"

"Malcolm would be better, but we can't use Malcolm right now."

Basinger nodded. "One scheduling matter. Kitty Crawford's funeral has been set for ten A.M. tomorrow morning. You're supposed to be meeting with Yanaga then."

"I want to go to the funeral. You get it sorted out with the Japanese."

"And I suppose we should be thinking what to do with Allen. Long-term, that is."

234

The President didn't answer. Instead he got up from his chair and walked slowly around the left side of the desk, his fingers traveling absentmindedly across the desk top. Then he folded his arms across his chest and, with his head down, moved toward the other end of the room, where two love seats were arranged in front of the fireplace. He paused when he got to the seating arrangement, then turned and walked to the door which opened into the Rose Garden. He leaned against the heavy molding around the door, put his right hand in his pocket, and looked out into the darkened garden.

Basinger felt extremely awkward. The President seemed to have forgotten he was in the room. He wondered if he should leave and let the President be along with his thoughts. But to leave without being dismissed was even more awkward than staying, so he finally decided to say something. "It's nothing we need to decide tonight," he said, continuing with the idea he'd been talking about before the President got up. "I just thought I'd mention it."

The President acted as though there had been no hiatus in their conversation. "No, no, you were right," he said, turning. "You were right to bring it up. I need to make a decision. It's just so damned hard." He paused. "You know, I thought the reason I brought him to the White House with me was to repay his loyalty to me. To be loyal to him because he's always been loyal to me. You know that, don't you? Oh, I suppose there's always been the possibility that some of his, uh, extracurricular activities might prove embarrassing to me, but he's always kept my best interests in mind." The President caught the skeptical look on Basinger's face. "No, he really has, at least insofar as he's been able to. Oh, I know he's played games with Morris and Latvala to build himself up, but practically everybody in Washington has done that. Using Morris and Latvala to make yourself look good is one of this crazy town's more popular pastimes. But in all the years I've known him, Allen has never done anything like that at my expense."

"Sir, I just think you're wrong," Basinger burst out. "When he cuts up anybody else on your staff in order to make himself look good, that is at your expense. If anybody who's working for you is made to look incompetent or untrustworthy, then you look like a fool."

"Dale, the reason I depend on you so much is because you understand that. But it's a point too subtle for most people. Most people can't see beyond their own self-interest. And you can't expect them to. You simply have to take it into account. Given his limitations—and they're limitations he shares with most of the population of the world—Allen Crawford has kept my best interests in mind. But I don't think I've done that for him. One of the crazy things about this job is the strange sort of ricochet effect there is sometimes. You make a decision with one goal in mind, and it glances off a hundred complicating factors until the end result is the opposite of what you intended. You have to keep the complicating factors in mind, or you make mistakes, like I did with Allen. The kind thing for me to have done after the election was the one which would have seemed brutally unkind at the time. I shouldn't have brought him over here with me. I should have foreseen the chemistry of the thing—the way this place and its power would react with his needs and weaknesses." Jenner walked back to his desk and sat down. "So I need to decide what's the kind thing now. Is it to move him out? Make him a minor ambassador someplace? Or would it be better to keep him here now? If he's forced to live with what's happened will he become a stronger man perhaps?"

"Why don't we put off resolving it for awhile? Maybe suggest he go on a vacation someplace quiet."

"Decide not to decide, hmm?"

"Give ourselves some time."

The President nodded.

"There is some good news," Basinger said. "Danny's son has been given permission to leave the Philippines and should arrive in Washington in the next couple of days."

"So Marcos blinked. Did you read the intelligence brief this morning?"

"Yes, it looks like they're really going to try to unseat him. Marcos seems aware the threat is there, but he still hasn't fingered the leaders. If he does, he's so damned clever, I'll bet he can put this thing down.

"You noted the CIA's opinion that Castillo's a tool of the New People's Army, a tool of the Communists?"

"But Malcolm was so sure . . ."

The President shook his head in frustration. "Is there anything else?"

"A report from a couple of people in my office that Stark was very upset when the demonstrators started shouting this morning."

The President was thoughtful. "So maybe this thing's going further than Boyston intended."

"Maybe. I didn't go out for the arrival ceremony, but the way I heard it, Stark ran out of the south grounds in a near-panic when the shouting started."

"Interesting. Boyston may do himself in yet."

"One last thing. Here are some suggestions for your toast tonight." He got up, handing the President a text the speech office had prepared. Then he gathered his papers together and walked through the anteroom and down the hall, looking at his watch as he went. He had exactly forty-five minutes to finish up everything and change into a black tie for the state dinner. There was no way he could tie up all the day's loose ends by then. Hell, in this job, he thought, maybe there was no way ever to tie up all the loose ends.

He made a mental check list of what he should be worrying about. It was all people, he realized. The Vice President and Allen Crawford. Danny and Danny's son and Marcos. And most of all, of course, Malcolm Ewing. So much depended on Malcolm Ewing.

Chapter 20

WHEN SHE unlocked the door to her apartment, Sarah was struck by how quiet it was inside. Wendy must have gone out, she decided. She closed the door behind her and walked down the hall into the living room. When she turned on the lamp, she saw a note propped against one of the pictures on the fireplace mantle. She held the envelope up to the light, and then tore off one of the ends.

> Dear Sarah:
> I want to thank you, first of all, for letting me stay with you. It was kind of you, and it was thoughtful of you not to pressure me these last few days.
> But I have told you more than I should, and I

can't tell you how much that disturbs me. Not just because I told you things I shouldn't have, but because it was so natural for me to do it. I think maybe I'm just not meant for this life that has to do with politics, with weighing words so carefully and keeping so much hidden. And if politics is what Malcolm's life is going to be, then perhaps I'm wrong for him. I don't know.

I do know I need to be by myself for awhile, and so I'm going back to my apartment. I've been away long enough, I doubt Nicholas Frye is still hanging about—and I thank you for giving me this respite from him.

Wendy

Sarah read the note over again. "Damn," she said, folding it and putting it back into the envelope. She laid it on the mantle and then went into the kitchen to pour herself a glass of wine. The chablis had been sitting out on the cupboard, so she put two ice cubes in her glass, poured in the wine, and went into her bedroom.

She turned on her television thinking she'd catch the first part of the CBC evening news before she dressed, but she had trouble concentrating on the news program. She was still thinking about Wendy Greene, feeling glad she hadn't pressured her any more than she had, but feeling guilty too. Part of what troubled her was that what she had learned from Wendy had been so important. Learning what Ewing had said in the note he had left had been absolutely crucial. Without it, she'd still be assuming that his absence had to do with his being the President's psychiatrist.

But she also felt uncomfortable because she hadn't been harder on Wendy. You didn't want people you'd interviewed thanking you for not being tougher. The people you interviewed weren't supposed to love you, for God's sake.

She sipped her wine and watched abstractedly as the evening news ran film of the Japanese arrival ceremony and the demonstrators on the Ellipse. "The President seemed untroubled by this morning's happenings," a correspondent was saying, "as impervious as he had been to the stories circulating in the Capital that one of his top aides, Malcolm Ewing, has been providing him with psychiatric counseling. Stay tuned for our special report in part three of our program on the growing number of Americans who are seeking therapy of one kind or another."

Well, there was one advantage the White House was getting from having refused to comment on Ewing, Sarah thought. If they had said something, no matter what it was, it would have fueled the story. As it was, CBC was struggling to find new reasons for bringing it up. Sarah watched as the CBC camera moved in on a group of young people, apparently naked, all sitting in a large, steaming, redwood tub. What did that have to do with the President of the United States? She doubted that many people would think it had very much. Still and all, she hoped CBC didn't get too desperate for angles on the psychiatric thing. They might start looking for other explanations of Ewing's activities and his absence, and it was almost a week before *Newstime* could be on the stands with what they knew. It was going to be a long week, a lot of it spent hoping that nobody else got onto the track *Newstime* was on.

Sarah set her wine glass on the wicker bedside table and walked across the room to the wardrobe. Out of it she pulled a very plain, long, black, jersey dress, her uniform for covering formal affairs. Some of the women reporters who covered social events in Washington dressed to the teeth for them. But Sarah thought there was something not quite right about that. It confused the matter of who were the guests and who the reporters, and she didn't think that was healthy. Reporters were there for quite different reasons than were the guests. Reporters certainly weren't in attendance simply to be polite and gracious.

But a few of the press corps women had so succeeded in blurring the line between guest and reporter that they entertained publicly the people they covered, and were entertained in their turn. They invited the senators and congressmen, the diplomatic corps and the Cabinet to lavish dinner dances, and when their hospitality was repaid, the reports of the events they were invited to inevitably glowed with enthusiasm. What guest, after all, would offend her hostess by writing in the newspaper that the rolls were stale or the dinner conversation dull?

Well, Sarah didn't intend to get caught up in any of that. She would keep on being businesslike about it, she resolved, slipping into her black dress, running a comb through her hair, and then, for good measure, putting on her glasses. They were a very weak prescription—she didn't even need them when she drove—but they would say to the world that she was at the White House for *Newstime,* not out of some desire to be considered one of Washington's social elite.

She took a cab to the White House, and at 7:45 was waiting in the mansion's lower hallway with the other reporters covering the dinner. Jane Minnick was next to her, and, from the looks of things, that was where Jane intended to spend the entire evening.

"I feel so embarrassed," Jane was moaning. "This old skirt—I should have gone home to change. I must stick out like a sore thumb."

Sarah thought to herself that Jane was much less conspicuous in her brown tweed skirt than she was in her usual state dinner getup: a tight brocade gown trimmed with false flowers. "Don't worry about it," she said.

"Oh, look at Dorothy's dress," Jane exclaimed, pointing to Mrs. Jenner's press secretary, who was wearing a coffee-colored silk gown and watching over the assembled reporters. "And look, there's Charlton," Jane exclaimed, as one of the movie stars invited to lend glamour to the White House event came out of the Diplomatic Reception Room, where guests entered, and into the hallway. "What's wrong with his neck?"

Sarah too was curious. Unlike all the other men present, who had on black bow ties, his neck was swathed in at least a yard of white satin. "I think it's an ascot or something," Sarah said. "Maybe it's the latest thing on the West Coast." Two Cabinet members and their wives followed, then several couples whom Sarah didn't know. She suspected, though, from the way they were looking around, that this was their first time in the White House.

As each couple entered the hallway from the Diplomatic Reception Room, they turned right, walked past the press corps, and up the marble stairs to the North Entrance Hall. At the top, Sarah knew, the White House doorman was identifying each guest and giving him or her a small envelope containing a table number. It was a rather slow process, so a line began to form on the stairway. Sarah watched the new guests who came into the hallway react in some confusion to the combined spectacle of the waiting press corps and the line on the stairs. It had to be a bit disconcerting, she thought, just being invited to the White House for dinner, and then to arrive and see the press corps turning their lights and cameras on and off, writing notes, jostling, whispering. And the line on the stairs, they must be asking themselves, what was that about? Some kind of security thing?

Sarah saw Dale Basinger and his wife approaching the gathered reporters from the right. They had apparently walked over from the West Wing rather than coming in through the canopied south entrance like the other guests.

"Hey, Basinger, where's your pal Ewing?"

Every head in the press corps turned. Sarah couldn't believe what she had heard. Frye? What was he doing here? She looked down to the other end of the group of gathered reporters, and sure enough, there he was. He hadn't come over from the press room with the rest of the group. He must have followed later. But how did he get in the press pool? Sarah looked around and saw that none of the reporters who usually covered social events for the *Post* was present. Frye must have convinced whichever of them was scheduled for the pool tonight to let him be his or her replacement.

"So where is he, Basinger?" Frye shouted again. Basinger's wife—was her name Marie?—looked horrified, as did most of those in the area. Frye's shouts were so incongruous in this setting, so out of place amidst the polite murmurs of the guests and the soft harp music floating out from the Diplomatic Reception Room. Sarah couldn't remember anything like this ever happening at a state dinner before.

Dorothy Stein whispered to one of the security guards standing in the hall, and then he and another guard went over and spoke to Frye. As Sarah and the other reporters watched, Frye, with surprisingly little fuss, let the two guards escort him toward the West Wing. When one of the guards put his hand on Frye's arm, however, the reporter angrily shrugged it off. Sarah watched until she could no longer see Frye and the guards, and then she began writing rapidly on her notepad.

ON THE STAIRS, Marie Basinger asked her husband, "Who let him in here?"

"Somebody who didn't know any better must have been minding the store," he answered.

From where they were standing, the Basingers could see down into the hallway where the press corps was gathered. Marie Basinger noted that her husband was looking at Dorothy Stein. "Do you think it's her fault?"

He didn't like the question, or rather he didn't like the avid way in which she asked it, as though she wanted nothing more than to hear Dorothy Stein declared guilty. "I don't know," he said. "It could be, but I just haven't worked with her enough to know what she might or might not do."

"After three years?"

He threw up his hands in mock despair, trying to lighten the mood. "Well, she's East Wing and I'm West."

"And never the twain?"

"And never the time is more like it."

They moved slowly up the stairs and received their table assignments from the doorman at the top. Then they went to the left where a military aide was waiting. He indicated to Marie that she was to put her arm through his, and with Basinger following behind, they moved through the Cross Hall, where the Marine Band, uniformed in red and blue, was playing, and toward the East Room. They paused before they went into the East Room until their names were announced, and then the military aide let them into the room, made sure they had an aperitif and their table assignments, and left them.

"Look over there," she said, indicating where a world-famous tennis player and a tall blonde were standing. "Isn't she the rich one who lives in Virginia? The one who's been in all the society pages?"

"I've never seen her before."

She looked at him. "You never read the society pages, do you? It must be her. She's dressed like a southern belle."

Both Basingers watched as a recently divorced and much-gossiped about senator approached the tennis player and his date. The senator concentrated his attention on the blonde, and within a few minutes, the tennis player was showing visible signs of irritation.

"The tennis player is much better-looking." Marie observed. "And younger besides."

"Ah, but he's not powerful," said Basinger.

"Oh, I see. It's power that does it. And you know this from personal observation?" There was an edge to her voice.

"C'mon now, you know better." He put a hand on her shoulder. "Hell, I work so hard, I don't have time for that stuff. And besides I'd be too tired." He was trying hard to keep the tone of their conversation light. He wanted her to have a good time. He wanted her to be happy. In the last year or two, there was so often a bitterness about her. It had become almost impossible for her to speak about anyone without being negative, especially when it was another woman. He knew that his being home so little was part of the problem. And part of it was jealousy. She resented the women he saw at work. She saw them usurping her place in his life, and no amount of arguing could convince her that was not the case. He knew the best way for him to help her have a good time tonight was to change the subject. "Did you ever notice how the politicians are the only ones who circulate at events like this?" he asked.

"You're right," she said, looking around. "The movie stars, the athletes, and the big businessmen sort of stand around by themselves, don't they? I guess they've just never acquired the politician's compulsion to introduce themselves to every stranger in sight."

"In fact, most of these people, these big names, spend a lot of time, money, and effort trying to insulate themselves from strangers. And how can they change years of behaving like that for one evening like this? And why should they for that matter."

"It would make state dinners livelier."

"True, but I really do think there's something unnatural about the way politicians behave, the way they have to behave. I suspect it goes against the grain of most human beings to walk up to somebody you don't know, stick out your hand, and tell them your name."

"Sometimes I think that feeling, that hesitation you have about forcing yourself on other people, is the only thing that keeps you from being a politician."

"It's not the only thing. It's important, but it's not the whole thing. There just have to be times in your life when you're not answerable to anyone but yourself, and politicians don't have many of those. They're always having to court this voter or pay tribute to that constituency."

Marie took a sip of her drink. "Your life isn't your own now."

"That's why I need to think it will be sometime."

"But I wonder if anybody's ever totally independent. When you were polling, there were clients you had to answer to. Is that any different from having to answer to voters? There are worse things."

"I agree with that." He pointedly looked to the door of the East Room where a short, distinguished-looking man and his wife were being announced. Both Basingers knew the couple. John Barone had been a White House staffer in a previous administration, and now was Vice President for Public Affairs—a lobbyist—for one of the nation's largest corporations."

"I don't see what you've got against money," Marie Basinger observed. Barone's salary was rumored to be in the $200,000 range.

"Hell, I don't mind money, you know that. But I do mind boredom. And the idea of staying around this town when you're not in power—damned if I'll be a ghost when this thing is over."

"Shhhh. Here they come."

The Basingers talked to the older couple until they heard the strains of "Hail to the Chief" and saw the Yanagas and the Jenners enter the East Room. Then they had to part as the reception line was formed. The Basingers, according to protocol, moving toward the head of the line, right behind the Cabinet members present, and the Barones staying farther back. After he had gone through the reception line, Dale Basinger saw Cecile Barone again. She was looking for her table in the State Dining Room, and when she saw him she came over and whispered in his ear, "What happened to Charlton's neck, anyway?"

A FEW minutes later, he saw with relief that the woman who would be on his left at dinner was an American. The woman on his right, an attractive Japanese, spoke very little English—which limited considerably the possibilities for dinner conversation. He remembered a state dinner in Rumania when no one at the table where he was seated spoke English. There had been much smiling and nodding and drinking of wine. And a hell of a hangover the next day.

So Basinger greeted the tall, older woman who was to be on his left with some enthusiasm. He recognized her name. It was associated with wealth and horses—hadn't her husband had a Triple Crown winner just a few years ago? As he helped her with her chair, he tried to formulate a few intelligent questions to ask.

But she responded to his efforts as though she were talking to him from the other end of a very long tunnel. It seemed to take forever for his questions to get through to her and even longer for her answers to get back. He found the exchange so disconcerting that at his first chance, he turned to the Japanese lady on his right. Smiling and nodding was better. He also spent more time than he ever had in his life studying the table in front of him, looking at the flowers on the china and trying to figure out which state flower was which. He concentrated on the dinner menu, which the White House calligraphers had elegantly inscribed, and tried to figure out what the exotically named courses would be. What the hell was a timbale, anyway?

He braced himself and made a few more efforts at conversation to his right and left. There was an attractive woman across the table from him, whom he discovered was a senior editor at one of the nation's major publishing houses, but she was far enough away so that any lengthy conversation with her was impossible. The black-coated butlers came and went, bringing new courses and taking old ones away. As soon as the dessert had been served, a group of violinists came into the room and played a medley as they strolled around the tables. Basinger was grateful for each interruption. Next time, he resolved, he'd have Joanie worry about *his* dinner partner, not Marie's.

The lights went up, the television floods were turned on, and the reporters from the press pool gathered at the doors of the State Dining Room. The President rose, formally acknowledged his Japanese guests, and began to speak as Basinger knew he would, about how world peace depended upon our constant readiness to defend it. His carefully chosen words were a way of emphasizing, without actually saying it, how important he felt it was for the United States to maintain its bases in Japan. The President raised his glass, the assembled guests in the State Dining Room rose to join in the toast, and then, when they were all seated again, it was the Japanese Prime Minister's turn.

The diminutive Yanaga, speaking through an interpreter, also paid tribute to peace, but his words had a different thrust to them. "Each country," he said, "must follow its own path to peace and security. Each country must pursue the dream of peace in its own way."

Basinger knew that Yanaga was a man trying to steer a difficult course. The pressure he was under from the left wing to get rid of American bases in Japan had mounted until there was the almost constant threat of riots, such as the one in Yokosuka last week. The Japanese Communist Party was gaining recruits from among Japan's socialists with the argument that the future of Japan lay in Asia, that it was there, not in America, that Japan ought to look for allies.

And, Basinger knew, when the issue was American bases in Japan, the left wing even had some support for the idea of closing them down from Japanese rightists. Many Japanese conservatives, bitter over the withdrawal of American ground troops from Korea and convinced that the erosion of United States power in the Pacific would continue, were certain that the proper course for their country was to cut free from the United States and develop an independent defense capability.

All of which made the Philippines and what happened there all the more important. If close ties to them were cut, if American bases there were lost, it was going to be impossible to convince Yanaga to resist the pressures being brought to bear on him.

Basinger stood with the other guests and raised his glass. Then the dinner was over. He said a few polite words to his dinner partners and looked around for Marie. She surprised him by approaching from behind and tapping him on the shoulder. "Did you enjoy yourself?" she asked.

"Mmm. And you?"

"I had the tennis player on my right," she said.

"Oh? How was that?"

"He drank all his champagne," she whispered, "so I shared mine with him."

They both laughed. It happened at every state dinner that one or more of the distinguished guests would drain his champagne glass as soon as it was filled. Then when the toast was offered, he would, with great embarrassment, understand what the champagne had been intended for. Some kind soul at the table would usually come to the rescue by sharing some of his own champagne with the chagrined guest.

The Basingers gradually made their way toward the exit of the State Dining Room which opened into the Cross Hall. Their progress was slowed by various people they stopped to talk with. Marie congratulated Pamela Whyte on how lovely the dinner had been. Basinger spoke a few polite words to Amos Jonathan, an aging Washington columnist, who managed at least once a month to mention Basinger disparagingly in his column. As Basinger made innocuous conversation, he thought to himself that Jonathan's trouble was the Kennedys. They had been nice to him, and Jonathan had never been able to forgive any administration since for not being Camelot, for not stroking him quite so pleasantly as the Kennedys had.

At the door to the State Dining Room, the Basingers got separated. As he tried to see what had happened to his wife, he nodded to various people he knew, including two reporters whom he considered a most unlikely pair: Sarah Hoff and Jane Minnick. Hoff moved to his side as he entered the Cross Hall, and, with Jane close behind, spoke to him. "Could I see you for just a few minutes after the entertainment? Just a couple of questions—important ones."

He smiled down at her. "I don't know if my wife will like my going off alone into a corner with you."

"I doubt we'll be alone," she said, glancing at Jane.

"You know I really don't much want to talk business tonight." It was true. What he really wanted was to be able to clear his head of all the problems, all the conflicts, even if only for a few hours.

"They're important questions that I want to ask." She paused, then smiled. "How about if I promise not once to mention psychiatrists or psychiatry."

He weakened. "O.K., you got yourself a deal."

"What did she want?" Marie asked, rejoining him, as Sarah walked off. She took a cup of coffee from a tray being passed by a butler.

"Some questions," he said, keeping his answer as short as possible. Her mood had been so positive the last few minutes, and he didn't want to risk getting her upset about Sarah.

Apparently she found his answer satisfactory. "Why don't you get a brandy," she suggested, "and let's go into the Blue Room for a minute or two."

"I think the President and the Prime Minister are sitting in there."

"The Red Room then. I like it even better."

He got a brandy, and they walked toward the Red Room. "It's quite a place, isn't it?" he said, looking around, speaking as much to himself as to her. When he was absorbed in his work, he sometimes forgot about his surroundings for hours at a time, forgot he was in the White House. But in the entire three years he had been working here, he couldn't remember that a whole day had ever gone by without his feeling at least once a heady amazement about where his life had brought him. He felt it now, with the lights dimmed, with people chatting and smiling in the stately rooms. But he felt something else too, though he wasn't sure how to name it. Dread, perhaps? It was a heaviness, a sadness that had to do with realizing that his time in the White House might be over sooner than he had thought. Five more years—before last week that's what he'd thought. But then the *Post* had printed the daily log.

Marie seemed to read his thoughts. As they sat down in the Red Room, she spoke. "Dale, how does it look for him?"

He knew she was talking about the President, and he wanted to reassure her. "He'll be fine. Don't worry."

"Cindy came home today and said that some of the kids at school were teasing her, saying that her dad was working for a crazy guy."

He shook his head. "I suppose that's the way kids are. How'd she take it?"

"I don't think it bothered her too much. She's a tough little girl. But it's not just kids. This last week I've heard adults say things much more vicious."

He was thoughtful. "In a way, it's like they're tired of him, bored with him, and so they're shouting 'off with his head' so they can bring a new entertainer on-stage."

"I just don't understand why he doesn't say something. Why he doesn't fight back."

He turned and looked at her. "Marie, he can't right now. He just can't."

"But if he waits too long . . ."

"I know. I know." He took a sip of his brandy. "It's a helluva job, the one he's got."

"You too," she said. "The one you've got's not so easy." There was sympathy in her voice, and it signaled a subtle change between them. For most of the evening, he'd been trying to keep her mood happy, but now she seemed to be comforting him. He found the change a relief. Not to have to work at keeping her spirits up was to be relieved of one more burden, one more responsibility. He took another sip of his brandy, leaned back in his chair, and studied the picture of Dolley Madison hanging high up on the silk-covered wall.

SARAH WATCHED the arrival of the guests who had been invited only to the after-dinner entertainment. They looked as happy, as full of anticipation as the dinner guests had—which never failed to amaze her. The invitations for the after-dinner entertainment seemed a bit of a put-down to her. They said, in effect, "We don't consider you quite important enough to be invited to dinner, but we'd like to have you come to the White House anyway." But then the White House was the White House. Most people were so thrilled to be invited that they were perfectly willing to overlook a minor detail like not being included for dinner.

Watching the dinner guests and the after-dinner guests file into the East Room for the entertainment, Sarah had butterflies in her stomach. What she was thinking about doing scared her. Should she go ahead and ask Basinger the questions she had in mind? Jack had said to be careful, but what could it hurt to talk to Basinger? Given the suspicions she had, the suspicions she meant to present to him as fact, he wasn't likely to spread around what she had to say. And if the suspicions were correct and she could catch him off-guard—well, that would be a story, indeed.

When all the guests had been seated for the entertainment, Sarah, along with Jane and the other reporters, crowded into the back of the East Room. Short as the entertainment was—it lasted no more than twenty minutes—Sarah had trouble paying close attention. She could see Basinger and his wife from where she stood, and she kept rehearsing in her mind what she would say to him.

After the cellist had finished and the President had stood and spoken a few words, the guests began to file

254

out of the East Room. Sarah found it difficult to maintain her place at the door where she planned to intercept the Basingers. For some reason, the military aides were moving the guests along faster than usual, and Sarah, along with Jane, who stayed by her side, had to give some ground. When she saw the Basingers, however, she was able to make her way to them. "What are the aides in such a hurry about?" she asked.

"There's not going to be any dancing tonight," he answered. "I think the Yanagas are leaving right now. The idea is to let everyone know the party's over."

Sarah felt a momentary panic. "Over? But why? You said we could talk."

He looked at her. "We'll talk. Don't worry. They're not having dancing because it's Kitty Crawford's funeral tomorrow."

Sarah felt a rush of embarrassment. "I'm so sorry. I don't know how I forgot."

He nodded, thinking to himself that her reaction was typical, not just of reporters, but of everybody around the White House. It was the way the place worked, with things rushing in on top of one another so fast that it was hard to keep anything—no matter how sad it was, or how important—in mind very long.

Sarah, with Jane still at her side, stood with the Basingers while Yanaga and his wife took their wraps from a butler standing by the North Portico. When the Jenners had said good-bye to the Prime Minister and his wife, the President and the First Lady went upstairs, and the other guests began to depart.

"Where can we talk?" Sarah asked, still worried that Basinger might change his mind.

"Let's walk over to my office," he said.

"Jane, too?" she asked.

He looked at her questioningly.

"She can wait outside your office while we talk."

He shrugged his shoulders, and with Sarah, Jane, and Marie following behind, he went down the stairs, through the mansion basement, and across the rose garden colonnade to the West Wing. Cleaning crews were vacuuming the halls, and Basinger stepped over one of their electrical cords to reach the door of his office. But when he tried the door, it was locked, and he remembered that his keys were in his suit pants, locked inside the office. So while the three women waited, he walked back down the hall to the guard outside the Oval Office. He returned in a moment with the guard's key, unlocked his office door, and then returned the key.

Once inside the suite of offices, he directed Jane to a small room just off the reception area. It had a comfortable sofa, a TV set, and a number of magazines arranged on a coffee table. Sarah felt a pang of guilt as Jane settled herself in the room. What she was working on was Jane's story, in a way, but as she watched Jane fumble nervously through the magazines, she told herself she would not be doing Jane a favor by asking to have her included. Basinger took his wife and Sarah into his office, and the three seated themselves in the green chairs in front of the fireplace. "I hope you don't mind if Marie sits in on this," he said to Sarah. He hadn't even asked Marie if she wanted to listen. It had just seemed to him like a good idea to give her a chance to be part of what he did.

"Of course not," Sarah said, though she was a little afraid Marie's presence might hamper the give-and-take of the interview.

Basinger looked at her expectantly. "Where shall we start?"

She decided to plunge right in. "I understand it has recently been discovered that the Philippine government has placed a spy in the White House."

"What?" he said, leaning forward in his chair. He could not have been more astounded. Despite her promises to the contrary, he had fully expected her to ask him questions about psychiatrists and the President's mental health.

She could see him deliberately check himself from saying anything further. "Moreover," she went on, "it is my understanding that the spy was placed in the White House in order to gain information about the imminent coup attempt in the Philippines. The coup being led by Francisco Castillo."

"Oh, my God," said Basinger, the words escaping from him involuntarily.

Sarah glanced over at Marie Basinger, who looked frightened, then back to Dale Basinger, and waited for him to speak.

It was several seconds before he did, and then he stood up. "Miss Hoff, I simply cannot allow this interview to continue, not tonight." He looked down at her. "And please don't assume that my unwillingness for it to continue is a comment upon the accuracy of your assumptions. You are probing into areas where I lack expertise, and I think I can only mislead you by commenting on matters when I am not fully informed."

Sarah was not going to be put off so easily. "My sources for this information are highly reliable, and the story will appear in *Newstime*." What would he say, she wondered, if he knew one of her sources was Jane, sitting in the next room. "I would like your comments."

He too was firm. "Not tonight," he said. "I'll get back to you on it, but not tonight."

From the tone of his voice, she knew further argument was useless. "I'll expect to hear from you then," she said, standing up.

He nodded distractedly, and she headed toward the door. "Wait," he said as she reached to open it.

She felt the adrenalin surge through her body. So he was going to talk, after all.

"Wait," he said again. "Marie and I will walk out with you. Otherwise you'll be stopped by one of the guards."

Concealing her disappointment as best she could, she leaned into the small office off the anteroom and told Jane it was time to leave. The two of them followed the Basingers downstairs and exited from the west basement.

ACROSS WEST Executive Avenue, in the old Executive Office Building, the lights were still burning in the Vice President's suite of offices. Robert Boyston was sitting at his desk, talking to Harold Stark, sitting across on the other side. The Vice President's manner was unusually subdued. "Do you suppose he knows then?" he asked.

"Probably he suspects. He knows you were working with the daily log on that efficiency study, and so at the very least, you'd have to be on his list of people who could have leaked it."

"And when the story comes out, he'll have it all laid out for him."

Stark nodded. "That's the way Hoff made it sound."

"And that damned demonstration today, that goddamned demonstration. How's that going to look on top of a story that we started the President's troubles? Couldn't you have stopped it?"

"I tried, sir."

"It's got to have pissed him off, and what do you suppose he's going to do when the story comes out?"

"I'm not sure. We can count on his being damned mad."

"But how mad, that's the question." The Vice President rubbed his eyes.

"You know, sir, that you've still got your same loyal supporters, and the President has to know that too." Seeming to take comfort himself from the idea he was presenting to the Vice President, Stark straightened up from the slumped position he'd been in. "I would imagine awareness of the support you have would temper his anger somewhat," he went on, even smiling a little now. "If he does anything to hurt you, he'll have to suffer their animosity. He has to know that. And he has to worry about it."

The Vice President seemed soothed, if not entirely comforted. "True, Harold, that's true. The odds are I'll be Vice President as long as he's President. But you know, for a while I thought . . ." His voice trailed off, and for a moment neither he nor his aide spoke. Both of them were thinking how their goals had shifted and changed over the past days. At first they had meant only to embarrass the President into making the vice presidency more important. They had meant only to ensure that Boyston would be Vice President again. But it had looked for a time as though they had the presidency within their grasp. A man who'd seen a psychiatrist and lied about it, a man who was probably seeing a psychiatrist now, couldn't hope to run again. And who would be a more natural successor than his Vice President?

But all that would soon be over. They could deny the story again and again. Nobody could ever definitely prove that they'd deliberately left a copy of the Oval Office log where that crazy woman reporter would pick it up. But reaching people with the denials and convincing them—both Boyston and Stark knew how hard that would be. The suspicions would remain for awhile, and even those who rejected a tainted President would be unlikely to pick as his successor the man suspected of revealing his difficulties. Nobody would want to reward Boyston for what looked like an act of disloyalty.

So they were left clinging to the vice presidency, a vice presidency under a President whose future was uncertain, a vice presidency which was likely to become more and more attenuated in its significance as Jenner's suspicions of Boyston increased. Both Boyston and Stark were avoiding the thought that the shakiness of their position had been increased a hundredfold by their own actions.

The Vice President let his hand fall onto his desk in a gesture of frustration. "What I can't stand is being passive on this thing. Isn't there any sort of action we can take?"

Stark shook his head. "We've already got so many tracks showing. He's going to know we leaked the log, and I'm sure he'll give us credit for the demonstration too. I think we ought to leave it all alone for awhile."

"There must be something, some way to strengthen our position. Maybe even distract him from the log and the demonstration."

Both men were silent, and then Stark spoke. "There's the Crawford thing," he offered.

"How can we use that?"

"I'm not sure. I just mention it because it's an area where the President's weak. Everybody knew what Crawford was doing, the way he was playing around. The President should have taken care of the matter before it got out of hand. He could have prevented the tragedy."

The Vice President was thoughtful. "It has possibilities," he said finally. "Cronyism of a kind. He gathers a few people around him, like Crawford and Ewing and Basinger, and he won't listen to anybody else. His Vice President tried to warn him of the dangers of putting his total trust in such a handful of men, particularly when at least one of them, Crawford, shows signs of instability."

"Do we want to say 'instability'? It underlines the

mental health thing and might weaken the President further. Might make it harder for him to work his way out of the hole he's in. And we are tied to him."

"He's in so deeply already, I don't think we can add to his troubles. But we can strengthen our position. We can improve my image and make it impossible for him to make any move against us.

Stark looked doubtful. "*We* can't do it."

"Of course not. *I'm* not going to say anything."

"Who then?"

"Why not Morris and Latvala? You can get hold of them. The basic hook should be my concern, my willingness to risk the President's wrath to warn him about his friends. 'The concerned Vice President willing to put self-interest behind him to show the President the error of his ways.' You know how it should go."

Stark stood, all the tiredness and frustration gone. This was action, a way of forging ahead. He'd like to call Morris and Latvala tonight, right now. But that might look overanxious. "I'll get on it first thing in the morning," he said.

Chapter 21

AS SOON as Sarah awoke, she reached for the phone, and then reached for it several more times before she got up her courage actually to pick it up. She felt more hesitant than she ever had about calling Rudy at home, though that was silly, she told herself, considering that as a homewrecker she had proved such a total flop. Finally, she dialed the number. She was relieved when Rudy answered. "Rudy, I need to see you. Soon," she said.

"What's the rush?" he asked.

"I talked to Basinger last night."

"About what?"

"About some of the things you and Jack and I discussed yesterday."

"You what? Why did you do that?"

"Don't worry. It's all right. The story's still ours."

"But what'd you go off on your own for?" He didn't wait for her to answer. "Never mind. I'll get Jack and meet you in the office at 9:00."

His abruptness upset her. The irritation behind it showed a certain distrust of her, she thought, a lack of faith in the way she might handle a story. And she'd never done anything to justify that kind of mistrust. She became angry as she thought about it, and her anger at Rudy's attitude continued as she quietly finished dressing and left a note for Jane, who had come home with her the night before. As she wrote the note, she thought to herself that her spare bedroom was full a lot lately. What was there about her that attracted people in trouble, anyway. Well, at least *they* thought her trustworthy.

She was still angry as she took the short subway ride to the office, and by the time she stepped from the elevator on the third floor of the *Newstime* building, she was fully ready to give Rudy a piece of her mind. What right did he have to assume that she didn't know how to handle a story? When she entered Jack's office, however, she found she had to be quiet. Jack was on the phone, and Rudy was listening intently to Jack's end of the conversation. "Yes," Jack was saying, "we'll be over as soon as we can. Yes, we'll leave right away."

As Jack hung up, he turned to her. "Well, well, what have you stirred up?"

"Damn it, I didn't stir up anything." She knew she was overreacting to Jack's question, using it as an excuse to release the anger with Rudy that had been building inside her. She tried to ease off. "I simply asked a couple of questions, and I thought about it long and hard before I did. We're not going to lose the story, if the two of you are worrying about that."

"That was Basinger on the phone," Rudy said.

"What did he want?" she asked.

"To see us, all three of us, right now. And apparently it has to do with the conversation you had with him last night."

"All three of us?"

"That's right."

In the normal course of events, Sarah knew, Rudy and Jack would be going off to see Basinger by themselves. She was seldom included in such gatherings. So at the least her questions to Basinger had accomplished her inclusion in their meeting, had made her a full partner in this venture. But the satisfaction she felt was tempered by uncertainty about what she had done. Christ, she hoped she hadn't ruined anything by giving away some piece of information she shouldn't have.

She hid her apprehension as the three of them walked the few blocks to the White House, and she repeated for Jack and Rudy the conversation she had had with Basinger. When they had heard the details, both men agreed that there didn't seem to be much harm in what she had done, though Rudy added irritably, "I still wish you'd checked with me."

Sarah was too caught up in the snowball of events she had started to pay him much attention. "I must have hit some button though," she said, "or why did he call us? He said it was about my questions, didn't he?"

"He wasn't that precise," Jack answered, "but he did mention he'd talked to you and he said he wanted to see the three of us."

They arrived at the northwest gate, showed their passes to the guards, and started up the asphalt drive. When Sarah started to turn left to go to the pressroom entrance, Jack stopped her, explaining that Basinger had asked them to come into the West Lobby. A marine in dress blues held the door for them, and they entered a small entrance hall which had a cloakroom off to one side. While Jack gave their names to the guard sitting at the desk just beyond the entryway, Sarah and Rudy took off their coats and deposited them in the cloakroom. Then they joined Jack in the lobby, "It'll be just a minute or two," he told them.

Sarah was nervous. However well she might hide it from the two men, there was no hiding it from herself. She clasped her hands together so that no one would notice they were trembling and walked over to look more closely at one of the large rural landscapes hung on the wall. As she bent over to look at the nameplate on the frame, she shivered, though it was not at all chilly in the lobby.

A heavy wooden door behind the guard's desk opened, and Basinger's secretary came into the lobby. Sarah had seen her only a few times before, but she knew her name was Joanie. Hadn't she impersonated her once when she called the military office? A fantasy flashed through her mind: could it be that the summons to Basinger's office was about that? Did they intend to arrest her for impersonating a White House secretary? She smiled to herself at the mental nonsense her nervousness was generating.

Sarah, Jack, and Rudy followed Joanie down a narrow hallway to Basinger's office. She led them straight through the anteroom into the large office where Dale Basinger stood to meet them. He shook hands with all three of them, then looked inquiringly at Joanie.

"Not yet," she said.

"Let's all sit down," he said, motioning them to the chairs in front of the fireplace. When they were seated, he spoke again. "I really got you here under somewhat false pretenses. It isn't really me who wants to speak to you. It's the President."

The knot in Sarah's stomach tightened, and she looked

at Rudy and Jack. Both of them had their full attention focused on Basinger.

"Could you give us some idea what he wants to see us about?" Jack asked.

But before Basinger could answer, the phone beside his chair buzzed loudly, and he stood. "Why don't we let him tell you?" he said, leading them out of his office and down the hall.

Sarah had never been in the Oval Office before, and her first impression was that it was large and cold. The walls and ceilings and moldings were all an off-white. Maybe on a sunny day, she thought, it would seem warmer. And where was the President? The chair behind the large, ornate desk was empty.

Basinger indicated that they were to sit in the mahogany armchairs scattered around the large desk, but no sooner had they arranged themselves, than a door to their right opened. Zern Jenner strode into the room, and they all jumped to their feet. The President nodded to them. As he sat down, indicating to them that they were to sit also, he looked at Sarah. "It's because of you, Miss Hoff, that I called this meeting."

Sarah found herself clutching the arms of her chair. She ought, she knew, to be flattered to be singled out this way by the President of the United States. It was, she supposed, beyond anything she could have hoped for this early in her career. But it was also damned frightening. She'd got herself into a high-stakes game, all right, and while she knew she had the nerve for it, everything seemed to be happening too fast. She made a conscious effort to relax her grip on the arms of the chair.

"What I'd like," the President went on, "is to talk to all of you about the questions Miss Hoff was asking last night. I understand there was some mention of the Philippines?"

"We understand that Marcos is in trouble, sir," Jack said.

Nervous as Sarah was, she didn't feel like having Jack take over the conversation entirely. "A coup is imminent, according to our sources, Mr. President," she said. She didn't dare look at Jack—after all, it was *his* source who had come up with the coup in the Philippines. Instead she stole a glance at Rudy. He saw her look at him, smiled, and winked.

Before Sarah had time to wonder why his attitude toward her had undergone such a change, the President spoke again. "Well, I know better than to ask who your sources are," said the President. "I don't suppose, though, you are going to be any more pleased with what I am going to ask." He looked at each of the reporters. "I'm going to ask you not to write your story."

Jack, Sarah, and Rudy all started to speak at once, but the President silenced them by raising his hand. "Now it isn't because of some whim of mine that I'm asking you what I am. And I know I can't expect your cooperation unless I give you good reasons. That's my primary purpose for having you here today. I want you to understand fully, on an off-the-record basis, of course, why I'm making this request. "Dale," said the President, turning to Basinger, who was sitting on his far right, "could you brief us on the background please?"

"Almost three weeks ago," Basinger began, "we received an intelligence report indicating that a coup was taking shape in the Philippines. Elements of the Army are involved, and according to the reports we have received, the takeover has a fair chance of success, partly because, although Marcos suspects something is afoot, he has been unable so far to determine who's leading the movement against him."

"If he knew," the President interjected, "he'd simply do with them what he's done with others who've opposed him politically—put them in jail and keep them there. And then the coup would be left leaderless."

"Even if the coup's leaders were to go into hiding, Marcos would, simply by knowing who they were and what their spheres of influence were, be able to take effective countermeasures," Basinger added.

"In other words," Jack said, "it looks like all Marcos needs to know in order to prevent the coup is who its leaders are. And I take it, Mr. President, that your intelligence reports have told you their identities?"

"Are you going to tell Marcos, sir? Do you plan to warn him?" Sarah blurted out before the President could answer Jack.

"That's one of our options, certainly," said the President, choosing to answer Sarah's question. "Marcos is an ally of ours, as you are aware, an ally whose importance has increased as our influence has declined in other parts of the Pacific. If it looked as though those who intended to make the takeover attempt would be hostile to us, then it would be in our best interests to inform Marcos of what we know.

"On the other hand, you know as well as I that the Marcos government is not ideal. There have been flagrant abuses of human rights under Marcos, and the indignation that various Filipinos have expressed has been justified. It may well be that the overthrow of Marcos is in the best interests of the Filipinos, and the right policy, as long as it doesn't violate our own national interest, may well be for us to let matters proceed, to let the chips fall where they may."

"As long as the revolutionaries aren't Communist, maybe we should let them have their revolution? Is that what you're saying, Mr. President?" asked Rudy, leaning forward.

"Basically, yes, that's what I'm saying. But I don't

know if I like the way in which you put it. It's a tough, mean, nasty world out there, Mr. Dodman. It's taken me awhile to come to this conclusion, but I'm convinced that there are times when we simply must use what power we have to influence the outcome of events. The principle of self-determination is important, but not so important that we can let the world become a place where we have no influence, no voice with which to argue for principles like self-determination."

"Surely, sir," said Jack, "you must have some idea of how much Communist involvement there is."

The President looked at him. "Yes, I have CIA information on that, and I suspect you do too. The questions Miss Hoff was asking tell me that."

Sarah looked at Jack. She saw him keep his eyes steadily fixed on Jenner, though she could tell that when the President mentioned the CIA report, it was an effort of will for Jack not to look away.

"The matter is complicated," the President was going on, "because I also have an unofficial source of information, and my unofficial source assures me that the coup leaders, Francisco Castillo in particular, are not Communist, nor are they about to let themselves be used by the Communists. Now, as I am sure you are aware, this conflicts directly with the CIA's report, and I have spent a great deal of time evaluating the contradictory information I have received. My conclusion is that the coup is the result of genuine outrage at the Marcos regime. It is not, in my opinion, an attempt at a Communist takeover."

The President paused, and Basinger began to speak. "That's why it's especially important that you not go with your story. If you do, if you let Marcos know about the coup and its leaders, you will, in effect, be ensuring the failure of the attempted takeover."

"A takeover which doesn't seem to pose a threat to our country and which may well be in the best interests of the Filipino people," the President added.

There was silence in the room for a moment, and then Jack spoke. "Mr. President, sir, I hope you will forgive me for what I'm about to say, but let me take just a minute to put the proposal you're making in the worst possible light.

"Let's just take as given that our intelligence community certainly doesn't need another scandal, another indication of its weakness or ineffectiveness. A news story based on top secret CIA information would be just that. A story about a planned takeover attempt in the Philippines—when it obviously was written from leaks in the intelligence community—would be one more blow to that community.

"Now I've watched you over these past months, and I've seen you become more and more concerned about America's role in the world, about what we must do if we're to remain the leader of the free world. And one of those things is to strengthen, not weaken, the CIA. And then what happens? Well, you suspect that a top secret report about the Philippines has been leaked to a national news magazine, and you realize what a setback that can be, how it can advertise our weakness to our adversaries, how it can demoralize our allies—as well as the intelligence community itself.

"Well, Mr. President, it's not farfetched to think that your reaction might be to come up with a strategem for keeping the particular national news magazine that has the information from publishing it."

The President shook his head. "You're wrong, Jack, though I have to admit there's plausibility in what you say. There have been times when I've wondered if the difficulty of governing isn't in direct proportion to the difficulty of keeping anything under wraps. It's impossible to govern if debate and discussion are enjoined, and yet that's practically the situation which exists. Anything that's talked about gets out, and anything that gets out, you publish, the consequences be damned."

"That's what freedom of the press is about, sir."

"I have to say, Jack, that from where I sit, it sometimes looks very much like irresponsibility of the press. It looks that way so much, sometimes, that I have been willing to stretch the truth on occasion—oh, hell, let's just say it, I've been willing to lie—to keep matters confidential that I believe should remain that way.

"But, Jack, this is not one of those occasions. I haven't told you anything which isn't true about the coup that is going to be attempted in the Philippines. I haven't stretched the truth, or violated it in any way."

"Sir, you've put me in a most difficult position. I simply cannot agree to kill the story we plan to do on the Philippines."

The President leaned back in his chair. "Well, I thought it might go this way." He nodded to Basinger who got up and walked toward the heavy wooden door through which the President had earlier entered the Oval Office. It was a door that the three newspeople knew led to a private study the President sometimes used.

Basinger knocked at the door, and in a moment it opened. Malcolm Ewing stood in the doorway and then entered the Oval Office.

Chapter 22

RUDY, JACK, and Sarah were silent in their astonishment. Although they had spent the last week worrying about Malcolm Ewing and what he was doing and where he might be, the conversation of the last few minutes had driven the thought of him from their minds. He was, quite literally, the last person they had expected to see.

The President got up from his chair, walked over to Ewing, and put a hand on his shoulder. "Gentlemen, Miss Hoff, I'd like you to meet my unofficial source. During the past week, Malcolm has been in the Philippines, assessing the situation there for me. Malcolm, why don't you sit down and tell our friends here about your conclusions."

Sarah looked at Ewing closely as he sat down. He was

of medium height and dark. He had a likeable face with the lines of it arranged into a seemingly permanent, almost shy half-smile. Wearing an oxford cloth shirt, open at the collar, a tweed sport coat, and heavy chino pants, he was, she thought, dressed very casually for a weekday in the White House.

"I think it would be best if I began at the beginning," Ewing said. "I first got to know Francisco Castillo almost twenty years ago when I was in the Philippines with the Peace Corps. He was then, as he is now, absolutely devoted to the idea of bettering the lot of his people. He was then, as he is now, one of the finest, most decent human beings I've ever known. As the President and I have talked over the years, I've mentioned Castillo to him. He's always seemed to me the perfect example of the selfless man, the man whose goal in life is to help others, not himself.

"When we first got the CIA reports—how long ago was it now?" He looked at Basinger.

"Three weeks," Basinger said.

Ewing shook his head. "I've lost track of time. But anyway, when we first got the reports about the projected coup attempt and Castillo's involvement, the President remembered that I knew him and called me in. I was quite surprised at the reports. Francisco is a man of peace, not a man of violence, and while he's often spoken out against Marcos, it was hard to imagine his participating in a plot to overthrow him.

"What I simply could not believe, however, were the reports that Castillo was working with the Communists. He is too much a man of God ever to throw in with them. I knew it couldn't be true, and so for a week or so there, the CIA was coming in every morning to tell the President that Castillo was a Communist tool, and I was coming in at one P.M. to present the other side. I drew together all the evidence I could and everything I could remember, and together the President and I went over the reports from the CIA. Every day at one P.M., we'd take their morning report and weigh it against what I knew."

"So that's what the one P.M. meetings were about," Sarah said.

The President nodded. "Yes, Miss Hoff, that's what they were about. Malcolm and I weren't in here practicing Freudian analysis or—what's that new one?—primal screams? No, we were talking about the Philippines."

Sarah smiled in spite of herself. Primal screaming had been around quite awhile actually, but that was not the kind of thing you expected a man like the President to know. He resembled Rudy in a way. He was just a little old-fashioned. Like the way he kept calling her "Miss Hoff."

Rudy spoke. "I know I'm getting a little off the track, Mr. President, but why did you let the psychiatry thing go on and on?"

"I didn't feel I had much choice. I couldn't indicate what Malcolm and I were really discussing without alerting Marcos to Castillo. If he'd known Malcolm and I were talking about the Philippines, it wouldn't have taken him long to check on Malcolm's old connections from the Peace Corps days. The 'psychiatry thing,' as you put it, Rudy, actually proved a pretty good cover for the discussions Malcolm and I were having—though I never intended for it to work that way."

"The press conference, Mr. President," Jack said, "the press conference where Frye asked if you'd ever seen a psychiatrist, that's what really opened up the idea that Malcolm was your psychiatrist." Jack looked a little embarrassed. "The fact that you tried to hide the truth about Dr. Brewer made it look like you were trying to hide the same kind of truth about Dr. Ewing."

"You mean the fact that I *lied* about Dr. Brewer, don't

you, Jack?" the President said. "You remember I said a minute ago that there have been times when I've been willing to stretch the truth to keep something confidential, something I felt it was essential to keep confidential? Well, this was one of those times. When Frye asked me that question about past psychiatric treatment, I had no idea he already knew the answer, and my first thought was that if I told the truth, it would focus attention on Malcolm, so much attention that what he was really doing might come to light. Of course, then the *Post* story about Dr. Brewer came out, and the pressure was on about Malcolm anyway. But ironically enough, all the attention on what he was doing was misdirected, so much so that no one's made the connection with the Philippines until now."

Jack looked at Ewing. "So all this while that we thought you were hidden away somewhere, you were in the Philippines."

Ewing nodded. "I spent hours with Francisco Castillo, then hours more interviewing the men around him. They're not Communists, not by the furthest stretch of the imagination. They're good decent men whose goals aren't any different from what yours or mine might be under the same circumstances. They want freedom; they want democracy. And they're willing to fight for it. That's the report I brought back to the President. I recommended that the United States adopt a hands-off policy toward the rebellion. We shouldn't be actively helping the rebels, and we shouldn't be helping Marcos either—which is exactly what any information published in your magazine will do."

There was silence in the room, and then Jack spoke. "Mr. President, I'd like to apologize for what I said a few minutes ago. I'd like to apologize for doubting your motives. But, sir, I still cannot kill our story on the Philippines."

Sarah looked at Jack in surprise, and then she looked at Rudy, who, to her amazement, was nodding his head in agreement with what Jack said.

"I remember," Jack went on, "at the press conference last Wednesday you spoke about 'executive privilege.' Presidents in the past, as you pointed out, have cited executive privilege when they wanted to withhold information from Congress or the Courts, and you used the same phrase when you talked about withholding information from the press. As you explained it, being able to keep something confidential is an important measure of independence, and you wouldn't answer certain questions because you think it's necessary to maintain the independence of the Executive Branch from the press, just as much as it's necessary to maintain its independence from the legislative or judicial branches of government. The parallel you drew made your refusal to comment on the log almost a constitutional matter.

"Mr. President, my refusal to go along with your request *is* a constitutional matter. Don't you see, sir, that if I did what you asked, I would be inhibiting the free flow of news and setting a precedent that there are circumstances under which freedom of the press ought to be suspended?"

"But I'm asking you voluntarily to withhold publication. I'm not trying to coerce you," the President said.

"Mr. President, I simply cannot let you decide the contents of *Newstime* whether you try to do it by persuasion or by force."

"As it stands, Mr. Sasser, you will be making the foreign policy of this country if you publish your story. You'll be determining the actions I have to take."

"If I didn't publish, sir, I would also be making foreign policy in a sense. I'd be making your hands-off approach possible."

"And you'd be saving the life of a good man," Malcolm Ewing burst out. "When you publish your story they'll go after Castillo and he'll rot in jail."

Jack looked down and said nothing.

The President stood. "Well, it would seem we have reached an impasse." He paused for a moment, then added icily. "It would seem there's nothing further to discuss."

As the others in the room got to their feet, Sarah spoke. "There is one other thing. The mess steward. The spy the Secret Service arrested."

"He was no spy, Miss Hoff," the President said. "Nor was there any arrest. He's just an ordinary man who was put under extraordinary pressure, and he came close to breaking, but he didn't." The President nodded his head curtly, dismissing the three news people. As they reached the Oval Office door, however, he added one more thought to what he'd been saying. "Perhaps you realize it, but if you don't, you should. Even if that man had broken, even if he had become a spy, the consequences wouldn't have been very much different from what they will be if you write your story."

He turned and walked quickly into his private study. Malcolm Ewing followed him. Dale Basinger walked out of the Oval Office with the three news people, and while Sarah and Rudy waited, he and Jack stood in the anteroom for a moment talking in whispers.

SARAH, RUDY, and Jack walked in silence out the northwest gate. As they stopped at the intersection and waited for the light to change, Sarah turned to the two men.

"I don't see how we can print the story," she said.

"I don't see how we can't," Jack answered.

The light changed, they crossed over to Lafayette Square, and Sarah spoke again. "Let's sit down for a minute, O.K.?" As the three of them found a bench,

Sarah thought to herself that autumn had passed and winter had arrived. It wasn't so much the cold—although it was cloudy, it wasn't very cold today—but the wind was whipping large numbers of leaves about. Sunday's light snow had taken its toll, and the trees around the square had a ravaged look about them.

"I heard what you said in there, Jack," Sarah said, gesturing to the White House across the street. "And I understood it all in an intellectual way. But emotionally it bothers me."

"Hell, it bothers me, too," Jack said. "I don't like playing God with this Francisco Castillo's life. I don't like having his fate on my shoulders."

"But there's no choice, don't you see?" Rudy asked.

"I guess it's your reaction that surprises me most," Sarah said to Rudy. "I've heard you talk about this same kind of thing when the *Post* did it. I remember when they wrote a story about one of our Mid East allies and how he'd been taking CIA money, and you went on and on about how the *Post* had too damn much influence. That story wasn't anything compared to what we're doing. We're responsible for keeping a foreign regime in power. All the *Post* did was embarrass one of our allies."

"I'm not backing off anything I said before, Sarah. They are too powerful, and maybe we are too. Nobody elected us, that's the key, I think. We don't have to answer to the people for what we do. There aren't any brakes except the ones we apply ourselves. And I don't think we apply them often enough."

"So shouldn't we put them on now?" she asked.

"Not now. Not now that we have the information. We can't let political considerations decide whether or not we go with what we know, we just have to go with it. Where the brakes come in, I think, is when we're deciding what we want to find out, where we want to look.

I'm beginning to think we look at Presidents too hard. We need to spread ourselves around a little."

"We could look at ourselves, for starters," Sarah said. "We could start right with the White House press corps. How about a piece on Clyde Lancing and the famous knife incident?"

"Or what about Jane?" Rudy asked.

"Oh, not Jane," Sarah responded immediately. "Though I guess the question is," she continued after a moment, "why not Jane? Since when has feeling sorry for somebody ever been a reason not to do a story?" She paused. "Oh, hell, we're just playing games. I wonder if we'd be drawing these distinctions if this wasn't our story? I mean, would we think it was so necessary to run it, if *we* weren't going to get the credit? How much does self-interest affect our thinking?"

Rudy was about to answer when Jack spoke. "In a way, that's an irrelevant question, Sarah. We've already lost the story."

Both reporters looked at him in surprise.

"Sure," Jack went on. "Remember when Jenner said something about our 'determining the actions he'd have to take'? He'll tell Marcos about the coup now. He'll have to because he knows Marcos is going to find out anyway, and if the United States is going to keep Marcos for an ally, then he has to find it out from our government, not from our press. Once that's done, and I imagine it'll be done in the next day or so—long before we come out with it—then Jenner will probably go public to try to patch up his wounds. He can explain that Ewing was in the Philippines assessing the situation. He can talk about how sensitive his mission was, and how he, Jenner, lied about Dr. Brewer to try to keep attention away from Malcolm."

"Will it work?" Rudy asked.

"I don't know," Jack said. "He's going to have to say

he lied, and the opposition won't let him or anybody else forget that if he runs again. I suppose it depends on how effectively he presents his case, and . . ." Jack's attention was suddenly drawn to the White House across the street. A presidential motorcade was pulling out onto Pennsylvania Avenue. "Where do you suppose he's going?" Jack asked, and then he answered his own question. "It's the Crawford funeral, that's right."

"Maybe that's one of those places where we should have paid more attention," Rudy said. "Crawford's life, Mrs. Crawford's life—they were a mess, and we didn't pay any attention."

"But why should we have?" Sarah asked. "I mean, shouldn't a man's private life remain private?"

"Not when it's so fouled up it's likely to affect his public functioning," Rudy said. "On the other hand, if it's something like he saw a psychiatrist twenty years ago, I'd say we ought to pass it up."

"There are different standards for Presidents and would-be Presidents," Jack said. "Teddy Kennedy's a good example. Nobody thinks about Chappaquiddick any more until we think Teddy's going after the big one. Then we lay it all out again."

"But that feels right," Rudy said. "Maybe Chappaquiddick's O.K. on a senator's record, but not on a President's. We *have* to expect more." He threw his hands up in exasperation. "Oh, hell, I know I'm going in circles."

Jack stood. "I'm going back to the office. I'll probably see you two this afternoon."

They both nodded. When they were alone on the park bench, Sarah looked at Rudy out of the corner of her eye. There were lines between his brows, lines she wanted to reach out and rub away. Instead she put her hand on his arm. Much to her surprise, he covered it with his own.

"You really held your own in the Oval Office," he said.

"Well, thank you."

"I had to keep myself from laughing when you jumped in to keep Jack from poaching on your territory—and then proceeded to poach on his."

"I take it you aren't irritated anymore that I went off on my own? That I went ahead and talked to Basinger at the state dinner?"

"No," he said. He looked down at her hand, took it in both his own, and seemed to study it. "Hell, I wish I could stay mad at you. This whole thing would be much easier, you know, if I didn't *like* you so much."

" 'Like' isn't exactly what I'm looking for. I was thinking more along the lines of passion."

Although she was smiling, he looked at her seriously. "You think I don't feel anything?"

"Not as much as I do. Obviously."

"You're wrong. It's just that there are more feelings with me. More things pulling me in different ways. Nancy's important, you know. My family's important."

"You make it too difficult."

He didn't answer for a moment, and then he stood. "C'mon," he said, struggling to change the mood of their conversation. "No more laziness. Let's get in there for the briefing and give 'em hell."

She stood too, willing for the moment to let him set things aside. But as they crossed back over Pennsylvania Avenue, she very deliberately slipped her arm through his.

Chapter 23

ZERN JENNER looked over at his wife and counted to himself how many days it had been now that she'd been having breakfast with him. This was the fifth morning, wasn't it? Yes, he decided, it was. It had been Saturday when she'd first appeared in the dining room at breakfast time. It was Wednesday now, and she hadn't missed a morning.

He took a sip of coffee and looked down at the news summary. One of the wire service reporters apparently had seen Malcolm, and his report that Ewing was in Washington had launched a fresh round of news articles. The report on last night's CBC News was typical. "The psychiatrist who works for President Jenner is back in Washington," was how the story had played, and the three-minute piece had touched on the log, on Ewing's "apparent" absence since its publication, and the fact that the White House had asked the networks for fifteen minutes of prime time Wednesday evening for a presidential announcement. "There is much speculation," the reporter concluded, "that Zern Jenner means to use the time he has requested to explain to the American public exactly what the mysterious Malcolm Ewing's role is in his administration."

Jenner leafed on through the summary, then stopped as an item halfway down a page caught his eye. He laughed aloud. "Well, Mary, there is some justice in the universe after all. You know Rita Walton?"

"The woman who worked for Dorothy Brewer?"

"That's it. The one who was Frye's source for the story about my seeing Dr. Brewer. She held a news conference yesterday afternoon, right in front of the *Post* building. Listen, here's what she said: 'Nicholas Frye made false promises to me. He said that if I talked to him about the times Zern Jenner came to Dr. Brewer's office, he'd bring me to Washington where I could meet lots and lots of people, maybe even some of the people who publish books. And I thought that was a good idea, because I could do a lot of people a lot of good if I would write down what I know and my ideas. Well, he hasn't let me talk to anybody since I got here, and I'm just going to take things into my own hands, I've decided.' "

Mary Jenner shook her head in disgust. "She'll have a book contract before the week is out."

Another summary item on the same page caught the President's eye. "Son of a bitch," he said.

"What is it?"

"Hell, I shouldn't get mad. It's kind of funny really. Boyston's using Morris and Latvala to cover his ass."

Mary Jenner reached over, took the summary, and began to read. "Did he ever warn you?" she asked when she was finished. "Did he ever say he thought Crawford was 'unstable' or that you were listening to too narrow a range of advisers?"

"The most he ever did was let me know he didn't think I was using *his* talents enough."

"Why is he doing this?" she asked, gesturing at the news summary.

"I guess he figures I've just about had a bellyful. And he wants to do everything he can to make himself look good. Everything he can to make me look so bad, if I decide to get rid of him, that I won't dare do it."

"So what are you going to do?"

"Get rid of him." The President smiled unexpectedly.

"But how? Why?"

"I'm going to ask him to come in this afternoon, and I'm going to give him two choices. He can either write me a letter in which he states that he has decided he does not want to be on the ticket next time, or I will announce on the air tonight that I have asked him not to be on the ticket. And if I do the latter, I'll accompany my announcement with a full explanation of how he leaked the Oval Office log."

"And how did he? And how do you know?"

"Jack Sasser told me. Or he told Dale Basinger, really. On his way out of the Oval Office yesterday he stopped Dale and told him that the log was leaked to Jane Minnick—you know, that rather strange woman in the press corps?—and that she in turn gave it to Frye. Remember? I thought Boyston had done it, but I couldn't believe he'd leak to Frye. Well, Sasser explained to Basinger how it all happened."

"But I don't understand why Sasser would do that. He hasn't been inclined to do you many favors lately."

"Oh, a little guilt was involved, I suppose." The President's mood became somber. "He knows exactly what the consequences are of that Philippines story—or the threat of it, anyway." He looked at his watch. "Sometime within the next eight to ten hours, Marcos will probably have Castillo under arrest, thanks to the United States government, and Sasser feels guilty as hell forcing us to get involved that way."

"But not so guilty he'd hold off on writing the story."

"No, but guilty enough so he'd try to even things out a little."

"What do you think Boyston will do when you call him in?"

"Oh, he'll sputter and stomp around and swear a bit, and then he'll agree to take himself off the ticket. I could destroy him by going on nationwide television tonight with the tale of how he leaked a confidential presidential document. The story will be in *Newstime* next week, but he can deny it, and hope everybody'll forget it eventually. Nobody'd ever forget, though, if a President, on national television, accused his Vice President of disloyalty and betrayal."

"But what about all those letters you've been getting. What about all those people who think Boyston walks on water?"

"Getting rid of him isn't going to win me any popularity contests, that's for sure. But one advantage of being down as far as I am now is that I don't have to worry about going down much farther. Things can't get much worse, so I might as well clear the decks while I'm here."

"About Dorothy Brewer too?"

"I'm going to lay it all out. Not just Malcolm's mission and my not wanting to draw attention to him, but all the years that have passed, and I've never said anything about seeing her. That was wrong of me. I made myself vulnerable by not airing this thing a long time ago. I might not have lied about it before, but I didn't tell the truth either, and I would have been a lot better off if I had." He paused. "And so would the American people."

He stood, walked over to the window, and pulled aside the curtain. "It's going to feel good to get it all out."

"What do you think the reaction will be?"

He shrugged, let the curtain fall, and turned around. "I honestly don't know. But, even more important, I don't care that much. Do you remember Maggie's freckles?"

She smiled and nodded. When their daughter was small, she had had a truly incredible crop of freckles, and her playmates had teased her about them endlessly. "They didn't bother her. She didn't care."

"Exactly. And what a gift that is. No matter what anybody said, she just went straight ahead on her own course, really not caring, not bothered in the least by what others might think. Well, that's how it is with me right now. I'm going to lay this thing out, and the press and the public can pick over it for the next twenty years if they want. But I'm going to walk away from it and do the best damned job I can for this country." He started walking back and forth the length of the dining room. "I'll get the Whitefeather dispute solved if I have to mediate it myself. I'm going to get our domestic house in order, and then I'm going to talk straighter to the Congress and the people than they've ever been talked to. I'm going to convince them that this country just can't retreat any more." He paused and looked at her. "You know, I just about got Yanaga convinced yesterday afternoon. I think I might even get him to defend the idea of our bases in Japan." He started walking again. "And I'm going to start worrying about the election. Maybe I'll let Malcolm head it up. What do you think of that?"

"It might work."

"And it might not."

"And we can always go back to the ranch."

"And watch the deer feeding while we eat," he said.

"And the calves in the spring. Remember how the

cows hide them in the tall grass when the winds blow?" She stood, walked over to him, put her arms around him, and laid her head on his chest. "We can go back to Montana," she said.

He closed his eyes. "Of course we can."

They stood holding one another until she felt him becoming restless. "What's wrong?" she asked.

"It's nothing."

"I know better," she said, looking up.

He took her arms from off his shoulders and sighed. "It's that priest," he said, rubbing his forehead. "That poor damned priest." He looked at his watch, then put his hands in his pockets and started walking again. Only now the excitement was gone. Now his pace was much slower.

THEY HAD decided to watch the President on one of the televisions at *Newstime*. Jack, Rudy, and Sarah were gathered in Jack's office waiting for seven P.M., waiting for the President to speak.

"You know," Rudy said, "maybe what I need is reassignment. Just a year or two someplace else."

Sarah looked at him, unable to believe what she had heard.

"Reassignment, hmmm?" Jack said noncommittally.

"Well, not right away, but maybe in six months when Nancy's finished her dissertation."

"It'll be the middle of presidential primaries then. You won't want to leave. And I won't want you to."

"I don't know. I just have a feeling there's a whole world out there where things are more in balance, more in perspective."

"It's no different," Sarah burst out. "It's no different at all."

"It's the Castillo thing, isn't it?" Jack said. "You saw it come in over the wires that Marcos has arrested him."

"Sure, that's part of it. We're responsible, and we did it without even considering whether his arrest was right or wrong."

"We were worried about something else," said Jack. "Freedom of the press is just as important."

Sarah could see that Jack's answer hadn't satisfied Rudy. "Maybe," she offered hesitantly, "maybe the most important thing is that we be aware that there are problems like this, that we stay concerned about them."

Rudy shook his head. "That's too easy, Sarah," he said. "That's just too damned easy."

For several moments, the only sound in the room was the inane jingle of a television commercial, and then there was silence as a picture of the White House came on the screen. In the quiet, Sarah thought to herself that Rudy was probably right. There weren't any easy answers. And maybe he was right too when he thought there weren't any easy relationships. At least not for him. And not for her, if he was what she wanted.

She heard a disembodied voice announcing, "Ladies and Gentlemen, the President of the United States," and she turned her attention to the television set.